NOTHING BUT NET

ALI SPOONER

Also by Ali Spooner

Single Books

Fairytail Farm

Sullivan's Trace

The Blank White Page

From the Cradle to the Stone

Holy Water and Whiskey Scars

The Ghost of East Texas

The Trophy Wives Club

The Bee Charmer

Forever Home

Ruined

Back in the Saddle

Open Your Heart

South of Heaven

Shotgun Rider

The Settlement

Love's Playlist

Cowgirl Up

Twisted Lives

The Epitaph

Terminal Event

Bailey's Run

Erotica

The Wolf and The Unicorn

Series

The Island Series

Neptune's Ring

Venus Rising

The Hunter Series

The Devil's Tree

Bound

Sasha Thibodaux Series

Sugarland

Bayou Justice

Line of Sight

Strong Southern Women Series

Diamond Dreams

Gator Girlz

True North

Footprints

Cast Iron Farm Series

The Mountain Whispers

The Star Child

Soul on Fire

The Sky People

Turn the Page

Songwriters Series
Six Strings and a Dream
Midnight in Nashville
Out and Loud

Co-authored with Annette Mori

Humbug- The Ultimate Lesbian Christmas Carol

Heart Strings Attached

Free to Love

Trouble in Paradise

Co-Authored with K.L. Gallagher

Hat Trick

NOTHING BUT NET

ALI SPOONER

Affinity
Rainbow Publications

2025

Nothing But Net
© 2025 by Ali Spooner

Affinity E-Book Press NZ LTD
Canterbury, New Zealand

1st Edition

ISBN: 978-1-991357-08-3 (paperback)

Editor: A Koenig
Proof Editor: Lisa M
Cover Design: Irish Dragon Design
Production Design: Affinity Publication Services

ACKNOWLEDGMENTS

I thank my readers for following my stories and providing great feedback and encouragement. Writing wouldn't be so much fun without you. Thanks to Affinity, Irish Dragon, for the cover art and the team of editors, readers, and publishers who continue to help me grow as a writer.

DEDICATION

This was a fun book for me to write, and I would like to thank my high school coach, Coach Williams, and college coach, Voorhees, who encouraged me to be the best I could be on and off the court. The game is so different today from my era, and I am thrilled to see how the quality of play and encouragement for support has grown on the college and professional levels. The fans are terrific, and I hope they will continue to help develop all women's sports in the future.

TABLE OF CONTENTS

Chapter One   1
Chapter Two   12
Chapter Three   27
Chapter Four   35
Chapter Five   47
Chapter Six   62
Chapter Seven   75
Chapter Eight   87
Chapter Nine   104
Chapter Ten   125
Chapter Eleven   143
Chapter Twelve   162
Chapter Thirteen   184
Chapter Fourteen   199
Chapter Fifteen   216
Chapter Sixteen   224
Chapter Seventeen   242
Chapter Eighteen   259
Chapter Nineteen   277
Chapter Twenty   292
Epilogue   305
About the Author   307
Other Affinity Books   308

CHAPTER ONE

Hunter James loaded her few possessions into a small duffle bag and closed her metal locker. It felt strange to wear street clothes again, and she was fortunate that they still fit. After tying her shoes and picking up her bag, Hunter left the cubicle that had been her home for five years. Hunter had already said goodbye to the few people she considered friends, so her walk to the discharge center was done alone. The loud buzzing of the locks on the heavy metal doors rang in her ears. Hunter turned briefly to look at her past. When the doors clicked open, she walked through quickly for the last time.

Sharon Collins escorted her to the parking lot gate. "I hope if our paths cross again, it will be under different circumstances. Good luck." She signaled for the gate to be opened.

"Thanks." Hunter walked through the gate and looked for her mother's car. She heard a car door open and watched her mother exit the vehicle. Elizabeth James looked much older than the five years that had passed, and Hunter knew that was partially her fault for the angst her family had experienced. Dropping her bag, she took her mother in her arms and hugged her tightly.

"You look good," Hunter said.

"So do you." Elizabeth smiled. "A bit on the thin side, but I know how to take care of that."

"Thanks for coming to pick me up."

"I hope you didn't consider for a moment that I wouldn't be here." Elizabeth ran her hands through her graying hair. "I would have been here much sooner if you had allowed visits."

Hunter felt the tears fill her eyes. "I couldn't stand the thought of you or Carson seeing me here. It was selfish but much too painful for me."

Elizabeth nodded. "Toss your bag in the back, and let's get out of here. We have a long ride ahead of us. What would you care to eat once we get on the road?"

"I will buy you a steak dinner if you find a spot."

"I think I passed a place not too far from here."

Hunter buckled her belt. "Dad couldn't make the trip today?"

Hunter saw her mom's tears wetting her cheeks. "We have a lot of catching up to do. I haven't seen your dad for four years."

"I'm sorry, Mom."

"Don't be. Let's talk about that later. Right now, let's get a decent meal together."

†

Hunter acknowledged her mom's request to keep the conversation light during the meal and focused on finishing every bite of her meal and the dessert her mom insisted she order.

"That was terrific," Hunter said. "I haven't eaten that much in ages." Hunter regretted the comment when she saw the painful look on her mother's face, but it was too late to take it back. She reached for the check when the waitress brought it, but Elizabeth handed the woman a credit card.

"I insist."

"Thank you for a terrific meal. I may have to nap after that."

"We've got a six-hour drive ahead of us, so kick back and nap. It won't bother me at all."

"I can help with the driving," Hunter offered.

"That's not necessary but thank you."

†

Hunter stretched three hours later when she woke from a nap. She wiped her hand across her face.

"I guess I was more tired than I thought. I'll admit, I didn't sleep much last night."

Elizabeth smiled. "You needed it, and you didn't miss much."

Hunter stared out at the passing landscape as they drove north. So much growth had occurred that nothing seemed familiar, so she turned back to look at her mom. "So, how have you been?"

"I've been well. I'm still working at the bank. A few more years and I'll consider retiring," Elizabeth said. "I've been dating Jim, a gentleman I met, for almost a year now."

"Do I know him?"

Elizabeth shook her head. "He moved to town two years ago. Jim's the new fire chief."

"How did you meet a fire chief?"

"We met at a support group for people who lost loved ones to crime. His wife was a murder victim in LA."

"I'm sorry to hear that." Hunter waited to see if her mom would elaborate.

Elizabeth smiled, "He invited me to coffee after a meeting, and we've been dating since. He's a good man and is excited to meet you."

"He knows?"

"Yes, he knows about Lilly. He understands your actions more than you could know."

Hunter let her mom's words sink in for a moment. She took a deep breath and slowly released it before asking, "What happened with Dad?"

"After you went away, he fell into a deep depression. He felt guilty that he wasn't the one to do what you did. He felt it was a father's duty, not yours."

"What I did was wrong. I know that now," Hunter replied.

"We didn't see it that way at all. You loved Lilly deeply and were hurt just as badly by what happened to her. I only regret that you lost five years of your youth because of him." She sighed. "Anyway, he started drinking, lost his job, and one night, he didn't come home. At first, I assumed he was out on a bender and would eventually show up. Six months later, I received divorce papers from an address in Texas."

"That was shitty of him. He couldn't even face you," Hunter replied.

"I know, but it was for the best for both of us. It gave me the freedom to move on in life."

"Still no excuse for being a coward. I'm sorry, Mom."

"Don't be. I'm happy and have become a stronger woman because of it."

"I'm glad that you've found someone who can appreciate you. Is it serious with him? Do you think you and Jim will marry?"

"Possibly in the future. We've talked about it a few times."

"I hope it happens. You deserve to be happy with someone who treats you well."

"Have you heard anything from Carson?"

"She wrote for the first year, but that faded quickly when I wouldn't allow her to visit. She's playing professional basketball in Las Vegas now. She's also moved on with her life and was married last year."

That should have been us playing ball together and getting married, Hunter thought.

"I'm sorry," Elizabeth said.

†

When they reached the edge of her hometown, Hunter noticed how things had changed in her absence. "This place has really grown."

"The population of California has increased significantly. Housing can barely keep up with the growth," Elizabeth said as she turned into their subdivision. She activated the remote for the garage and turned the car into the drive.

Hunter took a deep breath as her mom pulled into the garage. Her heart raced with excitement and trepidation.

Elizabeth turned off the engine. "Let's get you settled in, and we can decide on dinner."

"Is Franco's pizza still here?"

"Yes. Just as good as you remember." She smiled. "That was an easy decision."

Hunter exited the car and took her bag from the back seat. She walked through the house and stopped outside the door with a wooden sign, "Lilly's Room," hung on it. Hunter instantly felt an ache deep in her chest. She had dreaded this moment when she returned home to find the room empty. Hunter walked on and opened the door to her room. It was just as she left it when she entered college. Her sports posters still filled the walls, and her trophies filled several shelves. She tossed her bag onto the bed and sat down. Her eyes scanned the room. She was a much different person than the one who had left the room over five years ago. Hunter lay on the bed and stared at the ceiling until her mom entered.

"I know it's your first night home, but would you mind if Jim brought the pizza and joined us for dinner?"

"No, that's fine, Mom. I'm looking forward to meeting him."

"Thanks. Is 'meat lovers' still your favorite?"

Hunter offered her a smile. "Don't you know it? Anything else is a waste."

"I'll get it ordered then." Elizabeth stopped in the doorway and turned back to Hunter. "Welcome home, honey."

"Thanks, Mom."

†

When the garage door lifted, Hunter's eyes spotted a sizeable, covered item in the back of the garage, and hoped it was her cherished Indian motorcycle. She had worked hard in her last two years of high school to purchase the bike to take to college, and she was hopeful it was in good shape. Hunter knew she would probably need to replace the battery and perform routine maintenance, but the prospect of riding lifted her spirits. She had lain awake for weeks, failing to plan for her return home with no final decision, but suddenly, her plan began to form.

Returning to her room, Hunter opened her closet door. She smiled when her eyes landed on her motorcycle boots beside her helmet. Hunter placed her jacket and a few clothing items in the closet and left the room.

†

Jim had just arrived with the pizza when Hunter entered the kitchen. He kissed Elizabeth and turned when he heard Hunter enter.

"Hello," Hunter said, offering her hand.

"Hey. I'm Jim. Nice to meet you." Jim took her hand, shaking it firmly.

"Likewise. Mom has told me a lot about you today."

"All good, I hope," Jim said with a nervous smile. He shuffled his feet, waiting for her reply.

"Nothing but." Hunter returned his smile, hoping to put him at ease. Jim was only an inch taller than her six foot and had sparkling blue eyes. She could see why her mom was attracted to him. He was handsome.

Elizabeth pulled out three plates. "What do you want to drink?"

"Do you have a soda?" Hunter asked.

"I got your favorite," Elizabeth said, pointing to the refrigerator.

Hunter walked over and opened the door. A six-pack of Mountain Dew was chilling. "Perfect," she said, plucking a bottle from the shelf. "What can I get y'all?"

"A coke for me," Elizabeth said. "There's beer if you want one," she told Jim.

"Could I have a Dew?" he asked.

"Not a problem." Hunter carried the drinks to the table as her mom served large slices of pizza.

"That smells heavenly," Hunter said as she sat across from her.

"Still the best in town," Elizabeth said.

Hunter took a bite, closed her eyes, and moaned. "Tastes great, too."

†

They made small talk during the meal. "Hey, Mom, is that my bike covered in the garage?"

"Yes. I know how much you love that bike. Jim has been taking care of it for you."

Hunter's eyebrow shot up.

"I put a battery tender on it and have started it regularly to keep it charged. Changed the oil and refreshed the gas in the tank."

"Thanks. Do you ride?"

"I've got a Harley Roadster that I have managed to get your mom on back a few times."

"Mom on a motorcycle? This I've got to see. You always said that bike would be the death of me," Hunter teased.

"Jim has convinced me how fun it is to ride. It wasn't easy, but he was patient with me. We've taken a few rides down the coast."

"Very impressive. Thanks for taking care of my baby. I worked two hard years to afford it in high school."

"She's a beauty. I'd take her off your hands if you ever wanted to sell. That's a classic. They don't make them like that anymore."

Hunter chuckled. "Not a chance."

"I've kept your tags legal also, so if you've got a current license, you should be good to ride," Elizabeth said.

"I'm good for another year," Hunter said.

"Maybe we can take a ride this weekend," Jim suggested.

"I'd like that. Maybe I can take her out tomorrow to get used to riding again and see the town."

"I've got a board meeting in the morning, but I'll be home after lunch. Sorry, I couldn't get out of it."

"That's okay, Mom. Please don't feel like you must take time off for me. I'll stay busy."

"Your mom told me you were quite the athlete and had a full ride to play basketball. Have you considered going back to college?"

"I don't think I can get admitted with a felony conviction."

"You can if you are upfront during the admissions process. A one-time expungement program would allow you to have the felony removed from your record." Elizabeth smiled. "I checked if you wanted to consider that as an option."

"I have a lot to consider," Hunter said. "I've already had my record expunged as part of my release program. I need to decide where to go from here."

"I still have the college fund we set up for you and Lil...Lilly," Elizabeth stumbled, speaking.

Hunter reached over and covered her mom's hand. "I'll give it some consideration. I worked on electronics contracts and put some money away also."

"There's no rush for you to decide on anything," her mom said.

"Good. Right now, I want to take a nice hot bath and sleep in my own bed. Thank you for the pizza and for caring for my bike. And my mom," Hunter told Jim.

"It was nice to meet you finally. I'll see you this weekend," Jim said as Hunter left the table.

"Let's plan on a ride Sunday if that's good for you," Hunter suggested.

Jim smiled broadly at her suggestion. "That works for me."

"Goodnight then."

†

Hunter had finished bathing and was walking to her room when Elizabeth stopped her.

"I'll be home as quickly as I can tomorrow. I won't wake you, but there are plenty of options for breakfast in the morning."

"I'll be fine, Mom. Get some rest. You've had a long day, too."

"Goodnight, honey. I love you."

"Love you too, Mom." Hunter pulled her in for a hug. "It's good to be home."

CHAPTER TWO

Hunter dressed in shorts and a T-shirt for bed. She could still hear her mom and Jim in the kitchen as she closed her bedroom door. She was relieved that her mom had found someone to make her happy, and Jim seemed like a genuinely good man.

Hunter was lying in bed, still awake, an hour later when her mom walked past to her room. She heard her footsteps pause outside her door, then continue down the hall. When Hunter finally fell asleep, her dreams were filled with the image of the courtroom on the day of her sentencing. At two, she woke drenched in sweat when the judge banged his gavel to finalize her sentencing. Hunter sat up in bed, stunned by the proclamation of her sentence. Her eyes wildly searched the room until she realized she was back at home. Her heart was pounding in her chest as Hunter climbed from the bed and walked to her door. The house was silent as she stepped from her room and opened the door to Lilly's room. The small nightlight cast an eerie glow in the room as she walked over to sit at Lilly's desk. Lilly's most prized possession, her journal, rested on the desk's center. The room smelled of the sweet lavender scent Lilly had adored. Hunter placed a trembling hand on the journal and was surprised it felt warm. She assumed it was from the blood rushing through her body as her heart pounded.

Hunter had vowed never to open the journal again after reading the last entry Lilly had made. Tears began streaking down her cheeks as she sat staring at the book. "I am so sorry I failed you, Lilly." She wept until she heard a soft voice from the doorway.

"Hunter, it was not your fault, and you need to stop tormenting yourself with the belief that it was," Elizabeth said as she stepped into the room.

"Maybe if I had taken the time to return her call, she would still be here with us," Hunter said between sobs.

"Nonsense. Nothing that happened to your sister was your fault, and you paid your debt for your actions. Lilly would want you to move on and be happy with your life. She worshipped you as her big sister."

"I promised her I would always be there for her, but when she needed me most, I let her down," Hunter replied.

"What's done is done, and there's nothing we can do to change the past. We must concentrate on the future and how we will best live our lives." Elizabeth pulled Hunter into a hug. "It took me a year to realize that for myself after your father left. I felt like I had lost my entire family, and that's what you are facing now. You need to determine what you will do with your life."

"You make that sound simple. I have more questions than answers, and I am unsure what path to take."

"Would you join me for a cup of coffee and listen to an idea I had tonight?"

Hunter nodded and looked at her with eyes still full of unshed tears. She followed her from the room and carefully closed the door.

†

Elizabeth made them coffee and opened a container of freshly baked cookies. "I know they are your favorite, so I made them tonight after Jim left."

"He seems like a good man," Hunter said as she picked up a cookie.

"He has been my salvation, and we look forward to spending our retirement years together," Elizabeth answered. "He has brought me happiness I never thought I would feel again or even deserve."

"I'm glad you found each other," Hunter said. She bit into a cookie. "Just as good as I remember."

"When you and Jim were talking motorcycles tonight, I saw the spark of excitement in your eyes again, and I thought of an idea."

"I'm listening."

"There is no rush for you to decide your future. You will always have a home here, but you must do some healing and soul-searching before deciding on your course. What if Jim loans you his small trailer filled with camping gear that will attach to your bike, and you hit the road?" She smiled at Hunter. "Jim says there is no better time to think through problems than when you are cruising down an open highway."

"He's right about that."

"You've been confined for five years, and it's time to spread your wings and experience freedom again. You've always loved the outdoors; there is so much beauty to explore. Ride across the country if that's what it takes to find peace in your soul. Stop when you want to stay someplace for a while and take the time to find out who you are and who you want to become. You are not the same young woman who left this house five years ago. You are much stronger and more independent. If you choose to return to college or go in an entirely different direction, that's your decision. I will support you in anything you want to become."

"I have given that some thought, but I don't want you to feel like I am abandoning you, too."

"You won't be. Besides, I ordered an iPhone for you today that I will pick up tomorrow, so I can reach you as long as you have a signal. I will expect regular check-ins and pictures of your adventures."

"Thanks, Mom. I do like that idea. Can I give you a check to deposit and ask that you order me a new debit card on my account?"

"I can get both set up for you tomorrow."

Hunter glanced at the clock on the wall. "I'm sorry I woke you. I know you must work tomorrow, but you can get a few more hours of sleep."

"You didn't wake me. I sensed you were up, and we needed to have this talk. Sleep is overrated. A few more hours and I'll be fine. Jim wants to show off his grilling skills tomorrow night and cook steaks for us."

"That sounds delicious. Do I need to do any grocery shopping?"

"Nope. Jim's got everything he needs already. You can keep him company and talk motorcycles and camping while I prepare a few sides."

Elizabeth placed their cups in the sink. "I'll see you tomorrow afternoon."

"Goodnight, Mom." Hunter placed a final cookie in her mouth and sealed the container.

When Hunter returned to her bed, she was relaxed and quickly returned to sleep, this time without dreams.

†

Her alarm woke her at seven, and she stretched lazily before sitting on the side of the bed. The sun was shining brightly through her window. It would be a perfect day for a ride. Hunter relieved her bladder, brushed her teeth, and pulled her hair into a ponytail. She stared into the mirror and saw the sparkle had returned to her blue eyes. In her room, Hunter dressed in jeans, a T-shirt, and boots before removing the helmet from her closet shelf. She walked into the kitchen and brewed a cup of coffee while she made toast. She opened the fridge and found a jar of apple jelly, which she smeared across the bread.

Hunter found a note from her mom beside her bike keys on the table. *The garage door code is still the same. Have a great morning. I'll see you after lunch.*

After devouring the toast and coffee, Hunter picked up the keys and entered the garage, opening the door as she passed by the keypad. She planned to make a few laps around the subdivision to reacquaint herself with the bike before entering the morning traffic. Hunter slowly removed the cover, folded it, placed it on a workbench, and removed the battery tender. When Hunter straddled the bike, she felt at home. She started the motor and allowed it to idle for a few minutes. After securing her helmet and with her heart racing, she exited the garage. Hunter knew the door would close automatically after five minutes, but she dropped the kickstand and walked to the keypad to close it. She was ready to ride. The powerful motor purred as she twisted the accelerator, and Hunter felt the rumble of power between her legs. She maneuvered the bike as smoothly as ever and was ready for a long stretch of road. Her tank was full, so Hunter guided the bike toward Highway One. She would turn north and enjoy the salty air and bright sunshine along the Pacific Coast. The rocky cliffs reached out to meet the dark blue water and were as beautiful as she remembered. She opened her visor to welcome the air against her face, and almost immediately regretted not finding her sunglasses before leaving the house. The sun was bright as it kissed her skin. She rode north for an hour before exiting into a scenic turnout.

Hunter dismounted and stretched stiff muscles. It wouldn't take long for her body to adjust to riding again, but today, she enjoyed a brief respite to stare into the deep blue water of the ocean. Sailboats and fishing vessels dotted the horizon as Hunter's eyes followed a flock of seagulls flying to the south. They would coast into the nearest harbor with dreams of a handout from the many fishermen who would soon arrive with a morning catch. Memories of herself and Lilly playing on the beach as kids flooded her mind. Their mom took them to the beach at every opportunity, while her dad preferred to sit at home with his beer, watching whatever sport was in season. Hunter had loved those girls' days out. Hunter knew where she would ride next when she returned to her bike. She hoped there was still a flower shop not far from the cemetery.

Hunter found the shop and bought the yellow carnations that were Lilly's favorite to place on her grave. She had only visited occasionally before leaving, but Hunter drove to the correct spot without issue. Hunter discarded faded flowers before placing the carnations in the vase. She sat next to the headstone and touched the warm marble.

"Hey, Little Bit," Hunter said, using the nickname she had given Lilly all those years ago. "I returned home yesterday, and it's strange for you and Dad not to be there. So much has changed. However, Mom is happy and has found someone who makes her smile again. He seems to be a good man for her after Dad fled the coop. I have kicked myself every day for five years over not answering your call, but Mom is helping me to realize that it's time for me to release that guilt and move on." A cool breeze picked up, and some beautiful wind chimes began to play. Hunter looked for them and saw a female cardinal sitting on top of the shepherd's hook, looking at her. "I'm sorry I let you down, but I promise I will find a way to make something of myself. You always wanted to be a teacher, but I don't think I'm cut out for that." Hunter smiled. "I'll be going away for a while to do some soul-searching and determine my life's course, but I will return." Hunter felt her tears sliding down her cheeks. "I miss you and will always love you." Hunter leaned in to kiss the headstone, and when she turned toward her bike, a figure standing beside a car caused her to freeze in her tracks.

Hunter felt her face form a scowl as she approached the young woman holding a fresh bouquet. Rage filled her pores as she stalked toward her, and when Hunter saw the look of fear in her eyes, she stopped. Hunter couldn't hold Jen responsible for her brother's actions and knew Jen had loved Lilly since they were toddlers. Hunter felt her body relax as she continued her approach.

"I guess I'm the last person you thought you would find here today," Jen said softly.

"I must admit I was shocked at first, but Lilly meant a lot to you."

"Yes, she did. She had been my best friend since we learned to walk together," Jen said with a warm smile. "I visit every few weeks to freshen up her flowers, but you have beat me to it today."

"There is always room for more flowers," Hunter replied, trying to soften her tone. "How have you been?"

"I'm okay. I'll be starting college at Berkeley in the fall." Jen shuffled her feet nervously.

That had been Lilly's dream as well. "I hope you will enjoy your college days. They are much more fun than adulting."

"Will you be staying at home?"

Hunter shook her head. "I plan on traveling to get my plans for the future worked out."

Jen nodded and hung her head. "I know this is too little too late, but I am so sorry for what my brother did and what happened to Lilly and you."

"You are not responsible for his actions, nor mine, but I appreciate the sentiment. I know what I did was wrong and have paid that price. It's time to move on."

Jen's head snapped upward. "He deserved everything you did to him and more. I will never forgive him." Jen started crying.

Hunter did the only thing she could think of. She stepped forward and pulled Jen into a hug. "Lilly wouldn't want you to feel that way. She would want you to forgive him."

Jen shook her head. "I just can't. He is dead to me as a brother."

Hunter lifted her chin and looked into her eyes. "There was a time I wished I had killed him, but I wouldn't deprive you of your only sibling. I know what that pain feels like." She forced a smile. "Try to forgive him before it's too late. You must purge your anger toward him before it wrecks your life. He will never forget what he did, which is punishment enough."

"I'm just not ready to let go of it, Hunter. I feel like it would be another insult to Lilly if I did."

"Lilly would want you to be happy. She loved you like a sister. Remember the good things, and don't let your anger and hatred overwhelm that love."

Jen wiped the tears from her face. "I will try. I hope you find the peace and happiness you deserve."

"I'm going to give it my best shot," Hunter said with a smile. "You do well in college and make Lilly proud. She will always be a part of us."

Jen rushed back into Hunter's arms. "Thank you for not hating me."

"I would never dream of it," Hunter replied. She held her close for a long moment. "Enjoy your visit."

Hunter walked to her bike and quickly drove away before her tears could start to fall.

†

Hunter rode to a bookstore and scanned the selection until she found a small road atlas with plenty of detail that would be easy to store in her saddlebags. She drove home and parked her bike. Her mom hadn't made it home yet, so Hunter kicked off her boots and sat in a recliner to thumb through the atlas. She planned a stop in Las Vegas to see if Carson would speak to her. Hunter felt that she needed to apologize to Carson so they would both feel closure. Otherwise, her plans were wide open. She was still reviewing the atlas when her mom came home.

"I wasn't sure if you had eaten anything, but I can make some grilled cheese sandwiches," Elizabeth said.

"That would be fine. Light enough to save room for dinner tonight."

"What are you reading?"

"I bought a small road atlas and have been reviewing spots I want to visit."

"Jim has a book with all the State and National Parks. I talked to him earlier, and he suggested purchasing a pass allowing you to camp cheaply along the way."

"That's not a bad idea. I'll look into that."

"He said the lifetime pass is the best option and is a one-time fee. Would it be okay if I paid that for you?"

Hunter smiled. She had the money to cover it but felt like it was important to her mom for her to have one. "Sure, Mom. That would be great."

"Good. You can look it up on my laptop while I prepare lunch. Or, better yet, do it on your phone to download the membership card electronically for easy storage."

Elizabeth handed Hunter the bag with the phone, accessories, and her new debit card.

"Thanks, Mom." Hunter turned on the phone and found her mom had already programmed her contact information. She grinned and brought up the search engine to search for the park pass. Hunter chuckled when she pulled up the site.

"What's funny?" Elizabeth asked from the kitchen.

"The lifetime pass is for seniors only, but I can get an annual pass for less than a hundred."

"Well, you certainly don't qualify as a senior. Let me get you a card so you can make the purchase." Her mom brought her a credit card and handed it to Hunter. "You keep that one. It's in your name, but it's attached to my account. I want you to keep it for emergencies."

Hunter knew it was pointless to argue with her mom. "Only for emergencies." She tucked the card into her wallet with the new debit card.

"How was your ride?"

"It was a beautiful day, so I rode up Highway One for a while. Then I bought some carnations and visited Lilly. Do you want to guess who I ran into at the cemetery?"

"Who?"

"Jen. She arrived as I was leaving, and we had a nice talk."

"That doesn't surprise me. Jen visits often with flowers. How was she?"

"Good. She's excited about entering college at Berkeley. She and Lilly had always planned to go together."

"I'm thankful she will follow that plan. There was a time when I wasn't sure she would finish high school, but she came out of the funk and ended up at the top of her class."

"What about Allen?"

"Don't know and don't care. Allen left town soon after, and I haven't seen or heard about him since."

Hunter went to the fridge for drinks, and Elizabeth carried the sandwiches to the table. "Those look good," Hunter said as she sat across from her.

"So, have you decided on a first stop yet?"

"I have. I will go to Vegas first. I need to try to connect with Carson. There is so much I need to tell her. I hope that now that she's playing professionally and married, she will agree to speak to me."

"I don't see why she wouldn't. Do she and her wife play on the same team?"

"No. Carson's wife plays for Seattle. I checked her game schedule, and she will play at home in Vegas next Saturday."

"That still gives us a few days together. Do we need to do some shopping? I know you've grown taller."

"I could use some new jeans. Or at least something new to me. If we can find my size at a thrift store, they will be cheaper, and they are already broken in."

"Would you let me buy you at least one new pair?" Elizabeth asked.

Hunter smiled. "Yes, Mom."

"I've taken Monday off so we can spend the day together. We can do some shopping and maybe catch a movie or something."

"That would be great. I want to get a haircut. Maybe back to shoulder length. Anyone you recommend?"

"I will make an appointment for you next week."

"I've still got my army duffle bag I took to college, but I need to find a waterproof bag to cover it. We can find those at a sporting goods store. Do you know where my sunglasses are?"

Elizabeth smiled. "Top right-hand drawer on your desk in the case. What about a light coat?"

Hunter shook her head. "I've got several hoodies and a rain slicker. That should be all I need for now."

†

When Jim arrived carrying bags of groceries, Hunter joined him on the deck for a beer while they waited for the grill to heat up.

"Elizabeth says you're going to take a road trip."

Hunter took a sip of the cold beer. "I thought I would head out at the end of next week. I want to be in Vegas to catch up with an old friend."

"That will be a great ride. There are some great parks in Utah you can hit after Vegas. Have you ever been to Vegas?"

"No. This will be a first for me."

"Sin City is the perfect name for that place. There's nothing you can't find in Vegas, especially a lot of trouble." He chuckled.

"I don't plan on staying long. I'll visit the Hoover Dam and the Valley of Fire before riding to Utah."

"I'd like to visit Utah with your mom soon. Maybe in the fall."

Hunter shifted in her seat. "I think she would enjoy that. I promised to send her photos of my adventures, so hopefully, she will have a taste of what to look forward to seeing."

"I hope you will spend at least a week in Utah. There is so much to see there. Even a week won't be long enough to see all its beauty."

"I'm in no rush, so I can take whatever time I need to explore."

Jim stood to check the grill. "I can bring the trailer over tomorrow, then Sunday, we can all ride to get you used to pulling it. I've got all the camping supplies you should need."

"I'd appreciate that."

"I've got a book with all the State and National Parks you can borrow."

"I picked up a small atlas but didn't think about a book on the parks."

"It will come in handy and help you set up an itinerary. I'm going to grab the steaks. Are you ready for a beer?"

"Sure," Hunter said. She drained the bottle and handed it to Jim.

†

Dinner was excellent, and after helping her mom clean the kitchen, Hunter excused herself and went to her room to study the atlas and began making notes on the spots in Utah she would visit. Jim's book would help her determine a travel itinerary, but she searched a few sites on her phone. When her eyes grew heavy, she walked to the kitchen for a glass of water. Jim and her mom were watching a movie.

"I'm going to call it a night. Thanks again for a great dinner. Goodnight."

"I'll see you tomorrow," Jim said.

"Goodnight, honey. Does spaghetti sound good for dinner tomorrow?"

"I love your spaghetti," Hunter answered.

"I'll see you in the morning."

Hunter nodded before returning to her room. After changing and brushing her teeth, Hunter climbed between the sheets. The day had been good, and her excitement was growing along with her list of places to visit. She turned off her lamp and dreamed of miles of red rocks.

CHAPTER THREE

Hunter spent the next few days riding and preparing for her trip. By Wednesday, she was becoming anxious to leave, and at dinner, she told her mom and Jim she would leave the following morning.

"I'm envious of you seeing the Valley of Fire before us," Jim teased. "I hope you will have a wonderful experience on the road."

"Thanks, Jim. I appreciate you lending me your equipment. That makes travel so much easier."

"You'll have to highlight your travels so we know where the best parts are," Elizabeth said as she served dessert.

Hunter picked up her fork and cut a portion of cheesecake. "I will keep you posted on the prime spots and any to avoid. I hope there won't be many of those."

Jim smiled. "If you stick to the parks, everything will be a good experience. They don't tolerate mischief, and the tourism revenue pays their salaries."

"What time do you plan to leave?"

Hunter smiled at her mom. "I'll wait until after the rush hour."

"Great. I can make you a nice breakfast to send you on your journey."

Hunter nodded. "That would be fantastic."

Jim wiped his mouth. "Do you need any help loading up your gear?"

Hunter shook her head. "Thanks, but I'm all set."

†

Hunter shared the plans for the first leg of her trip with Elizabeth.

"I hope you will send my regards to Carson. I liked having her visit."

"I will. I know Carson enjoyed the time we spent here together. She's happily married now and living her dream of playing professionally. I hope to reconnect and not cause her any more regrets."

Elizabeth smiled warmly at Hunter. "I think Carson will be happy to see you and appreciate your efforts to reconnect. She was at a loss like I was when you refused to have visitors, but you had a reason for doing that at the time. Now, it's time to move forward with your life."

"I pray daily that she will forgive me for carelessly treating her feelings. I'm not proud of that, and I hope she will understand how much chaos I was dealing with."

"You are giving her a chance. I'm sure you both have changed so much in five years."

Hunter nodded but remained silent. A few moments later, she lifted her head. "I think I'll call it a night. Goodnight, and thanks again for everything."

"Goodnight, Hunter. Enjoy your travels.

"Thanks. Goodnight."

†

Hunter climbed into bed and slept peacefully through the night. When she awoke the following day, she could hear her mom in the kitchen. She quickly dressed and freshened up before walking into the room. Her mom was preparing a monster-sized omelet. "I hope you intend to split that with me?" Hunter wrapped her arms around her mom and kissed her cheek.

"I don't want to send you off hungry."

"I'll be doing good to eat half of that. It looks like you used everything but the kitchen sink."

"Fine, we'll share," Elizabeth replied. "Grab a coffee and pour some juice if you want. Food will be up in just a minute."

Hunter poured a coffee and a glass of juice. "Do you want some?"

"No, I'm good," Elizabeth said while plating the food.

Hunter grinned when a plate appeared before her with a noticeably more significant than half portion. "Did your knife slip?" she teased.

"I took all that I can eat."

Hunter took a bite and moaned. "This is heavenly. Thanks for cooking."

"It's nice to have someone to cook and eat with." Her mom smiled. "I know you're excited about your trip, but you just got here, and now you'll be gone again."

Hunter reached over and covered her hand. "The big difference is now I can come home anytime I want. I promise not to become a stranger again."

"Oh, honey. You were never a stranger."

Hunter felt her emotions catch in her throat, and she felt guilty for leaving her mom so soon. When she was able to speak, she looked at her mother. "I know it's soon, but I desperately need to figure things out."

"I understand. You know you can return home anytime you're ready. I'll always be here for you."

"Thanks, Mom."

Elizabeth finished eating and glanced at the clock. "I hate to go, but I will be late if I don't."

"Everything's good, Mom. I'll pick up the kitchen before leaving and call you soon."

"Don't worry about the kitchen. I can do that tonight."

Hunter stood and hugged her mom close. "I love you, and we'll talk soon." She could see the tears in her eyes.

Elizabeth nodded and kissed her cheek. "I love you, too. Be safe and call me."

"I promise," Hunter replied, crossing her heart. She walked her mom to the door and watched her back out of the garage.

Hunter washed the breakfast dishes and returned to the bathroom to prepare to leave. After making the bed, she slipped her keys into her pocket and reached for her sunglasses. Hunter felt her heart pounding as she walked through the house to start her journey. She pulled the bike out of the garage and closed the door. Checking the security of her gear, Hunter climbed onto the bike and drove away.

✝

The sun shone brightly as she drove through town, heading to the highway that would take her east. The heat was comfortable on her face and arms as she rode through the brisk morning air. The ride to Las Vegas was over nine hours, so Hunter had planned to cut the drive in half to allow for some discovery time and fuel stops. She hoped to make it to Cave Lake State Park or a similar park with time to set up her campsite for the night. After crossing into Nevada and turning south, Hunter found her eyes surveying the landscape. She felt herself grinning when she turned off the highway. *If I stop whenever I see something picture-worthy, I will never reach Vegas.* Hunter snapped a few photos and continued her route.

Stopping to fuel up, Hunter pulled out her atlas to check her route. She was making good time, but the distance she had traveled on the map looked less significant. *I'll be good if I make it to Vegas for Carson's game Saturday night.* Hunter had already purchased a ticket, and her excitement to see Carson grew with each passing mile. She felt the temperature increase as heat waves danced on the asphalt ahead of her, and a trickle of sweat rolled down her spine. *Maybe I should find a hotel near Vegas to shower and look presentable when I see Carson.* The idea held some merit, but Hunter didn't need to decide yet.

When she reached her turnoff for the highway to take her to Cave Lake, she had one hundred miles remaining for the day. She stopped to fuel up, ate a large sandwich, and drank cold water before continuing. She added a bag of snacks to her trailer and cold water to her cup holder. Hunter was not prepared to cook at a campsite yet, so she felt the snacks would hold her over until the morning when she would find an excellent breakfast on the road. She would heed the warnings to stay hydrated and resupply once her case of bottled water began to diminish. The last thing she needed would be dehydration. That would be a horrible way to start a trip.

The traffic to Cave Lake was light, and Hunter arrived with plenty of daylight left. She decided to set up her tent and then tour the area before darkness fell. Her plans changed when she reached the crowded campsite, and Hunter quickly rode through the park. Her experience over the last five years had taught her not to trust people, and she worried about having her gear stolen. *Hopefully, my trust in people will return one day.*

†

Over the next two days, Hunter visited the Valley of Fire and the Hoover Dam. She was driving through the red rock desert when one of the biggest rabbits she had ever seen darted across the road in front of her. Hunter slowed to watch it pass safely. "That's certainly nightmare-worthy," she said as she watched the jackrabbit lope across the red sand. She drove slowly through the park and pulled over to the side of the road to photograph an unusual red rock formation. When the movement caught her eye, Hunter zoomed the image on her phone to find several bighorn sheep leaping across the formation. After capturing several images, she drove out of the park and headed into Vegas. She stopped for lunch, sent her recent pictures to her mom, and decided it was time for a call.

After giving her mom an update, Hunter decided to pull into a truck stop for a hot shower. The shower facility at the park had offered only lukewarm water, and she felt she needed another to be more presentable for the game after driving the park's dusty roads.

Taking her hygiene kit and fresh clothes, Hunter walked into the truck stop to pay for a shower and wait her turn. It didn't surprise her that slot machines were everywhere inside the truck stop, so she smiled and placed a ten-dollar bill into a machine to play. She drank a Gatorade bottle while waiting, and when her number was called, she hit the payout button on the machine and walked into the shower facility. Her ten-dollar bill had grown to twenty-five, more than enough to pay for the shower and Gatorade. She smiled as she tucked the slip into her hygiene bag and entered the shower.

Forty-five minutes later, she emerged from the bathroom looking presentable, cashed out her winnings, and decided on a ride through the strip before heading to the arena for the game. The traffic moved slowly, allowing Hunter to observe the diversity of people on the strip. There were throngs of tourists walking from one venue to another and gatherings of young people her mother would call modern-day hippies who were surrounded by clouds of smoke from the marijuana they were smoking. Hunter smiled at them. If she parked too close, she was sure to get a contact high from the malodorous smoke drifting toward her.

People on a zip line flew above her on her journey down the strip as she passed the Eiffel Tower and row after row of beautiful hotels and casinos. She wondered about the millions spent, earned, and paid out on the strip daily. Her short stay in front of a slot machine showed Hunter how easily it could be to become hooked on the search for immediate gratification. She wondered how many lives were destroyed by the variety of addictions so readily available in Sin City.

When she reached the turn for the highway that would take her to the arena, she welcomed the faster speed and the slightly cooler wind as she rode.

CHAPTER FOUR

Hunter was nervous when she pulled into the lot at the Michelob Ultra arena. The moment she had waited so long for was about to arrive, and she was anxious about her interaction with Carson. She wouldn't blame Carson if she turned her away, considering how Hunter had broken off their relationship, but she hoped for at least a lukewarm reception. Hunter had paid dearly for her behavior and wanted a clean slate in order to start fresh. Mending things with Carson was a big first step.

After parking her bike, Hunter secured her helmet and walked toward the ticket office to claim her pre-ordered ticket. She had arrived early, hoping to watch Carson's team warm up before the game. Hunter wasn't sure how she would approach Carson and would let that reunion wait until after the game. The office was busy as fans filed into the arena. Hunter picked up her ticket and walked inside to find her seat. She had purchased a spot close to the players' bench to allow for an opportunity to communicate with Carson after the game.

Hunter was surprised when her seat was three rows behind the players. A few of Carson's teammates were already on the floor stretching when she took her seat. Her heart was hammering in her chest when Hunter saw Carson and a teammate walking out of the tunnel toward the court, talking animatedly. Carson was even more beautiful than she remembered. Her blonde hair was still curly and just below shoulder length, but she knew Carson would pull it into a small ponytail before she hit the floor. When they arrived at the bench, Carson looked up, and her deep blue eyes locked onto Hunter.

Hunter watched as Carson's hand flew to her chest, and her teammate asked if she was okay. Carson did something that Hunter would never have expected in her wildest dreams. Carson parted the chairs and climbed over the railing, rushing to meet her. Carson enveloped her in a powerful hug, and Hunter could tell that Carson was crying. When she pulled away from the hug, she wiped her face.

"Hey, you."

Hunter's knees felt weak. "I hope it's okay for me to be here. I wanted to have a chance to talk with you afterward if you're up for that. Maybe over coffee or something stronger?"

Carson grabbed her for another hug. "Of course, it's okay for you to be here. I hoped one day we would meet again. Wait for me here after the game, okay?"

"I will." Hunter finally smiled.

"It's so good to see you. You look terrific," Carson said.

"Thanks. You look beautiful, and I can't wait to see you play."

"I'd better get back down there. Promise you won't leave?"

"I promise," Hunter replied. She settled back in her seat, wearing a big smile from the reception Carson had given her. *I did not expect that.*

†

When Carson returned to the court, she was approached by an older woman whom Hunter recognized as the head coach. She spoke to Carson briefly, nodded, and looked back in Hunter's direction. Carson nodded again and began a shooting drill. Hunter found she couldn't pull her eyes off Carson. Watching her warm up brought back so many memories of the short time they had played together. They had been rivals in high school, but their attraction instantly sparked when they got to college, and they soon became lovers. They had only been together a few months before Hunter's world was turned upside down. That painful memory made her heart ache from loss. She hadn't noticed that the arena had filled rapidly, and the crowd booed when the team from Chicago took the court. Hunter glanced at the opposite end of the court and briefly watched their opponents. She knew it would be a hard-fought game, but she was confident Carson's team would win.

The teams returned to the locker room before the start of the game, and Hunter purchased a soft drink from a vendor and settled in for the contest. Las Vegas won the opening jump and never looked back, sinking the first ten shots they took. Carson's laser focus on the game enabled her to find open players for easy baskets as the defense shifted to keep her away from the three-point line. Hunter knew that, eventually, the opponents would have to drop back on defense, and then Carson would light them up. She had witnessed it on many occasions and felt proud of her friend. Carson hooked up with a power forward for some easy baskets, and the defense shifted. Hunter looked at the program and learned the player was Michelle Thomas from Oregon. *A tall drink of water at six foot five, and not hard on the eyes either.* Hunter found herself chuckling at the thought. She was attractive, though. Hunter wouldn't deny that. The woman had some moves, too. She seemed to be Carson's favorite target as she quickly threaded passes through the defense. By halftime, they had pulled in front by ten points. Carson smiled as she walked past on her way to the locker room. Carson wasn't the only one smiling. Michelle looked in her direction and flashed a brilliant smile. *Did I imagine that?*

Hunter took advantage of the break to go to the restroom and stop at concessions. The aroma of the soft pretzels was too tempting to resist. Her mouth watered in anticipation as the vendor handed her the treat. She hadn't thought she was hungry until she took the first bite and considered returning for another. Lunch had been long ago, and she had been too nervous to eat before coming to the arena. Maybe she and Carson would go for a late dinner after the game.

Carson's shooting caught fire in the second half as she drained shot after shot beyond the arc. The player guarding her was obviously frustrated by her inability to stop Carson from scoring, and Hunter felt sorry for her momentarily until she gave Carson a hard shove, sending her flying across the court. The crowd roared in protest, and Thomas stormed across the court and rushed at the offender. A cooler-headed teammate caught her before she could light into the defender. The referee issued a flagrant technical foul as another player helped Carson to her feet. Carson winked at the player, walking to the foul line to shoot free throws. Hunter laughed. That was so vintage Carson. She drained both shots and inbounded the ball to Thomas. Thomas passed the ball back to her, and Carson launched a long three. The crowd erupted as the quarter ended, and they were up by twenty.

Carson was rested for most of the fourth quarter but entered to score another five points, which Hunter later found to be her season-high of thirty-five points. Carson shot Hunter a thumbs-up when the game ended and made her way to the tunnel. She was surrounded by young girls who wanted her autograph, and Carson took time for each of them.

Hunter rested back in her seat while she waited for Carson. The crowd thinned out, and Hunter watched the staff collect the towels and water containers left on the bench.

†

Carson felt an arm around her shoulder as Michelle caught up with her. "Great game tonight. I don't know who she is, but you should ensure she gets tickets to every game."

"She's an old friend from college. We played together briefly."

"Cute. Was there more than basketball going on?"

"Yes, but that's a long and tragic story. I haven't seen Hunter in five years and had no idea she would show up tonight."

"Hunter? As in Hunter James?" Michelle asked.

39

"Yes," Carson answered.

"I know she disappeared, but she had a promising future in the game."

Carson nodded with a frown. "We hoped we'd get drafted together after college."

"Cool. Have fun catching up. I'll see you tomorrow at practice." Michelle jogged ahead into the locker room.

When Carson entered, the coach tossed her the game ball. "Great game tonight. It's a season high for you."

"Thanks, Coach. Hey, guys, can I ask a favor? I have a special friend at the game tonight. Would you mind signing the ball so I can gift it to her?"

"She must be special if you're giving away your first game ball," one of the players teased.

Carson felt herself blush. "She is special, and her college career was cut short. She was a great player back in our day."

Thomas was the first to reach for the ball. "I do love being first," she teased.

After everyone signed the ball, Carson headed for a shower, then dressed in jeans and a pullover. She picked up the ball and left the locker room. Hunter was still in her seat, and when she looked up, Carson tossed her the ball.

"What's this?"

"My first game ball, and I had the team sign it for you," Carson said.

"I can't take your first game ball," Hunter said, offering it back to Carson.

"I insist," Carson said. "Come on. Let's get out of here. I'm hungry."

Hunter tucked the ball under her arm and followed Carson from the building through the player's entrance. They walked to a beautiful Land Rover.

"Sweet ride. Can you drop me around front?"

"Sure. Hop in."

Hunter climbed into the passenger seat.

Carson chuckled when she pulled to the front of the building, and Hunter pointed to her bike. "Oh my gosh. You still have your Indian."

"Yeah. Mom kept her when I went away."

"That's awesome. Are you up for some breakfast?"

"I can always eat breakfast," Hunter answered.

"Follow me then."

Hunter nodded and stored the ball inside the trailer before retrieving her helmet and mounting her bike. She started the motor, nodded to Carson, and pulled forward to follow her. It had still been light outside when Hunter arrived at the arena, but now that complete darkness had fallen, the city's lights glittered against the sky. Hunter was sure the skyline could be seen miles away as she followed Carson. Hunter followed and when Carson pulled into an all-night diner, Hunter parked beside her.

"Best breakfast in the city," Carson said.

They were led to a booth, and after placing their orders, Carson looked at Hunter. "I am so glad you came tonight."

"I stayed with Mom a few days after I was released, but I decided to spend some time traveling to figure my life out. I wanted my first destination to be visiting you. I realized all too late how much of an ass I was to you, and I wanted to apologize for mistreating you."

"Oh, Hunter," Carson reached to stroke down her face. "Lilly was your world, and when you lost her, your life was in total chaos. I can never begin to realize the devastation you felt when that happened. You have nothing to apologize for. My life has been good. I found another great woman, and we got married. Unfortunately, Stacy plays in Seattle, but we've made it work. She'll be home on a break next weekend. I hope you'll consider staying to meet her."

"I'd like that. I'm glad you found each other. You deserved better than I could give you."

When the food arrived, Carson said, "Dig in."

"This is a ton of food," Hunter said, looking at the plate Carson had ordered for her.

"Where are you staying?"

"I've been camping in parks on my bike," Hunter said.

"Well, you're coming home with me. I have two bedrooms and won't sleep well knowing you are in a tent somewhere."

"It's not all that bad."

"Nonsense. You know you can't win an argument with me."

"Never could." Hunter grinned and took a bite of pancakes. "It won't cause any problems?"

"Stacy's not the jealous type. She's heard me talk of you and knows a little about you. Not the whole story, but that we were together for a while in college." Carson took a sip of juice. "Something weird happened tonight, though."

"Besides me showing up out of the blue?" Hunter asked.

Carson nodded. "Coach recognized you and wanted me to invite you to watch practice tomorrow if you're game. She never allows visitors, which is odd."

"I'd like to watch you practice."

"She might offer you season tickets. I scored my season high tonight, and she saw us together before the game and put two and two together."

"Does that make me your lucky charm?" Hunter smiled at Carson.

"I guess it does. You always had a way of bringing out the best in me."

Hunter blushed. "You're a fantastic player. You always have been. I noticed you and Thomas have a lot of chemistry on the court. She played awesome tonight, too."

Carson smiled. "She thinks you're cute."

"What?"

"You heard me. Michelle said you are cute. Would you like to meet her?"

"She's not hard on the eyes either. So, yeah, I would."

"Dinner tomorrow night? Michelle thinks she's a pit master. I have to admit, she cooks a mean steak."

"I never pass on steak."

"She'll be on cloud nine. I'll text her in the morning. Practice isn't until three, so she'll have time to shop."

"Digesting this breakfast will take all night, but it's terrific."

"I like to come here after games to do some carb loading." Carson cut a bite of ham. "So, tell me more about this adventure you have planned."

"I was able to expunge my record as part of my prerelease, so I don't have that hanging over my head. I need to decide what the rest of my life will look like. Mom hopes I'll go back and finish college. She was the one who suggested I do some traveling to learn to enjoy freedom again and sort out my future." Hunter sipped her coffee. "Her boyfriend loaned me his motorcycle trailer and camping equipment. So, I thought I would ride until I found a spot to stay a few days and do some heavy soul-searching. I spent a few days at Fire Valley and visited the Hoover Dam. I think Utah will be my next destination."

"I've done some exploring there. It will take you months to see everything it has to offer."

"I'm in no rush. I saved up some money and have enough to keep me going for six months without tapping into my college fund money."

"Do you think college is in your future?"

"Honestly, I don't know. I worked on an electronics project and was quite good at it. Maybe a technical school for some advanced training. I'm not sure about diving back into college just yet."

"Are you interested in playing again?"

Hunter laughed. "I'd be the oldest freshman in history to play."

"Not college ball. Professionally. The league is expanding and adding three more teams next year."

Hunter hadn't considered that as an option. "What is the likelihood of getting drafted after not playing college ball?"

"The league drafts international players who did not play in college every year."

"Yeah, but they've been playing on professional teams in their home country."

"That's also true, but you must think of this. Every player coming out of college that gets drafted doesn't make a roster. It's a big jump from college to professional ball, and some kids don't have the makeup for it. Undrafted or interested players can be invited to training camps and, if they perform well, can make a roster. With a minimum of thirty-six new players needed for the new teams, it could be a great opportunity for you."

"It is something new to consider."

"You look like you're still in great shape."

"I can still hoop, but not sure about being competitive. I still love the sport."

The waitress came to check on them, and when Carson handed her a credit card for the check, she looked at Hunter. "It's getting late. Let's go home and get settled. We'll have plenty of time to catch up this week."

"Thank you, Carson."

"For what?"

"Making me feel welcome even after the way I treated you. And for a fantastic meal."

Carson reached over and covered her hand. "You will always be a special person in my life. My hope for you is that you will break out of this heartbreak hell you're stuck in and have a happy life. Lilly would want you to be happy."

"I hadn't thought of it like that, but you're right. I must move beyond my past and start living for myself. The guilt is still a heavy burden, but I'm trying to process it."

"I am and will always be here for you. What happened was beyond tragic. I'm sorry it happened to your family."

Hunter cringed at Carson's vow to always be there for her. Those were the exact words she had spoken to Lilly, but she failed to live up to them. Luckily, Carson missed her pained expression as she leaned down to sign the credit card slip.

"I'm not far from here. There is room in the garage for your bike, so pull in beside me," Carson said as she slid out of the booth.

†

Carson gave her a condo tour and got her settled into the guest room for the night. "I usually sleep in a bit after a game. If you're still an early riser, there is coffee and food for breakfast in the kitchen. Make yourself at home."

"I'll try to be quiet if I wake up early," Hunter replied.

Carson pulled her into a hug. "I'm so glad you're here. I'll see you in the morning."

"Rest well," Hunter replied as Carson closed the door.

✝

Hunter changed into a T-shirt and shorts to sleep in. The curtains were open in the bedroom, and she gazed at the neon skyline of Vegas. Fireworks filled the night sky, making Hunter question if she was missing a holiday, but she soon learned this was a regular event for Vegas. When she turned away from the window, she was surprised it was almost two. She yawned and climbed between the cool sheets. "Much better than a sleeping bag on the ground."

Her mind returned to the conversation with Carson. Heartbreak hell was a good name for the torture she had put herself through for the past five years. "Time to change," she spoke into the quiet room.

CHAPTER FIVE

The sunshine pouring through the window woke Hunter. She was surprised to have slept until eight as she crept from the bed and relieved her bladder. When she opened the bedroom door, the condo was quiet. Hunter made a cup of coffee and walked onto the balcony to enjoy the morning sun. She finished her coffee and relaxed when she heard the sliding door open, and Carson walked out.

"Good morning. I'm making coffee. Do you want another?"

"Sure." Hunter handed Carson the empty cup. "Did you sleep well?"

"I did. How about you?"

"Much better than a tent." Hunter smiled.

"I'll be right back," Carson said, stepping inside.

"It's a beautiful morning."

"It will heat up quickly," Carson said. "The heat here is almost unbearable sometimes. Much different than California."

Hunter nodded. "No ocean breeze to cool things off."

"You must stay hydrated here. The results are harsh if you don't," Carson warned.

"I've already been through a case of bottled water," Hunter replied.

"I've invested in Dasani stock."

"I'll have to remember that."

Carson sat next to Hunter. "You said your mom had a boyfriend. What happened to your dad?"

"He couldn't deal with everything that happened. Turned into an alcoholic and left Mom to deal on her own. She finally got divorce papers from him from Texas. Jim, her new boyfriend, is a vast improvement; they are so cute together. He's the new fire chief in town. He dotes on her, and I think he will propose soon. They will retire in a few years, and I can see them traveling a lot."

"That's good to hear she's found someone who treats her well."

"Yeah. Jim's a great guy."

"I sent Michelle a text, and she's excited to cook for us tonight."

"I look forward to that. I find it hard to believe that someone with her looks is single."

"We've tried to hook her up with others, and she's never found someone who she thought was right for her. She's been good about going on the dates, but it's been a one-and-done every time."

"Kudos to a woman who knows exactly what she's looking for," Hunter said.

"Michelle refuses to settle, and I'm proud of her for that."

"You seem pretty close."

"We both came in as rookies and bonded quickly. We've been thick as thieves since. I think of her as a sister. Her family doesn't have much to do with her. They disagreed with her sexual orientation announcement in college. Her pastor father swore it was just a phase she would grow out of when she found a good Christian man." Carson scoffed. "It was devastating to her, but she's such a happy person. She moved on quickly. The team is her family, and she would do anything for any of us."

"I noticed she was about to beat the brakes off the player that dropped you last night."

"She's very protective of her team and won't tolerate anyone getting bullied. Did you see the shot she blocked right into her face a few minutes after that?"

"Not a coincidence, huh?"

Carson grinned. "Uh, no. She would normally have blocked it to one of us, but she wanted to send a message. I think Harvey got it loud and clear."

"I'd say so, too, from the blood on her jersey," Hunter chuckled. "There's no room for that bullshit on the court. You were eating her for lunch, and she should have checked out and gotten her shit together versus landing a cheap shot."

"That's still an issue on the pro level. A lot of fans want to see aggressive play. I hate it, especially when someone is injured because of it."

"Does the league issue fines for that type of behavior?"

"On occasion, but not often enough, in my opinion."

"That's sad, but I'm glad you have Michelle on your side. I'd hate to cross her."

"Me too. Michelle could do some damage if she were that kind of player. She's aggressive, but it's always clean play."

"Will we go for dinner after practice? How do I need to dress?"

"Casual shorts and a light shirt. We will probably eat out on Michelle's deck unless it's still scorching outside."

"I can do that," Hunter said. "Mom wouldn't let me buy all my clothes from a thrift shop."

"Hey, you can find some great bargains there," Carson agreed.

"I tried convincing her, but she still insisted on a few new outfits."

Carson drained her coffee. "Since we slept through breakfast, are you good with brunch? Some grilled ham and cheese sandwiches, chips, and fruit?"

"I'm all in. What can I do?"

"Keep me company. It won't take long to throw it together. Then we can shower and head to practice.

"I'll need time to shave," Hunter joked. "It's been a few days."

Carson laughed and pulled the door open. "We have plenty of time for you to clean up." Carson reached for her cup. "Have you grown taller? Something looks different."

"Nope. Still a shade over six. I've put on a few pounds of muscle since college."

"You look great, and you sure filled out those jeans nicely last night."

Hunter blushed. "Kind of you to notice."

"Oh, those weren't my words. Michelle said she followed out behind us last night and enjoyed the view. She said your smile wasn't your best asset."

"You're kidding me, right?"

"I swear I'm telling the truth. You have definitely caught Michelle's eye. She would be a fabulous catch for anyone, but you two could hit it off well."

"Playing a matchmaker?"

"Can you blame me for trying to bring my two best friends together?"

Hunter felt it was time to change subjects. She was excited to get to know Michelle better but still insecure about dating. Especially someone Carson thought of so highly. "Do you have another game this week?"

"Yes, Friday night. Then we are off for the weekend, just in time for Stacy to come home. She plays Thursday night, so she'll be here for Friday's game."

"I look forward to meeting her."

"Stacy's excited to meet you, too."

"Would it be better if I get a hotel this weekend since you have limited time together?"

"Hell no. Don't be ridiculous," Carson said. "Stacy wants us to spend time with you."

Carson plated the sandwiches and cut them in half. "Will you grab the fruit bowl from the fridge?" After walking to the pantry for chips, Carson picked up two forks and napkins. "Grab two bottles of water, too, please."

Hunter carried the fruit and water to the table. She smiled when Carson placed the bag of chips on the table.

"Still a Fritos kid, huh?"

"I haven't found anything better with sandwiches," Carson said, smiling.

"You will be pleased to know that I now add them and shredded cheese to my chili," Hunter said.

"That sounds terrific. I will have to try that."

"Pretty hard to beat." Hunter took a bite of the sandwich. "You still grill a mean sandwich."

"It's my favorite on the weekends. I give myself this pleasure as a reward for eating healthy during the week."

"Let's enjoy every bite of them then," Hunter said, crunching on a corn chip. "Did you buy stock in these too?"

"No, but that's not a bad idea."

"Is this your permanent home?"

"At least for now. Stacy has a small apartment in Seattle, but we call this home."

"Do you think she will be traded to Vegas?"

"That's a hard call. Our starting five is pretty solid. You never know what the future might bring, though. Especially once the league expands. It may open up an opportunity for us to play together."

"Who's coming into the league you are interested in?"

"Golden State and Toronto will be first. I wouldn't mind being back in California. Toronto could be interesting, too."

"I'm glad to hear the league is growing. There is room for many more teams."

"I think this is a very positive move, and as the game's popularity grows, the league will also. We are drawing more media attention and attendance than most of the NBA teams."

"The game has come a long way." Hunter ate the last bite.

"Did you get enough to eat?"

Hunter nodded. "I'm saving room for steak tonight." She looked at Carson. "Do you have an iron and board I can borrow? My clothes tend to get a bit wrinkled in my duffle."

"Bring me out what you plan to wear, and I'll do them while you shower and shave," Carson offered. "Starch?"

"Light, please," Hunter said.

"I need to press an outfit for tonight, too. I'll shower at the gym after practice."

"Thank you. Do you mind if I hit the shower?"

"No. If you want to save yours for the road, there are products in there. I think there's a fresh razor or two in the drawer."

"I'll be right back. Thanks for brunch." Hunter returned to the bedroom to search through her clothes. She decided on a pair of tan cargo shorts and a red pullover. Hunter carried them back to Carson. "Will this work?"

"That should look yummy on you. I'll put them on the bed when I'm done."

Hunter nodded and walked into the bathroom. Soap, shampoo, and conditioner were already in the shower. She opened a drawer and removed the razor. Hunter looked at the stubble on her legs. "Yeah, it's time for a shave."

Hunter was shaving her legs when she heard the bedroom door open. Carson placed the ironed clothes on the bed and left the room. She finished showering, and after drying her body, she applied some lotion and dried her hair. Hunter brushed her teeth and went to the bedroom to dress. She checked her appearance in the full-length mirror and thought she would be presentable. Hunter spritzed cologne on her neck and wrists. She looked at the bottle in her hand that she had found in her bathroom at home. "Ah, nice to smell good again."

"I'll second that," Carson said.

Hunter turned to find Carson leaning against the bedroom floor.

"That scent always smells so good on you."

"Thanks."

53

"I almost feel sorry for Michelle."

"What?"

"She's going to get one whiff of you and be a goner."

Hunter shook her head. "You are too funny."

"Give yourself some credit. You are beautiful, and that scent drives lesbians wild. It certainly drove me crazy when we first met."

"You never told me that."

Carson shrugged. "A girl's entitled to a few secrets. You look great, but you might be a distraction at practice."

"I'll do my best to make myself a wallflower," Hunter promised.

"No chance of that. Be warned. Michelle isn't the only single lesbian on the team. There could be some major flirting today."

"Noted," Hunter said. She slipped her wallet in her pocket. "Remind me to get my shades from my bike."

"Will do. Are you ready?"

"Right behind you," Hunter answered.

Carson picked up her bag and walked out through the garage. She started the car and AC while waiting for Hunter. Hunter slipped her shades onto her face.

"Holy fuck," Carson spoke aloud.

†

Carson pulled into the practice facility, walked inside, and showed Hunter around. She introduced her to the coach.

"Thanks for allowing me to watch practice," Hunter said.

"You're very welcome, but I must confess I have an ulterior motive. Would you mind talking with me a bit after practice?"

"Sure," Hunter replied.

"I'll see you later then."

Carson walked her into the gym and got her settled on a small set of bleachers. "I've got to get taped, but I'll see you soon."

Hunter pulled out her phone and scrolled through the messages from her mom. When the players began entering the gym, she put the phone away to watch them stretch. Carson and Michelle came in together, and both smiled at her.

Hunter smiled and nodded back at them. She noticed some of the players were male and dressed in red instead of black, and she assumed they were the scout team that scrimmaged against Carson's team. As the team warmed up, the players in black uniforms fed balls to shooters around the court and mocked a defender trying to alter the shots.

The coach called them into a huddle when they warmed up and explained the new plays they would add for the next game. "Dallas may be short-handed by injuries, but they will be a force to be reckoned with from the outside. The interior play is hampered by their bigs being out, so that's where we will focus our offense. We outsize them and should control the boards with ease. They will probably add a third guard, so if we tighten up our perimeter defense, we will be successful."

She looked around the group. "Let's run through the new plays a few times before we go live. Any questions?" When no one needed clarification, she said, "Group one on this end, and group two on the far end."

Carson dribbled the ball from half court and called out 162 as her teammates went into action. "That's it, Thomas. Hold that screen until Carson or Joy rub off the guards and pivot to the goal. Look for a pass as you cut, and if it's not there, crash the boards for a short-range jumper. Again."

Hunter watched as they ran through each of the new plays several times. "Very good. Are you ready to go live?"

"Yes, coach," they all called out.

"Scout team, let's go. Make them work."

Hunter watched as they skillfully ran the new plays. She moved with the passes and flinched when a pass was tipped or didn't work to perfection.

"Carson," Coach barked. "If the rebound goes long or the pass is tipped, don't hesitate to put up a three if you're open. We won't force a shot if it's not there."

"Got it, Coach," Carson answered.

They ran a few more plays, and when the man guarding Michelle tripped over a screen, she was wide open under the basket when Carson fed her the ball. She caught it and made an easy lay-in.

"Thomas."

"Yes, Coach."

"If you find yourself that damned wide open in the game, I want you to slam that ball home. I know you are aching to dunk, and it drives the fans crazy."

"Yes, Coach." Michelle grinned.

When she found herself open again a few plays later, Michelle slammed the ball through the goal with enough force to shake the backboard.

"That's what I'm talking about." Coach clapped. "Hell, yes. Take a water break. Then we'll do a ten-minute full court and a thirty-minute shoot-around."

Hunter smiled at Carson. "Coach doesn't hold back, does she?"

"This is mild. She's going easy on us today," Carson replied.

"Okay, B Team up first. I want to see you run the new plays first."

Carson and her teammates sat on the sidelines and cheered for the players. The plays and passes weren't as crisp as Team A, but they successfully ran them. After five minutes, Coach barked out, "Team A."

"Communicate on the screens, Joy," Coach called out.

Carson dropped a three-ball in transition and fed Michelle, and the other bigs precision passes just beyond the defender's reach. "Good job!"

Carson stole the ball from the scout team and placed a lob pass perfectly for Michelle to dunk.

"Fantastic. After thirty minutes, I must meet the group at half-court for an announcement."

Carson worked on her short-range jumper and three-point shots before practicing her free throws. Hunter watched as Michelle concentrated on her footwork and gained position on one of the male players. She noticed she tended to force up a contested shot when she could take one step back for a short jumper. It had been one of Hunter's favorite shots, but she was envious of Michelle's ability to dunk. *What a difference three inches makes.* She grinned at the thought.

After the shoot-around finished, Coach hollered, "Huddle up." She waited until everyone stood around the center court logo and then walked to the middle of the circle.

"Today, I have some fantastic news to share with you." She smiled at one of the scout team players. "Kelsey, will you join me?"

Hunter watched a young woman stand beside Coach. "Today, Kelsey hangs up her scout team uniform."

"Awww," came a course from the group.

Coach held up her hand. "This is a happy occasion. Kelsey has just been called up on a two-month waiver to replace a player in Los Angeles. Let's all give her a big hand."

The team erupted in congratulations.

"The next time we see this amazing young woman, she will be playing against us." Coach paused. "Three weeks from now, we will travel to LA. Good luck to you for every game except when we play you," Coach joked.

"Thanks, everyone. I appreciate the opportunity to learn from the best, and I will give this shot everything I have."

"Safe travels and we'll see you soon. Hit the showers, and I'll see you at four tomorrow."

Hunter watched as the players hugged Kelsey and wished her luck before heading into the locker room.

When the gym was empty except for the coach and herself, Hunter smiled as she approached. "That was a great send off."

The coach eased down beside Hunter. "She's worked hard and deserves a spot to play."

"I wish her well," Hunter said.

"You probably don't remember seeing me at any of your high school or college games, but I've had my eye on you for many years. I was disappointed when you left the college game. I had high hopes of drafting you and Carson."

Hunter's eyes grew wide. "I never knew that. Thank you for being so interested. Carson is a great player."

"You are, too. You may think you're done with basketball, but the game is still in you. Last night and again today, I watched you shift in your seat to the plays and saw the fire of competition in your eyes. I know you are here to visit Carson, and I don't know your plans, but I'd like to make you an offer. I need a post player for three months to replace Kelsey for the rest of the season. The pay isn't that great, but it will get you into great shape. The league is expanding, and more players will be needed to join professional teams. If you have the fire and want to make a team, I will gladly invite you to our training camp next spring."

Hunter sat in silent shock.

"I don't know why you left the game, and it doesn't matter. You are too talented not to be allowed to make a roster somewhere."

"Thanks for your vote of confidence, Coach. What does the position require?"

"Working out with the team on an almost daily basis. Traveling with the team to assist with warm-ups and pregame practices."

"I planned to travel these next few months to determine where I am going in life, but that can be put on the back burner. I'm traveling on my motorcycle, so I don't have any equipment or workout gear."

"You will have seven days of practice uniforms, three pairs of shoes, and game-day apparel provided by the team. All I need is a commitment from you. If you need a place to stay, my wife and I have a rent-free pool apartment that can be yours. We can also help you find part-time employment if you need it. You will travel, eat with the team on the road, and pregame meals for home games."

Coach placed her hand on Hunter's shoulder. "After the season, you can continue your journey or work out with the team in the off-season and prepare for training camp. Some choose to play international ball, but most stay and work out a few days a week to keep in shape. You have access to all the facilities the team offers."

"I'd be a fool to pass up this offer," Hunter said.

"You're no fool. Be here at one tomorrow, and we can do the paperwork and get you equipped to start work. Should I tell my wife we will have a young'in in the house again? Our daughter is in college back east."

"Can I get back to you after talking with Carson? I don't want to cramp her style when Stacy visits."

"You can move into the pool apartment when Stacy is in town if that makes you feel better. Our door is always open for you."

"Thank you for the opportunity. I promise I will work the team hard."

"Fantastic. I'll see you tomorrow at one, then?" Coach offered her hand to seal the deal.

"Yes, ma'am, you will. Thanks again."

Hunter's heart was pounding as she watched Coach leave the gym. She couldn't believe what had just transpired. Hunter was studying the team roster when Carson walked into the gym. She looked up with tears in her eyes.

"Pinch me." She jumped to her feet.

Carson pinched her arm. "What's going on?"

"Coach just hired me to join the scout team to replace Kelsey. She said she'd also invite me to her training camp next spring."

"Oh, Hunter. That's fabulous news." Carson hugged her tightly.

"She even offered me a place to stay."

"What? No way. You're staying with me," Carson insisted.

"I don't want to cramp your space when Stacy visits, but I can use the pool apartment when she's home."

"Okay, but not this weekend. You two need to get to know one another. When do you start?"

"I have to be here at one tomorrow to fill out paperwork and get geared up."

"I can drop you off, and you can ride home with me after practice," Carson offered.

"I still can't believe this," Hunter said.

"Come on. We must celebrate. Michelle is going to be so stoked. Kelsey was her primary defender."

"Coach told me that she expects me to push her hard."

"Michelle will love that. She dominates Kelsey and needs a challenge."

They walked out and drove to Michelle's desert home.

CHAPTER SIX

Hunter could smell the smoke from the grill when she stepped out of Carson's car. Carson led them through a side gate into the backyard, and Hunter gasped when she saw the view.

"That is a gorgeous view."

"Yeah, much different from living in town," Carson said.

Michelle stepped out the back door and saw them approaching. "Hey. I didn't hear you come up. Welcome, Hunter."

"She was just admiring the view from your backyard."

"Not a neon light in sight," Michelle said.

"Why don't you show Hunter around? Then we need to crack open a cold one. We got celebrating to do tonight."

"I'm always up for that. Come on in," Michelle told Hunter. "Grab some cold ones, and we'll be right back."

Michelle gave Hunter a tour of her home. "It's not flashy or elegant, but it's home. I'm a country girl at heart, and the city sucks the life out of me too much to live there."

"This is wonderful," Hunter said. "It fits you. I didn't have you pegged for a condo person."

Michelle smiled. "I like my space and the freedom to walk out into fresh air, not exhaust fumes from the traffic."

"The view is fantastic. Have you explored much in the area?"

"Every chance I get, I hop in my Jeep and visit someplace new. I can reach a lot of beautiful spots tourists can't access. I'd gladly share some of them if you plan to stay for a while."

"I'd like that."

"You look great today, and you smell delicious, too," Michelle said, blushing at her boldness.

Hunter felt mischievous. "I heard you enjoyed the rear view, too," Hunter teased.

"I'm going to strangle Carson for sharing that with you."

"Please don't. Carson's going to be my landlord for a while."

"What?" Michelle asked, looking confused.

"Let's go have that beer, and I'll tell you about my conversation with Coach today."

"You've got my attention. This way, please," she guided Hunter back down the hall.

Carson was sitting at the table when they arrived. She handed them a beer and raised hers. "Congratulations to the newest member of our scout team."

"For reals?" Michelle cried out.

Hunter nodded and smiled. "For reals, I start tomorrow, and you are my assignment." Hunter grinned. "Be prepared to work hard."

"I look forward to that. I think." Michelle took a sip of her beer. She stepped forward and hugged Hunter.

It was Hunter's turn to blush. She enjoyed the feel of Michelle's arms around her and gasped softly.

Carson didn't miss the interaction but remained silent. Hunter was grateful for that.

"Is anyone hungry? I can go ahead and put the steaks on. How do you like yours, Hunter? Carson likes her hockey pucks."

"Medium rare for me, please."

"I do not like hockey pucks," Carson pouted.

"When we'd go out to eat, she would send her steak back at least twice to be cooked more," Hunter teased.

"I finally just started ordering chicken," Carson laughed.

"You did, didn't you?" Hunter said.

"That way, I could eat with you," Carson replied.

"Good point. I'd better go ahead and start yours. I've got a tossed salad chilling and some macaroni salad. I'm grilling corn with the steaks."

"That all sounds delicious," Hunter said. She watched Michelle remove a platter of meat. "I thought you were cooking steaks. Those look more like roasts."

"That's a good one. I'll send you home with leftovers if you can't finish."

"We ate brunch to save room for tonight. Go for it, Hot Shot," Carson told Hunter.

"I love a good challenge," Hunter replied, wiggling her eyebrows.

"Just save room for dessert. I made brownies for brownie Sundays."

"Oh, hell yes," Carson said. "You can go ahead and make my steak to go."

"Nope, you have to eat at least half," Michelle said.

"Half?" Carson pouted.

"Yes, half."

"That's cruel."

"Will you get the door and our beer and join me outside?" she asked Hunter.

"I need to use the restroom before I join you," Carson said.

†

Hunter opened the door and then followed Michelle out to the deck. She placed the steaks beside the grill and opened the lid, placing Carson's steak to cook and adding three ears of corn.

When Michelle turned around, she smiled. "I am so happy you will be working with us."

"I'm excited. It may open a possibility for me to attend training camp next spring and maybe make a roster somewhere."

"I hope it will be here with us," Michelle said.

"That would be awesome. That's a long way away right now. I've got work to do to get back into playing shape."

"We will help you with that," Michelle stated.

†

Hunter found herself staring into Michelle's unusual light-gray eyes. She hadn't noticed that her short-cropped hair had the same tint to it or if it was natural or light hair frosting. *I'd like to run my hands through it, though. Whoa, where did that come from?* Hunter felt a smile creep into her lips at the thought. She knew she needed to divert her thoughts from Michelle and decided to return to basketball.

"What are the team's workout schedules beyond the court?"

"We lift weights three times a week when we aren't traveling. Nothing weighty, mostly lower body. I try to run a few extra miles whenever possible to build my stamina."

"I think that will be my biggest challenge, to increase my stamina and upper body strength."

Carson smiled. "We can get you up to speed between the three of us. You look like you've stayed in decent shape."

"Thanks. I'd appreciate any advice you can give me."

"We can start tomorrow after practice. Maybe get some extra miles in," Michelle suggested.

"I can't tomorrow. I've got an appointment," Carson said.

"You and me then. I'll drop you at home afterward," Michelle suggested.

Hunter felt her smile broaden. "That would be great. Thank you."

"My appointment won't take long. What if I brought some Chinese home for dinner?" Carson recommended.

"You know I love Chinese," Michelle replied.

"Me, too," Hunter added.

"It's a date then," Carson grinned at Hunter.

Michelle stood and placed the remaining steaks on the grill. "Are you comfortable out here, or do you want to eat inside?"

"It's cooled off, and I'd hate to miss that beautiful sunset," Carson said, pointing to the west.

"That works for me," Hunter said. "What can I help with?"

"You can bring our plates, utensils, and napkins. Also, bring out the salads if you would. It won't take these steaks much longer."

†

Carson held the door for Hunter. "What do you think of Michelle?"

Hunter felt a blush rise to her cheeks. "She seems pretty amazing, and I get lost in those eyes."

"They are gorgeous." Carson chuckled. "A girl could do much worse than Michelle."

"I still find it hard to believe she's single."

"I told you she was selective but seems very interested in you. Roll with it and see what happens."

Hunter shook her head. "She could do much better than me."

"Will you stop that shit? You both deserve someone great. You would make a very handsome couple and turn many heads." Carson let out a giggle. "Hearts would be broken to see the two of you together."

"You are so full of crap, but I love you anyway," Hunter said.

"Come on then. Lighten up and give Michelle a chance to creep into that big heart of yours. You wouldn't be here tonight if she weren't interested."

Hunter nodded and followed Carson out to the deck.

Michelle looked up from the grill. "What do you want to drink? There is more beer, water, or sweet iced tea."

"You have sweet tea?" Hunter asked, cocking a brow. "You're from Oregon, right?"

"Ha! Yes, I am. I had a teammate in college from Georgia, and she got me hooked on sweet tea." Michelle smiled. "Don't knock it until you try it."

"I love it," Hunter said. "My father is from the South."

"Cool. Will you pour us a glass?" Michelle asked.

"Sure. Carson?"

"Why the hell not?"

"Glasses are to the left of the sink," Michelle said.

"I'll be right back."

†

"That's gorgeous," Hunter said, nodding toward the sunset.

"I never get tired of the sunsets here. It's even better to have good company to enjoy them with."

"Thanks for the invite. This meal is terrific. I'm trying my best to eat half of this steak," Hunter replied. "It's delicious. Who knew a power forward to cook so well?" she teased.

"I rather enjoy cooking," Michelle answered with a playful pout. "I do, however, tend to get a bit messy in the kitchen while I cook."

"I'd gladly clean up after a meal like this," Hunter praised.

"I've got this," Carson said. "I need to make room for dessert. You two relax, and I'll be done in a few."

"I've already placed to-go containers on the counter for you two. Please feel free to take salads along with your steaks."

"Lunch for tomorrow." Carson smiled.

Hunter watched Carson disappear inside and turned to find Michelle watching her.

"You still love her, don't you?" Michelle asked.

"I always will. Carson was my first real relationship, but I messed that up. I'm happy she's found Stacy."

"They are perfect together, and I think Carson thinks the same about you. She speaks very highly of you."

"She deserved better than how I treated her. That's the main reason for my visit. I hoped to make amends with her for my behavior."

"Did you?"

"Yes, I think so, and because of her, I'm getting another shot at a dream."

"I'm pretty sure that was Coach's doing. She remembered what kind of player you were. She's a good judge of talent," Michelle added. "Coach sees something in you, even if you don't."

"Thanks for the offer to help me get back into shape."

"I'm sure I will enjoy every minute of it."

"Just don't laugh if I pass out after running. It's been a while."

"I won't. I'll help you up and get you going again," Michelle smiled. "Now that you will be staying here a while, can I offer my guide services to show you around the area?"

"I'd appreciate that."

"We don't have practice on Saturday or Sunday next week. Coach is giving us a few days off. Maybe Saturday or both?"

"That would be good. I want to give Stacy and Carson some time together."

"Maybe we can explore and meet up with them for dinner?"

Hunter smiled. "That sounds like fun. Thank you."

"It will be my pleasure. So, how hard do I push you this week on workouts?"

"Until I beg you to stop," Hunter said. "Damn, I can't believe I said that."

Michelle's laughter filled the night. "That is the most aggressive answer I could have hoped for." She winked at Hunter, who was now blushing. "I promise to push you hard, but not over the edge. We travel to Dallas next week, and you need to be able to move."

"I'm looking forward to practice and seeing more games."

"The next few weeks will be crazy. We will travel from coast to coast with a home game in between."

"I guess I should look up the schedule," Hunter said. "I may have to buy more clothes since I've been traveling with the bare minimum."

"Let me know if I can help. I'm not a fashionista like Carson, but I can pass as decently dressed." Michelle chuckled.

"I can't afford designer clothing, but I think I'll be presentable."

"A few pairs of Chinos and shirts would be sufficient. A comfy pair of loafers, too. Something you can kick off on the long flights."

"That, I can handle. I've got a few decent pairs of jeans and shirts for traveling."

"Maybe we can make a shopping trip this week before practice. See if Carson wants to go with us," Michelle suggested.

"Go where?" Carson asked as she returned.

"On a shopping trip for a few outfits for Hunter," Michelle said.

"Girls, you know I love to shop," Carson teased. "I'll even offer to drive."

"What, you don't want to be seen in my Jeep?" Michelle teased.

"I'm afraid I might pull something climbing into it." Carson grinned. "I don't have Amazon genes like you two, remember?"

"Okay, shorty. You can drive. I call shotgun. I don't think I'll fit in the backseat."

"That's fine with me," Hunter replied.

"I also plan on kidnapping Hunter next weekend to go exploring. Maybe we can meet up with you and Stacy for dinner?" Michelle grinned at Carson.

"Just don't keep her all weekend. I want Hunter and Stacy to spend some time together. You are always welcome, too."

"I promise," Michelle agreed. "Who's ready for dessert?"

"I am," Carson admitted. She looked at Hunter.

"Me, too."

"I shall return," Michelle said and went inside.

"Are you having a good time?"

"Yes. I like Michelle."

"Good. You haven't stopped smiling since we got here."

"I think you make an excellent Cupid," Hunter stated.

Carson nodded. "I think so, too."

✝

"What a crazy but exciting day," Hunter said when they returned to Carson's condo. "If you don't mind, I'm going to call it a night and give Mom a call to share the good news."

"You go ahead. I need to call Stacy, too. I'll see you in the morning. Get some rest for your big day tomorrow."

"Thanks, Carson. I am so excited."

"I'm excited for you, my friend. You will be great."

✝

When Elizabeth answered the phone, Hunter said, "Mom, you won't believe what happened today."

For the next half hour, Hunter shared all of the details with her mom, and even speaking of them still sounded like a dream to her.

"Your decision to reconnect with Carson has led to an excellent opportunity for you. I am excited and proud of you for accepting the offer. I can't wait to tell Jim."

Hunter frowned. "Speaking of which. I need to find a way to get his trailer and equipment back to him since I won't need it in the future."

"Don't you worry about that. I'm sure Jim will gladly suggest a road trip to Vegas to pick it up, so keep me informed of your travel schedule. Maybe we can catch a game and win a few bucks there."

Hunter laughed. "I stopped at a truck stop for a shower before the game Saturday, put a ten in a machine, and cashed out at twenty-five dollars. I can see why the quest for immediate gratification can be so addicting."

"Have you visited a casino yet?"

"No, but we probably will this weekend when Stacy comes home for a visit."

"Are you doing okay for money? I can transfer money into your account," Elizabeth offered.

"I'm doing good, Mom, but thank you. I should start drawing a paycheck soon."

"Oh, honey. I am so happy for you. You sound excited."

"This is a dream-come-true opportunity I thought I had lost forever. I never thought I'd have a chance to walk onto a WNBA court. I won't be a player yet, but I'll have a chance to prove myself and hopefully make a team's roster."

"Did you mention earlier you are coming to California?"

"Yes, in two weeks on the twenty-third."

"Plan on seeing us there then," Elizabeth said. "I miss you, but I'm glad you are happy."

"I miss you. I look forward to seeing you both. I'll keep in touch while we're on the road. The next three weeks will be crazy, going from coast to coast."

"Get some rest then and enjoy your first day tomorrow. I am so proud of you, Hunter."

"Thanks, Mom. I love you. Talk soon."

†

Hunter took the time to unpack her clothing and selected a pair of shorts and a shirt to change into after practice to go shopping with Michelle. She would press them in the morning before heading to the practice facility. Just thinking about Michelle brought a smile to her face. *I hope I'm not overthinking things and rushing toward a heartache. Maybe she's just being nice to me because she's Carson's friend.* Hunter laughed at the outrageous thought. The way Michelle looked at her was much more than friendly. The interest was definitely there between them, and Hunter would see where it led.

CHAPTER SEVEN

When Carson entered the kitchen, Hunter was awake, sipping coffee and pressing her clothes. "Good morning. Do you need anything pressed for today while I have the iron out?"

"Good morning. No, I'm good for today." Carson poured a coffee and sat at the table to watch Hunter. "Excited about today?"

"Extremely," Hunter answered.

"I'm excited for you. Is there anything you want to have tonight from the Chinese place?"

Hunter nodded. "I'm good with most anything Chinese."

"I'll get a variety of items then. They have great Rangoon there. I know that is one of your favorites."

"I haven't had that in ages. Can I pitch in some money for dinner?"

"Nope, I've got this. Do you want some breakfast?"

"I thought I'd wait a bit and have an early lunch from our leftovers. I can cook you something."

"I'm not a big breakfast person during the week, but lunch around eleven sounds good. Did you have a good call with your mom?"

"Yeah. We talked for a half hour. She is almost as excited as me. When we return to town, Mom and Jim will ride here to catch a game and pick up Jim's trailer. I won't need it for a while."

"That's great. I would love to see your mom again. Maybe we can hit a casino while she's here."

Hunter chuckled. "That's exactly what she suggested. Do you go often?"

"Not really to gamble, but they have some great restaurants, and the shows are good, too."

"I'll look at our schedule and see what shows are in town and what we can plan." Hunter finished ironing and poured fresh coffee. "Any advice for my first practice today?"

"Work us hard. The more the practice squad pushes us, the better we play in games."

"I hope I can keep up."

"Don't forget to hydrate well so you don't cramp up. Plenty of Gatorade and water will be on the bench, so hit it every opportunity."

"Got it. Does the practice squad run plays, or is it free play from our side during scrimmages?"

"Freestyle, so we never know what you're coming with. Occasionally, Coach may ask you to run a particular play our opponents run to ensure we defend it well. We expect Dallas to attempt many perimeter shots since their interior play is nonexistent with the injuries they've had."

"That sounds doable," Hunter said.

"You will be just fine," Carson assured her. "Be prepared for some trash talk. Especially at practice."

"That goes both ways?" Hunter asked.

"Oh yeah. Get inside our heads and distract us." Carson grinned.

"I'm loving this already."

"It will be right up your alley, but it's only fair to warn you that Michelle can hold her own."

"Noted," Hunter said, carrying her outfit to her bedroom and packing a small bag before laying out an outfit to wear to the practice facility. Carson had her head buried inside the fridge when she returned to the kitchen. "Are you hungry already?"

"Yeah. We could eat, shower, and dress. If you get done with Coach quickly, maybe we can do some shooting to get you warmed up."

"I'd like that," Hunter replied. "I played recreationally, but it's not the same."

"Wanna bet you pick it right back up?"

"No. I'd hate to lose money on my first day back." Hunter chuckled. "Hand me the steaks to warm up, and you can serve the salads. I wish we had some of Michelle's sweet tea."

"We'll have to get her to teach us how to make it. I'm sure she would love that. Especially if you asked her." Carson winked.

"How can you eat a steak like this?" Hunter teased as she placed the steaks inside the microwave.

"I don't like it mooing at me," Carson said.

†

77

Carson leaned against the bedroom door. "Cologne for practice. Really?"

"It feels good to get back into old habits," Hunter said.

Carson shook her head with a smile. "Grab your bag, and let's roll, hotshot."

"Right behind you," Hunter said and whistled at Carson.

Carson turned to shoot her a look.

"Just practicing," Hunter laughed. "That is a mighty fine swing you have."

"Good grief. Let's go," Carson said, struggling to keep from laughing. "Please promise me you won't break out dad jokes."

Hunter screwed up her face. "I promise to do my best."

†

When they arrived at the practice facility, Carson pointed toward Coach's office. "I'm going to change into practice gear and meet you in the gym later."

"Thanks," Hunter said and stopped outside Coach's door. She lifted her hand and knocked.

"Come in," Coach called. Her eyes lit up when Hunter entered.

"I know I'm early. Is this a good time, or should I wait?"

"No. Please come on in. I'm glad you're early."

Hunter noticed a young woman sitting across from Coach. "This is Sandy, our locker room manager. She will be getting you outfitted today and will need your measurements.

"Waist and inseam, please." Sandy smiled.

"Thirty-inch waist and a thirty-four-inch inseam."

"Shirt size?"

"Extra large," Hunter answered. "Size nine shoes."

"Perfect. I will get your practice uniforms and game wear together in the locker room. You can meet me there once you are finished with Coach. Can I take your bag? You'll find it in locker fifteen."

"Thanks, Sandy." Hunter handed the bag to her.

"That was your college uniform number, wasn't it?" Coach asked.

"Yeah. Is that coincidence or an omen?" Hunter asked.

"Maybe a bit of both. Let's move over to the conference table, shall we?"

Hunter followed her to the table, where several documents were spread out. She sat next to Coach and listened carefully as she explained each.

"The first ones are easy. They are the payroll documents Human Resources needs to get you on the payroll. This is your salary for the remainder of the season."

Hunter's eyes grew wide at the salary number. Much more than she expected.

"Do you have a bank account established for direct deposit?"

"Can it be in California?"

"It can be anywhere you need it to be. We will need the routing number, account number, etcetera. Payroll is every two weeks, but we can do an advance now if you need one."

"I'm good, thanks," Hunter said as she filled out the banking information.

"Next is the contract. Fairly standard confidentiality statements, codes of conduct, etcetera. Please read each of them carefully before you sign them."

"Hazardous activity?" Hunter asked. "My motorcycle is my main means of transportation."

"I will waive that requirement, but if you sign a professional contract, that will be a non-negotiable clause."

"I understand. I think I can stay away from skydiving, too." Hunter smiled.

"Players tend to be adrenalin junkies and many careers have been cut short due to reckless behavior."

"A second shot at playing basketball is more important to me. I'll ride with Carson whenever possible. I know I'm a safe rider, but I must be worried about others."

"Will you require the use of the pool apartment?"

"Maybe when Stacy is home for visits to give them space. Otherwise, Carson insists I stay there."

"She probably enjoys the company."

"I think so. I imagine it's not fun to live by yourself so much."

"Probably not."

"I want you to press Michelle hard in practice. She needs someone to challenge her, and I know you can do it."

"I'll give it my best. We will do extra workouts and run to get me into shape."

"That will be good for her, too."

"I've noticed a few things she could improve on. Would you mind if I shared them with her?"

Coach smiled. "That is exactly why you will be perfect. Don't sugarcoat anything. What have you noticed?"

"She tries to force herself inside too much, especially if she gets a double team. She would do better to take a step back for a short jumper especially when she gets trapped along the baseline. She needs to either pass out of it or take a step back. With her height, I'd recommend a step back unless she's got a guard open for a three."

"That's a fair assessment. I'd also like to see Michelle develop a midrange jumper or a decent three to expand her skills. She can be more than a strong post player."

"We can work on that, as well. Some time going one-on-one would be good for both of us."

"Go get suited up then and work with Carson until the rest of the team arrives and stay hydrated."

"Yes, Coach. Thank you."

"I'll make a copy of everything and put it in your locker."

†

Hunter made her way to the locker room. Sandy was stocking lockers when she arrived. "I've got you all setup. Welcome aboard."

"Thanks, Sandy."

"Whenever you're done, drop everything in the hamper, and they will be washed and ready to go. You have seven sets of everything. I rotate them so the freshest is on top. You have three sets of game-day attire, three pairs of shoes, and a dozen pairs of socks."

"Will I need to take these home to pack for road trips?"

"Not unless you are gunning for my job." Sandy smiled. "We take care of all the apparel, so everything is set up for you when you arrive in the locker room."

"I could get spoiled."

"Your job is to support the team, not worry about packing clothes and uniforms. You're on your own with street clothes, though." Sandy winked.

Hunter stripped out of her clothes and dressed in a practice uniform. She thought the fit was perfect. Hunter placed the socks and shoes on her feet. They were so comfortable she didn't worry about breaking them in.

"Looks good on you."

"Thanks. I'll see you later."

†

Carson was shooting free throws when she arrived. "Get stretched out, and we can start shooting."

Hunter drank water and sat on the floor to begin stretching. Her muscles were tight, and it would take days for her to get used to the strenuous activity again.

"Black looks good on you," Carson said.

"Thanks. Do these shorts make my butt look fat?"

Carson broke out laughing. "I'll wager there is very little fat on your frame. You have always been lean and mean. Have you grown taller?"

"How kind of you to notice. I'm now six foot two," Hunter replied.

"I wish I had grown a few more inches. I got stuck at five-ten."

"You are perfect the way you are."

"Reckon I'll have to be content with this height."

Carson waited for her to stand, passed her a ball, and watched her dribble in for a lay-up.

"That part was easy. Will you set me up for a few short-range jumpers, and then we can switch?"

"I'm pretty warm, so let's focus on you."

Hunter nodded, caught Carson's pass, and drained a ten-foot jumper.

"You still have a sweet stroke. So natural. How does it feel?"

"Pretty good."

"Head to the corner, and let's try some threes."

Hunter jogged to the left-hand corner. She missed the first two shots. She adjusted her shot, and the balls started falling.

Carson was smiling. "Move ten toward midcourt."

She fed Hunter balls until she reached the top of the key, at which point she called for a water break.

"How does it feel?"

"Good, but then again, they are open, uncontested shots. It will be much different when we go live."

"I have a feeling you will be just fine. It will be like riding a bike. Do you need to take a few laps before we continue?"

"That probably wouldn't hurt," Hunter agreed.

"I'm going to get rid of some water." She tossed a ball, and Hunter dribbled as she headed down the sideline. When she reached the corner, she smiled when Hunter pivoted, shifting the ball into her left hand, just as they were taught in high school.

†

Carson passed Coach as she was returning to the gym.

"How's she doing?"

Carson shook her head. "She looks like she walked off a court yesterday instead of five years ago. Her shot is as smooth as ever."

"Good," Coach said. "I'll see you in a bit."

Hunter was shooting from the top of the key, draining shot after shot as Carson stepped in to rebound. "Ten more, then you need to rest until the others arrive. Once Michelle is stretched, you can start feeding her some balls."

"Not a problem. It feels good to have a ball in my hands again."

"Okay, take a break. I'm going to shoot some free throws until everyone else gets here. Be sure to grab some water."

Hunter drank a glass of water and watched Carson as the team and scout team started arriving to begin stretching. She stepped back onto the court and rebounded for Carson.

†

When Coach arrived, she introduced Hunter to the players and announced they would work on shooting drills and then have a full-court scrimmage. "Michelle, since Hunter will be working with you, please show her your shooting drills."

"Sure thing, Coach." Michelle picked up a ball. "Let's go, Rooks."

Hunter chuckled and followed Michelle to the opposite end of the court.

"Pretty simple. You pass me the ball on the low post on both sides first, and then you can pass and contest those shots. We'll finish up with some short-range shots in the paint."

"Sounds easy enough." Hunter got into position, passed the ball to Michelle, rebounded, and continued for a dozen shots on each side. Hunter passed the ball to Michelle without warning and moved into a defensive position.

Michelle smiled and started a drive toward the baseline, only to be cut off by Hunter. Michelle was trapped and threw up a weak shot. Michelle's smile quickly faded, and she drove the ball more aggressively, making the next shot.

"That's better. I will trap you every time you try to go baseline. Give me a fake toward the baseline, and then drive to the basket."

"Perfect," Hunter praised. "This time, I've cut you off at the baseline, and a second defender has dropped into double coverage. You have options. You can try to drive and split the defenders, hoping to be fouled, or take a step-back jumper. Lean in so we think you'll drive, take one step back, and fire."

It took several attempts, but Michelle was a quick learner and began consistently dropping five-foot shots. "Not bad for a big," Hunter teased. "You can do that from any position, not just on the blocks. Try one dribbling in from the foul line."

"That feels pretty good," Michelle said.

"I noticed in the game the other night that you always try to force your way to the basket. Your height helps, but a step back is the perfect option if you face a taller opponent or get doubled."

"You spotted that in one game?"

Hunter nodded. "That was the only issue I saw in your last game, but Coach wants us to work on developing a midrange jumper and a three-point shot. You will be unstoppable if you perfect those."

"I've never worked on those. My college coaches worked me hard on the inside, but not much from the perimeter."

"That was successful for you in college, but now the competition is bigger and stronger, and we've got to outthink them. Once a team realizes you have those skills, it will force them to defend you farther away from the basket, and if they double-team you, it opens up a teammate for an easy shot. If you have someone open for a three, pass and crash the boards for a rebound or follow up if necessary."

"I probably need to improve my passing skills, too," Michelle replied.

"We will," Hunter said. "Maybe we can enlist Carson's help with that. She has laser focus when it comes to passing." Hunter tossed her the ball. "We'd better get your free throws in before Coach starts barking."

After two dozen free throws, Coach yelled, "Water break."

"Ready to scrimmage?" Hunter asked Michelle.

"I'm always ready."

"Try the step back if you can. It will be more effective when simulating a game situation."

"Got it."

Hunter dribbled the ball to the water station and drank a large cup.

"Does anyone need a bathroom break before we scrimmage?" Coach asked.

Dan raised his hand. "I do, Coach."

"Take five, and then be ready for full court."

Hunter followed several players into the bathroom. She was washing her hands when Simone, one of the practice team guards, stepped beside her.

"Welcome to the team. I'll admit I envy you working with Michelle, but I know you are more capable of challenging her than I am."

"We will all have the opportunity to work her hard," Hunter replied as she reached for a paper towel. She smiled at Simone. "Let's do this."

CHAPTER EIGHT

Carson took the ball from the tipoff, and Hunter closed in on Michelle, making body contact to prevent Michelle from getting position down low. *This physical contact may be more challenging than I expected. It is not the contact, but being closely pressed into Michelle's body will be problematic. Suck it up, buttercup.*

Michelle stepped back from the contact and received a pass. Hunter anticipated her driving the baseline and cut her off. *Come on, Michelle, step back and shoot.*

Hunter smiled when Michelle pivoted, took a giant step backward, and made a short jump shot. She turned to watch the ball through the nylon. "That's what I'm talking about."

Michelle smiled, and they began jogging down the court. Dan and Simone inbounded the ball, and Simone passed it to Hunter, who faked a drive on Michelle and passed it back to

Simone. She put up a shot. Dan caught the long rebound and found Hunter in the corner. Hunter grinned when Michelle didn't come out to defend her. She took the wide-open shot and sank a three.

"I can do that all day if you don't challenge me," Hunter teased Michelle on her way back down the court.

Coach barked. "Perimeter defense means you go out to challenge shots, Thomas. Don't let her use you like that."

"Yes, Coach," Michelle answered. "Nice shot, Rooks."

"Come and get me and see what happens," Hunter said, hoping to get into her head.

When Michelle received the ball, Hunter and Simone collapsed to double-team her, and she wisely passed the ball to Carson, who took the shot.

"That's it. Good choice," Hunter praised.

The scrimmage lasted for twenty minutes before the Coach called for a break. "Don't forget to try out those new plays," she told Carson. "We need more live action on them."

Hunter was winded from the game's fast pace and was thankful for a break. She downed a cup of water and went for a refill.

"Good job," Dan said, giving her a fist bump. "You look like you never left the game."

Hunter smiled at him. "Except for sucking wind, it feels pretty good. I've got to work on endurance." She sat beside him. "Where did you play?"

"UNLV for my last two seasons. I wasn't drafted, but I hope to make a roster one day. Running with these ladies keeps me in shape, and I've learned a lot from Coach."

"She's a great coach. I appreciate her giving me a chance to work with y'all. I thought my basketball days were behind me."

"She sees a fire in your eyes that she hopes will be contagious," Dan said. "I like what you've done with Michelle so far. She's got finesse but doesn't use it. Power is not her only strength."

"Agreed, and I hope I can help her with that."

"I have faith," Dan said, pulling her to her feet.

†

The next opportunity Hunter had for a corner three, she hesitated to see if Michelle would come out on her. She moved quickly but didn't guard the baseline. Hunter faked a shot, drove past her along the baseline, and found Dan cutting through the lane.

"Footwork, Hot Shot." She winked at Michelle.

Michelle shook her head and hustled down the court. When she got the ball, she took two steps toward the basket and took a ten-foot jumper. Hunter came out on her too late and was nowhere close enough to affect her shot.

She bumped Michelle's shoulder. "Hell yeah."

When Coach ended the practice, she said, "Good job, everyone. Same time tomorrow. Plan to watch some new game film before we start practice."

Michelle looked at Hunter. "You still up for some extra work?"

"Yes, I am."

"I'll be back in a few minutes."

"I'll be right here." Hunter picked up a ball and began dribbling down the court. She was on her fifth lap when Michelle returned.

"Are you up for a few more?"

"Grab a ball," Hunter said.

Michelle laughed and took a ball from the rack, chasing after her. She watched the pivot turn Hunter made and followed suit.

After five laps, Hunter slowed and stopped at the hydration station. She poured a cup, handing it to Michelle, and then drank one.

"Thanks. Do you always run with a ball?"

"Always when I'm in the gym," Hunter answered. "It's a distraction from the boredom of running and helps work on ball-handling skills, especially when you get tired. The tendency is to get careless as fatigue sets in," she explained. "I grew up with a red, white, and blue Harlem Globetrotters outdoor ball that I eventually wore the color off running the neighborhood streets."

"Has basketball always been your first love in sports?"

"Always, since I got that first ball and Dad hung a goal for me."

"What are we working on next, Coach?" Michelle teased.

"I want to see what you can do with a three-point shot."

"I don't think I've ever hit one," Michelle said.

"You will, and your opponents won't know what to expect. They will rush out to defend you if they fear you can drop the shot. You can catch them off balance, drive past them, or take the shot. It would be rare for anyone to be tall or fast enough to block you, but it gives you other options." Hunter rolled a rack of balls to the foul line. "What side are you most comfortable with?"

"Left," Michelle answered.

"Okay, we can start there. Let's see what you've got." Hunter stopped passing balls to her when she missed three shots. "What are you doing wrong?"

"Besides missing short?" Michelle said.

"You can't rely on your height out beyond the arc. It would help to bend your knees to get the lift you need to reach the basket. You are shooting too flatfooted." Hunter dribbled a ball to where Michelle had been shooting. "Like this." She moved slowly so Michelle could see the bend in her knees and the lift of her jump. The ball sailed through, barely moving the nylon.

"Damn. You make that look so easy."

"When you've shot as many of them as I have, it becomes a natural stroke. You have some catching up to do. I don't think Coach wants you to shoot a lot from behind the arc, but it will throw defenses off if you take and make a few. Keep them on their heels." She jogged back to the ball rack and tossed Michelle a ball. "Bend and lift."

The next shot bounced off the far rim, hit the backboard, and dropped in.

"Shooter's touch." Hunter smiled and tossed her another ball.

When the rack was empty, Michelle had hit two in a row.

"Not bad for a rook." Hunter winked. "Up for another rack?"

"Sure, then I'll set one up for you."

"Let's move up the court a bit. You can use the backboard to bank from that spot. Same principle as shooting down low. Kiss that top left corner, and it's almost certainly falling in."

Michelle focused on the basket for the first few shots and the backboard for the others. Hunter watched the smile grow as several shots fell for her. "That's it. Kiss that sweet spot." When she realized what she'd said, Hunter was glad her back was to Michelle as her face turned red. She took her time retrieving the next ball, passing it to her.

Michelle was grinning. She hadn't missed the sexual innuendo in the comment. Unintended or not. She drained the shot.

"Good job," Hunter said when Michelle made the last spot. They hustled to retrieve the balls, and Hunter shot a rack, missing only three. "I think I've had enough for today."

"You did well in the scrimmage," Michelle said as they collected the balls.

"It felt good," Hunter replied.

"Let's shower and do some shopping," Michelle suggested.

"I'm right behind you," Hunter said as she pushed the rack to the end line.

†

The locker room was empty when they entered. Hunter couldn't help but stare when Michelle pulled the jersey over her head. Her eyes were riveted to Michelle's ripped abs, and without the shirt, she could see how the shorts hung low on her hips. She swallowed hard and pulled her eyes away.

"Like what you see?" Michelle teased.

"What's not to like?" Hunter replied. "You have a beautiful body. How did you get abs like that?"

"Lots of work in the weight room." She looked at Hunter's flat stomach. "It wouldn't take much to get you there."

"Oh, please." Hunter chuckled.

Michelle sat down to remove her shoes. "I'll show you how if you teach me those jump shots." She tossed her jersey and socks in the laundry bin. "My journey will be much less painful."

Hunter tossed her jersey in the bin. "You have a deal."

"Come to practice an hour early tomorrow and we'll get a workout in," Michelle said.

Hunter nodded and stripped out of her clothes. She was used to showering with women, but Michelle wasn't just a woman. Hunter felt her heart race when she observed Michelle fully naked. *Dear Lord, help me.* Hunter left the locker room quickly and walked into a shower stall. She knew her face was on fire and didn't want Michelle to see the effect she had on her.

†

They finished showering simultaneously, and Hunter was relieved when Michelle pulled on a sports bra, panties, and shorts before walking to the sink to dry her hair and brush her teeth. As she dried her short-cropped hair and ran her fingers through her hair to add a product to style it, she still gave Hunter the view of Michelle's arm muscles. Once more, Hunter wondered if the coloring in Michelle's hair was natural or a dye. It reminded her of the mercury color of her eyes. She brushed her teeth and dried her hair while Michelle finished dressing and packed her gym bag and waited patiently as Hunter finished dressing and packed her bag.

"Ready?"

Hunter grabbed her belongings. "Let's roll," she said, taking a cross-body bag from her locker.

When they walked to the parking lot, Hunter chuckled. "I see what Carson meant about climbing into your Jeep. How much is it lifted?"

"Only four inches. Do you need a leg up?"

"Hardly." Hunter tossed her gym bag behind the passenger seat and climbed inside.

"I could use a snack before we start shopping. How about you?"

"What did you have in mind?"

"Do you like frozen yogurt? There's a great shop close to the outlet."

Hunter smiled. "That does sound good."

"My treat," Michelle said and started the Jeep.

Hunter pulled on her seat belt and watched Michelle drop shades over her eyes. *Good idea.* She reached inside her bag and pulled out a pair. The glare from the intense sunlight went right away.

†

Michelle held the door open and led her inside. "You build your own concoction here." She handed Hunter several souffle cups. "If you want to sample a flavor."

Hunter made her way down the bank of flavors and sampled a few. Michelle headed straight to her favorite.

"What are you getting?"

Michelle smiled. "I'm addicted to the salted caramel."

"That does sound good." Hunter tasted the flavor. "Oh yeah."

"Grab a cup and start creating," Michelle said.

Hunter filled her cup and followed Michelle through the topping selections, adding several to her cup. When they reached the cash register, Michelle placed her cup on the scale.

"Pony up," she said. "It's sold by weight."

"Hey, Michelle," the young cashier said. "I haven't seen you in a few days."

"Hi, Reba. I've been busy. How are you?"

"Better now that I get to see your smiling face."

Hunter watched the interaction, and the twenty percent discount Hunter received.

"Will you be working the game Friday night?"

"I sure will. I hope I can sneak in to watch a few minutes of the game. Maybe after the halftime rush."

"It will be a good game," Hunter said, taking her card back from Reba.

Michelle led Hunter to a table.

"Come here often?"

"Almost every week. We get a twenty percent discount, and I love frozen yogurt, especially on hot days."

"Which is almost every day." Hunter smiled.

"October through April is usually tolerable."

"Do you remain here after the season?"

"Yep. This is home for me now."

Hunter took a bite of her treat. "This is really good."

"I know some other players play in Europe to supplement their salaries here."

"I'm not greedy. I have my home and everything I need. I work out to stay in shape. There's a rumor that a new three-on-three league may be starting up this off-season. I may try out for that."

"That sounds pretty interesting and fast-moving."

"An incredibly intense ten-minute game or the first to twenty-one. One point for anything inside the three-point line and two from deep."

Hunter nodded. "That would make developing a three-point shot and a midrange jumper even more important."

"That it is." Michelle smiled. "Would you consider teaming up with me? Maybe we could rope Carson into playing point for us?"

"That's something to consider."

"It would be good exposure for you and probably garner some interest from pro teams if you play well."

†

"I'm going to take you to my favorite store first." Michelle parked in front of Tommy Hilfiger. "His men's clothing fit me well."

"I like the preppy look, and I bet it's delicious on you. Shit, did I say that out loud?" Hunter's face turned scarlet.

"Yes, you did. You are good for my ego. Thank you for the compliment."

"You're welcome."

Hunter held the door for Michelle. A woman behind the counter smiled when she saw Michelle.

"Welcome back. What can I help you with today?"

"Thanks, Susan. My friend needs a few game-day outfits. This is Hunter."

"Nice to meet you, Hunter. Thirty-inch waist and thirty-four inseam?"

"Damn, you're good. Shoe size?"

Susan looked at her feet. "Size nine and a large to extra large shirt, depending on the cut."

Hunter chuckled. "I need four outfits. What do you recommend? You've been spot on so far."

Susan looked at Michelle. "You know the drill. Go relax, and I'll bring some outfits for your inspection."

"You heard the lady. Follow me." Michelle led Hunter to a row of comfortable chairs and sat beside her.

"Susan is amazing."

"Yeah, she is." Michelle grinned.

Within minutes, Susan returned carrying several outfits. "Let's try these for starters."

Hunter took the clothes Susan handed her and walked into the dressing room. She started with a tan pair of chinos and a solid black oxford. The fit was perfect. Hunter walked out to model for Susan and Michelle.

"Oh yeah, that's a keeper," Michelle said.

Susan nodded in agreement. "Try the blue pants and pinstriped shirt next."

"That one, too." Michelle smiled.

Hunter returned, tried on the two other outfits Susan had selected, and decided on all of them. When she walked out, Susan showed her two belts. Hunter nodded and watched Susan open a shoe box.

"These will go nicely with all four outfits and are half-priced."

"Damn, I like those. Do they come in boat size?"

Susan chuckled. "Eleven, right? Let me check." When she returned, Susan handed Michelle the shoes to try on. "The jeans you like so well are on sale, too."

"I guess I should get a couple of pairs. Would you allow me to buy you a pair?"

Hunter smiled. "Sure."

"I'll be right back."

"Do I need to try them on?" Hunter asked.

"Need to? Probably not, but I'd like to see how they look on you."

Hunter shook her head and put the shoes back in the box. She took the jeans from Susan and returned to the dressing room. She had never had jeans that fit her body that well. *I may have to come back for more of these.*

"Turn, please," Michelle said when Hunter returned to them.

"Very nice," Susan said.

Michelle smiled and nodded. "They look like they were designed for you."

†

After they checked out, Hunter placed her bags in the back seat. "Do you get discounts everywhere in this town?"

Michelle looked at her. "The city is very supportive of its sports teams. We get discounts at most businesses as a thank you for the revenue we bring in."

"That's great to hear. Women's sports are gaining in popularity. It's about damn time, too."

"Our attendance records have skyrocketed in the last few years. We rarely play in anything under a sold-out crowd, even on the road."

"Anything else you need to do before we head home?"

Michelle shook her head. "Not unless you need something."

"I'm good. I'll text Carson and let her know we are on our way. She may be done with her appointment and can bring the food home. Thank you for taking me shopping. That was a fun trip."

"My pleasure. You looked great in the outfits, and I got some new jeans, too."

Hunter sent the text, and Carson replied. *Good, I'm starving. I'll see you soon.*

†

When they returned to the condo, Michelle reached into her bag and handed Hunter two pairs of jeans.

"Oh, you're sneaky."

"I couldn't help it. The jeans looked so good on you and were on sale."

"Thank you."

"Let me help you with those bags," Michelle offered.

Hunter was hanging up her new wardrobe when Carson returned with bags of Chinese food. She stuck her head in the bedroom.

"Dinner is here, you two." Carson looked at the closet. "Y'all did good shopping. The closet isn't so bare now. C'mon, let's eat."

"You heard the lady." Michelle grinned.

They entered the dining room, and Carson started unloading bags. "What does everyone want to drink?"

Hunter smiled. "We made a pitcher of sweet tea."

"Let's give it a try then," Michelle said.

"You were hungry." Hunter chuckled when Carson finished unloading her bags. She poured three glasses of tea. "What else do we need besides plates and forks?"

"I got egg drop soup for anyone who wants some, so bowls and spoons."

"On it," Hunter replied, handing Michelle the tea.

†

"Someone, please make me stop eating," Michelle groaned. "It was all delicious, and your tea was excellent."

"Not bad for a first batch." Carson winked at Hunter.

"Your hair looks great," Hunter said. "Got your nails done, too, huh?"

"I'm looking forward to Stacy coming home."

"Speaking of which," Michelle said. "I plan to kidnap Hunter this weekend to do some exploring. Maybe we could all go to dinner on Saturday night and try our luck at a casino?"

"I'm sure that can be arranged. There's a great new sushi place I've been dying to try out." Carson looked at Hunter. "Don't feel like you have to disappear the whole weekend just because she's home."

"Are you kidding? I have a personal tour guide in a monster Jeep. How can I pass on that?"

Michelle smiled at Carson. "I promise to return her in one piece."

"I know she'll be in good hands." Carson smiled. "Will we see you in one of your new outfits Saturday night?"

"New jeans, yes. I'm saving the others for game days. So you'll see one Friday night."

"Good enough for me."

After placing the few leftovers in the fridge, Michelle looked at them. "Thanks for a great meal and a fun day shopping. Do I need to pick you up tomorrow?" she asked Hunter.

Hunter looked at Carson. "We are going to hit the weight room before practice starts, so I agreed to meet her an hour before practice."

"I could use a good workout. I'll make sure Hunter's on time," Carson said.

"She's promised me washboard abs if I teach her to shoot three-pointers."

"That sounds like a great deal."

"We have an ulterior motive," Michelle said. "We want us to team up for the new three-on-three league next year. We need you for a point guard. Hint, hint."

"I bet that would be fun. We'll have to see how the schedule works out. Stacy wants to do some traveling during the off-season."

"I'll see if I can find more information," Michelle said. "I'm going to head out, so I'll see you both tomorrow."

"Sounds good. Thanks for a great day," Hunter said.

"We'll see you tomorrow afternoon," Carson said, walking her to the door. Carson whispered, "Did you have fun too?"

Michelle nodded. "I did," she whispered back and then laughed. "Have a good night."

"You too, and drive safe."

†

"Are you up for a beer?" Hunter asked.

"Yeah. Let me see if we can get Stacy's game on television. They play Chicago tonight."

Hunter walked to the refrigerator and pulled out two beers while Carson surfed the channels.

"Here we go," Carson said and reached for the beer. "Do you mind?"

"Not at all. Which one is Stacy?"

"Number twenty-three," Carson said.

"Oh, she's cute," Hunter replied.

"Thanks," Carson said. "So, what did you and Michelle do?"

"We worked out for an hour after practice, showered, and stopped for frozen yogurt before shopping."

"Sounds like fun," Carson said. "I'm glad you two get along so well."

"Michelle is terrific. Everybody loves her, and even vendors know her by first name."

"Michelle is extremely popular in the community. I bet we can't make it through dinner before someone asks for her autograph and a selfie."

"Don't sell yourself short. I saw you after the game, and you had a crowd waiting for you."

"It's so much different from college. We never played in front of a crowd like this."

They watched the game, and Seattle finally pulled ahead.

"Chicago plays pretty rough, don't they?"

"They are very aggressive, which I don't mind, but some of them use cheap shots to their advantage and don't always get called out for it. It drives Michelle crazy. She's got a long fuse, but she won't tolerate anyone bullying her teammates."

"I've seen that already. I wouldn't want Michelle to come after me."

Carson nodded. "I've only seen her lose her shit once, and that was enough. She gave them a dose of their own medicine, and the player went off with a broken nose after taking an elbow to her face. Michelle was mortified once the adrenalin calmed down, but I'm sure the offender learned a lesson."

"We worked on a three-point shot and a midrange jumper today, and I think she shows great potential. Because of her size, she's always encouraged to play the low blocks, but I think she will surprise some folks soon. Including herself."

"You looked pretty sharp out there today, too. Coach smiles every time you sink a shot."

"I love playing again and appreciate the opportunity."

"Are you serious about playing three on three?"

"Yeah, I am. If I'm allowed since I'm not a professional."

Carson looked at Hunter. "If you want it, Coach will make it happen for you. It's supposed to be an excellent salary boost. A way to keep our players local instead of going to Europe to play there."

Hunter fell silent as she contemplated Carson's statements, and when the game was over, she dropped their bottles in the trash. "I think I'll call it a night. It's been a long day."

"Get some rest. We'll make breakfast in the morning since we're leaving early. I'll wait on Stacy's call and then crash."

"Goodnight then. Thanks for dinner."

"Goodnight, Hunter."

CHAPTER NINE

Michelle wasn't kidding when she told Hunter she would work hard in the weight room. There was no way Hunter could keep up with Michelle's rigorous routine.

"This will take some working up to," she told Michelle.

"You did well for the first day, but you will feel it tonight." Michelle grinned.

"I feel it already," Hunter said with a grimace.

"You can relax while we watch the game film. Just be sure to stretch out well before practice."

"Does the practice team watch film with you?"

"Of course. You are a critical part of the team and can mimic some of the moves our opponents will make."

Carson had her earbuds in as she rode an exercise bike. Michelle tapped her wrist and nodded toward the film room. "Let's get something to drink and get a good seat."

"No popcorn?" Hunter teased.

"Too distracting," Michelle replied. "Coach expects our full attention."

As soon as all the players took their seats, Coach moved to the front of the room. "Good afternoon, team. I fully expect Dallas to play three guards and two bigs. That means they will be lighting up the three-point line. I expect us to dominate the glass, but our perimeter defense will win the game for us. Pay attention to their guard play and see if you can pick up on some tells on when they will take a shot. They have several spectacular shooters that we need to manage. We won't stop them completely, but we can make it difficult for them to get shots up." Coach took a breath and surveyed the room. "We will be rotating guards frequently to keep everyone fresh, so we will only have a long shoot-around on Wednesday and Thursday. Normal pregame warm-up on Friday. Any questions?"

One of the second-string guards raised her hand. "Will we stick with our normal starters or match them guard for guard?"

"We will start our usual team, but if the defensive effort isn't effective, we will make some substitutions. We need this win, and we will be favored by fifteen points. I want that doubled."

"Yes, Coach."

"Anything else?" The room was silent, and Coach started the film.

Hunter noticed their shooting guard was a catch-and-shoot player. Once the ball was in her hands, she shot immediately, passed off, or drove toward the basket. There was no hesitation if someone wasn't in her face. She also noted the point guard only shot well when she was on the right side of the court. She rarely put up a shot if she was forced to go left. That would be Carson's assignment. She leaned over and whispered into Carson's ear. Carson nodded and smiled at Hunter.

Hunter zeroed in on their defense next. The player that would likely be assigned to Michelle would be significantly shorter, which would allow her to score easily over her. This would be the perfect test for a midrange jumper. She had two bigs that would crash the boards for rebounds. Hunter just needed to convince Michelle that she could consistently make the shot. *Maybe she could even shoot a three if the opportunity presented itself. One step at a time.*

When the game ended, Coach asked if anyone had any feedback to offer. Hunter was proud when Carson raised her hand.

Carson smiled at Hunter. "Hunter picked up on this. The point guard only shoots effectively from the right side. If we can trap and force her to go left, her shooting percentage should be lessened."

"Great observation, Hunter, and spot on. Anything else?"

Several players noted a few observations, and Coach looked directly at Hunter. "I think you noticed a few other things. Would you share with us?"

Hunter blushed but nodded at Coach.

"Their top shooting guard is a catch-and-shoot player. If she doesn't have room to shoot right away uncontested, she passes or drives down the middle of the lane, sometimes pulling up at the foul line for a jumper. I don't think she will successfully drive to the basket unless our bigs are spread wide."

"And." Coach nodded.

"Whoever is defended by the third guard will score easily over the guard, or if their bigs come to assist, they can pass to an open big or take a midrange jumper or a step back from close range."

"Maybe I should give you a whistle," Coach teased. "Good observations."

"Thanks, Coach."

"Okay, get warmed up, and we'll have a final scrimmage for thirty minutes and a short shoot-around."

†

Michelle, Hunter, and Carson walked to the gym. Michelle slipped an arm around her shoulder and winked at Carson. "I think we should name her CJ."

"CJ?" Hunter asked.

"Coach Junior. Those were great observations," Michelle told Hunter.

"Let's see if they work. Shoot some midrange jumpers in the scrimmage today. Remember to kiss the sweet spot."

"What?" Carson said.

When Michelle explained the comment, Carson broke out laughing. "If it helps, use it. If nothing else, it should make you smile when you shoot and keep you loose."

"That it will. If you hear me yell 'kiss it,' you know what to do," Hunter teased.

†

Coach called the practice team into a huddle when the players were ready. "I want you to light them up from behind the arc at every opportunity. Let's see how well they can defend the three."

Hunter drained two three-point shots and drove inside on Michelle, who quickly cut off her drive.

"Good job," Hunter praised. As they trotted down the court, Hunter continued, "Come out quicker on my threes. You're waiting too long to contest. That shooting guard will eat your lunch if you don't act quickly when she's in your zone. You have backup under the basket, so go for it."

Michelle received a pass, and Hunter grinned. "Kiss it," she said.

Michelle pulled up for a ten-foot shot and banked it home. She smiled when the ball dropped through the hoop.

"Hell yeah," Hunter said.

Carson and Simone coordinated a trap well for the point guard that cut her off and forced her to move to the left. She was forced to pass the ball to Dan, who missed a three. Michelle raced down the court, beating Hunter, and caught a pass from Carson for an easy layup.

"Damn, I didn't know you could move that fast," Hunter teased.

On the next trip down the court, Hunter and Dan trapped Michelle. Without prompting, Michelle took a step back and dropped a shot. Hunter nodded her approval.

Hunter faked a three-point shot and attempted a jump shot that Michelle blocked from behind.

"Good enough for today. Hydrate and work on some shooting. Good job," Coach called to them.

Hunter and Michelle worked on her three-point shot and midrange jumper. When she missed two contested shots, Hunter turned to her. "What are you forgetting?"

"To bend my knees and lift," Michelle said.

Hunter tossed her a ball. "Focus." She rushed toward Hunter to contest the shot. "Coming for you," she said.

"Bring it," Michelle said and executed a perfect shot.

"That's it," Hunter said, tossing the ball back to Michelle. She rebounded several more shots until Coach called an end to the practice.

"Do you want to stay late today to run or shoot? I'll give you a ride home. Maybe after some frozen yogurt?" Michelle asked.

"That's cruel," Hunter said. "What the hell. I'm already going to be sore. I'll tell Carson I'll be home later."

"I'll shoot until you return." Michelle smiled.

†

Hunter found Carson in the locker room. I'm going to get some laps in. Michelle said she would bring me home later."

"Invite Romeo for dinner then. I was planning on some baked chicken and vegetables. Don't encourage her to run; we are on limitations until Friday's game. She can shoot. Coach would be okay with that."

"I'll remind her. Thanks. Do we need to bring anything for dinner?"

"Nope, I've got it all planned. Thanks. I'll see you later."

†

When Hunter returned to the court, Michelle was talking with Coach. Their conversation ended, and Coach walked by her. "Great job today, Hunter."

"Thanks, Coach." Hunter took a ball from the rack and walked to Michelle. "Carson said to remind you about physical restrictions. Why don't you shoot while I run? I

109

don't think I'll run more than ten laps. You're also invited to dinner tonight."

"Okay, I'll work on some shooting. Dinner sounds great."

"Kiss it," Hunter said and started jogging.

Michelle watched her run away and resumed shooting.

When Hunter's shirt was soaked, Michelle called her to the hydration station. "You are soaked. I think that's enough for today." She handed Hunter a cup of water.

"Agreed. I've pushed enough for today." Hunter drained the cup and handed it to Michelle for a refill. "Are you getting more comfortable with the new shots?"

"I am. I plan to try those out in the game. Coach thinks it's time, too."

"You'll continue to get better with each practice."

"She also said she wanted me to dunk early in the game if an opportunity arose. That always gets the crowd fired up."

"It will bring me out of my seat," Hunter said. "I dream of dunking one day."

"What's stopping you?"

"About three inches." Hunter chuckled. "I've got to improve my vertical jump before I can get to the rim."

"You can do that. We can work on your leg strength in the weight room. Three inches should be easy for you. The core training you started today will help, too."

"We'll see," Hunter said. "Ready to hit the shower?"

"I thought you'd never ask," Michelle replied and laughed at the shocked look on Hunter's face. "Sorry, that was mean."

"Yes, it was," Hunter said and started walking to the locker room. She hid the smile on her face from Michelle.

†

"Two days in a row. I could get used to this," Reba teased.

"It's so danged hot out there. This is the perfect spot to cool down a bit," Michelle replied.

"I've heard that a lot today. It's been a busy day." She handed Michelle her card back.

Michelle smiled when she saw Hunter with the salted caramel again. "That's hard to beat, isn't it?"

"It really is. I was tempted to try the banana split today."

"They have dividers over by the cups if you want to try half and half next time," Michelle said.

"I may do that. My turn to buy next time, okay?"

"Fine with me," Michelle answered.

†

Dinner was fantastic and filling. After sharing a beer, Michelle turned to Hunter. "Do you plan to run after shoot-around tomorrow?"

"Yes, I do. I'll come early for a workout in the weight room and run afterward."

"Will you need a ride home?"

"Not tomorrow. I will drive my bike. I think it's time for a ride," Hunter answered. She saw the look of disappointment on Michelle's face. "I could drop by afterward if you plan to be home."

"How about I cook for you then? Carson, you can come out, too."

111

"Stacy has an early game tomorrow, so I plan on getting take-out and call it an early night. But thank you for the invitation."

"Who do they play?" Michelle asked.

"They are down in LA."

"That should be a good game," Michelle said. "We can watch it together if that's not too late for you to be out on your bike."

Hunter chuckled. "I've been known to ride after dark."

"The game should be over by eight, so it won't be too dark," Carson said.

"I've got lasagna ready to bake with a salad and garlic bread."

"That sounds great," Hunter replied.

"Cool. I'll see y'all at practice tomorrow. Have a good night."

"You too." Hunter smiled, walking her to the door. "I'd invite you to ride, but I know your contract has a hazardous activity clause."

"Maybe once the season is over." Michelle smiled.

"You have a deal. Drive safe."

"Will do."

†

Hunter returned to the living room and placed her hand on Carson's forehead. "Are you feeling okay?"

"Yes, why?"

"I've never known you to pass on homemade lasagna," Hunter said.

Carson turned toward Hunter. "Did you see Michelle's face when you told her you were riding your bike tomorrow?

I think she's becoming fond of you and enjoys spending time with you."

"I enjoy her company, too. I need a long ride to get my head straight."

"Please don't toy with Michelle if you aren't interested."

Hunter recoiled from Carson's comment. "I can't believe you would say that."

"I'm sorry. That was harsh, but Michelle is my best friend. I see her falling hard for you. She deserves someone who will be good for her, and I think that's you if you quit overthinking your past."

"That's easier to say than do, but I'm trying hard to put it behind me. I planned to talk to Michelle this weekend about what happened with Lilly. I want to be perfectly honest with her about whether we can take things further." Hunter sighed. "I don't want to have any secrets between us, and there is always a threat of someone who knows my past to drop a bomb and ruin what I've got going."

"I can appreciate that. Even though I don't know the whole story, I still love you. Differently than before, but not because of what happened. How we ended things was painful, and it took months for me to quit being selfish and move on with my life."

"You know I never meant to hurt you. That was as painful as losing Lilly, but I thought it was best for you at the time."

"I understand that now, and I hope you can find happiness with Michelle or someone else. Lilly would want you to fall in love again."

"Yeah, she would."

"You should probably consider having that conversation with Coach, too. I don't think it would change anything. She thinks the world of you but doesn't like surprises either."

"Let me start with Michelle. She's the most important right now, but I owe that to Coach, too."

Carson stood and pulled Hunter into a hug. "I'm sorry if I hurt your feelings. I am so proud of you and love you dearly. You deserve more than life has given you." She kissed Hunter's cheek.

"I love you, too, and appreciate everything you have done for me when it would have been easier just to turn away."

"I would never do that to you. I hope you know that."

"I do now. Coming here to see you was a huge risk, but I'm glad I did."

"I am, too." Carson released Hunter. "Will you cook French toast in the morning?"

"Do you have bacon to go with it?"

"Already thawing in the fridge."

"You have a deal then. I'll lock up and hit the sack in a few."

"Goodnight then."

Hunter nodded. "Goodnight."

†

Hunter locked the front door and walked to the garage. She unhooked the trailer and moved it to allow her to get her bike out in the morning. "I haven't forgotten you," she said as she ran her hand down the seat. "Tomorrow, we will ride."

Hunter turned off the lights, brushed her teeth, and climbed into bed. She looked out the window and watched the now-familiar fireworks display until she fell asleep.

†

Carson woke to the smell of bacon cooking. She stretched and freshened up before walking to the kitchen. "You've got it smelling good in here."

"Pour a cup. Breakfast will be ready in a few. I'll take a refill, please," Hunter said, handing Carson her cup.

"How'd you sleep?"

"Pretty good. You?"

"Like a rock," Carson said, setting Hunter's coffee on the counter.

"What time are you heading to the practice facility? Practice is at one."

"It's just a shoot-around today and tomorrow, right?"

"Yep, no scrimmages for you, so it should be an easy two days."

"I'll leave at eleven. That will allow me to get a hard workout and some laps in."

"Will you take a break for a sandwich for lunch if I bring it?"

"Sure."

"I'll be there around twelve thirty then. Any special requests?"

"Nope. I'm pretty easy." Hunter grinned.

"You are far from easy, but I know what you like."

"Will three slices be enough for you?" Hunter asked as she plated three slices of French toast.

"Plenty. Damn, this looks good. I still suck at cooking it. My slices still fall apart."

"You get them too soggy. You've got to dredge them fast." She handed Carson the plate. "Get started, and I'll be right there."

†

Carson cleaned up after breakfast while Hunter showered and dressed. She needed to fuel her bike before she went for a long ride. When Hunter entered the kitchen, Carson sat drinking coffee. She arched an eyebrow. "Damn, you look hot."

Hunter chuckled. "Thanks. I can clean up well on occasion."

"I never knew anyone who could make jeans and a T-shirt look so good."

Hunter spun around and laughed. "I'll see you for lunch."

"Drive safe."

"Always," Hunter said, pulling on her crossbody bag.

†

After fueling, Hunter drove to the practice facility. When she walked inside, Coach was coming down the hall. "You're early."

"I thought I'd get a workout in since we're only doing shoot-around the next two days."

"Come to my office first," Coach said, stepping into her office.

"What's up?"

"Smile into this camera for me," Coach said, pointing to the camera lens on the computer. "Security is much different at the arena and on the road, so you need a team pass to enter the player's lot and get inside. This won't take long. I'll stick it in your locker when your badge is ready."

"Thanks, Coach." Hunter left the office and walked to the locker room to change. Sandy was in the room storing freshly laundered gear. "Hey, Sandy."

"Hey, Hunter. You're early."

"I wanted to get a workout in before practice. Do I need to take my game-day uniform home tomorrow for Friday's game?"

"No. My team and I will set up the locker room for you Friday morning, so all you need to do is come in and change."

"Thanks, Sandy."

"You're welcome. Have a good workout."

Hunter changed into her practice uniform and ran first to loosen her muscles. After stretching, she picked up a ball and began jogging. She was ten laps when she looked up to find Coach watching, and Hunter slowed when she approached her.

"I'm going to run out for some lunch. Can I bring you anything?"

"Thanks, Coach, but Carson is bringing me a sandwich."

"Good. Enjoy your workout."

Hunter nodded and resumed her run. She changed her routine, passing the ball between her legs and behind her back to sharpen her dribbling skills as she ran her final twenty laps. Hunter drank some water and walked to the weight room to find Michelle sitting on a bench on her phone. She looked up when Hunter entered.

"Hey. I thought you might need a spotter," Michelle said.

"Thanks for being so thoughtful," Hunter replied.

Michelle handed her a bottle of Gatorade. "Drink. You look like you could use some."

Hunter opened the bottle and drank a large swig. "That's good."

"Do you want to start on your abs or your legs?"

"Might as well continue on the abs. The run helped relieve some soreness."

"Good. It shouldn't last long. Abs first and then squats."

Michelle put Hunter through the paces on the machines while watching the clock. "That's good. Carson will be on her way. Finish that drink, and let's head to the break room. How are you feeling?"

Hunter laughed. "My legs feel like jelly, but I'm good."

"Your lower body strength is solid. Those three inches are going to come fast," Michelle said. "I saw your bike outside. She's a beauty."

"Thanks. I bought her when I graduated from high school. I love wide-open rides."

"I understand that. I feel the same way when I put the top down and drive."

They walked into the break room, where Carson was laying out sandwiches. "Honey ham for Hunter and turkey, bacon, ranch for Michelle."

"Perfect," Hunter said. "Thanks."

"Good workout?"

"Yeah, I'll blow through these calories quickly."

"I'll load you up on carbs tonight," Michelle said.

"My mouth is already watering."

†

The shoot-around was fantastic. "If you shoot like that Friday night, Dallas won't have a chance," Hunter praised Michelle.

"I was on fire today, wasn't I?" Michelle smiled proudly.

"The more repetitions you get, the better the shot will feel."

†

Hunter showered and dressed in her riding clothes. She couldn't help but enjoy how Michelle's eyes appraised her as she leaned down to slip into her boots. A hunger in her eyes made Hunter's knees feel weak. It had been forever since anyone had looked at her that way.

"I'm going straight home, so come whenever you finish your ride," Michelle told her.

"I will. See you later, Carson," she said as they walked out together.

"Stay safe," Carson said.

Hunter nodded and slipped her helmet over her head after putting on her sunglasses. They watched her mount the bike and drive away.

"Not a bad look for her, is it?" Carson teased Michelle.

"Not at all. See you tomorrow."

"Have a good night," Carson said with a wink.

†

Hunter left the lot and headed for the desert road she had selected from the map. Traffic was non-existent, so she opened up the bike. The rumble of the powerful motor between her legs made her grin. *It's not a harmful side effect of riding.* The rock formations were excellent, and she stopped several times to send pictures to her mom. She pulled in and parked when she came upon a small gas station and removed her helmet. A weathered older man sat on a bench beside an ancient drink machine. Hunter nodded to him as she bought a drink and opened it. He looked at her bike and then at her.

"Would you mind sharing your bench?"

"Not at all, young lady. That's a beautiful bike. I had an Indian about forty years ago. I loved that bike."

"They are wonderful. What happened to it?"

"Had to sell it when we had too many kids." He laughed.

"How many did you have?" Hunter asked.

"Six and the wife threatened me with scissors if we had any more." He made a snipping motion with his fingers.

"Ouch." Hunter chuckled. "Is this your place?"

He nodded. "Has been for fifty years. Me and the Missus run it. We don't see much traffic this time of the year, though."

"Is she inside?"

"Yeah. Watching her soaps behind the cash register. Do you need something?"

"I'll top off my gas tank. Would you like to go for a short ride with me?"

Hunter saw the man's head snap up. "You'll take me for a ride?"

"As long as your wife doesn't shoot me," Hunter teased. She finished her drink. "I'll top off my tank if you will talk to her about taking a ride."

He stood and walked inside faster than Hunter would have guessed he had in him. She rolled her bike to the pump, filled the tank, and stepped inside. She handed the woman a ten for her fuel.

"My Walter said you wanted to offer him a ride. Is that right?"

"Yes, ma'am, if you approve. My name is Hunter. I promise to bring him back safe."

"He had a bike like that years ago and missed it every day until we grew old. He's in the bathroom, getting ready. Are you sure you don't mind?"

"Not at all. I couldn't ride for a few years, so I know how Walter feels."

"I'm ready." Walter approached them, running his hands through his hair.

"Take Hunter to the falls, Walter. I bet she's never been there."

"No, I haven't. Are you ready?"

"You two be careful," the woman called to them.

"We will," Walter said as he lifted his hand to wave to her as he led Hunter outside.

Hunter pulled on her helmet and mounted the bike before turning to offer him a hand to climb on behind her. She could feel the frailty of the bones in his hand as he climbed on behind her.

"All set?"

"Yes, I am. We're going that way." He pointed. "I'll let you know when to turn. It's a few miles ahead."

"Hold on then," Hunter said and felt his hands on her waist.

Walter's wife waved to them as Hunter eased away from the pump and pulled onto the road. When they were out of sight, she asked, "Faster?"

"Oh yeah," Walter said.

She could hear the giddiness in his voice as she accelerated quickly, and they roared down the highway. It was ten miles before they reached a side road, and Walter motioned for her to turn right.

"The road's not as smooth, so you might want to go slow," he warned.

Hunter drove until Walter pointed off to the left, and she pulled to the side of the road. She saw a small trail. "Can we ride down that to get closer?"

"Yes, ma'am," he answered.

Hunter drove a half mile until a small waterfall came into view. She pulled to a stop and turned off the motor. She helped Walter off the back, set the kickstand, and dismounted, pulling off her helmet. "That's beautiful."

"I proposed to Betty here a million years ago," he said. "Remarkably, she said yes."

"How long have you been married?"

"Coming up on sixty years soon." He stared at the falling water.

Hunter pulled out her phone and took several pictures. She looked at Walter. "May I get a picture of you in front of the falls?"

Walter pushed his wiry hair back on his head and stood tall. "Yes, ma'am."

Hunter took several shots and showed them to Walter.

"Damn, I've gotten old," he said. "Time passes so quickly."

"Any regrets?" Hunter asked him.

"Maybe our kids were closer so we could visit more. Betty has been the love of my life since we first met. I wouldn't trade a second of my time with her."

Hunter could feel his genuine love for his wife, and her eyes were filled with tears. She was glad she was wearing her sunglasses.

"Do you have someone for your own?"

"Not yet, but I may have found someone."

"Don't waste a minute when you decide. The years pass all too quickly. Latch on and hold them close for as long as you can," Walter advised.

"I hope I will be as lucky as you and Betty," Hunter said.

"Don't dwell in the past. Grab ahold of your future and hold on tight. It will be a wild ride, but one you'll never regret."

Hunter was shocked by his comment. That was precisely what she needed to do, and to hear it from a total stranger was jolting. "I will," she said.

"I reckon I should get back to Betty. Thank you for the ride. It made my day," Walter said with tears in his eyes.

"I may be in the area for a while. Would you like to ride again?"

"I'd love that. My heart feels twenty years younger, but these old bones remind me I'm no longer a youngster."

They mounted and drove slowly back to the main highway. When Hunter pulled into the store, she stopped by the door. "Thank you for sharing the falls with me."

"Did you enjoy the ride?" Betty asked Walter.

"I did," he answered with a huge smile.

"The falls were beautiful."

"Hunter said she'd take me for another ride when she's able."

"I've got a busy few weeks, but I'll be back, so keep an eye open for me."

"I will. Thank you, Hunter."

"It was my pleasure. I'll see you again soon."

Hunter started the bike and drove away. She saw Walter waving in her mirror and lifted her hand to wave back at him. She hadn't planned on that side trip, but Hunter knew she was destined to meet Walter and hear his sage advice. Hunter opened the throttle and drove to Michelle's home.

CHAPTER TEN

Hunter's short exchange with Walter inspired her to talk to Michelle. She felt herself falling quickly and didn't want to prolong another heartbreak if Michelle turned away from her. Hunter parked in Michelle's driveway and walked to the front door to ring the bell.

When Michelle opened the door, Hunter felt herself melting. Michelle was wearing a black muscle shirt and workout shorts. *Delicious.* That was the first thing that came to Hunter's mind at the sight. *Focus.* She chastised herself for letting her hormones take over briefly.

"Welcome," Michelle said, swinging the door wide to invite Hunter inside. "Did you have a good ride?"

"Yes, I did. I picked up a passenger who directed me to a beautiful hidden waterfall."

"Really? This I've got to hear. Can I get you something to drink?"

125

"Some tea would be great. Thanks."

"Do you mind if I have a beer?"

"Heaven's no. I just don't drink when I'm on my bike."

"Good. I was just about to put the lasagna in to bake," Michelle answered.

"How long will that take?" Hunter asked.

Michelle turned and saw a worried look on Hunter's face. "At least an hour. Are you starving?"

"No. I need to talk with you about something," Hunter said.

Michelle poured a glass of tea and took out a beer before joining Hunter on the couch. "The look on your face is serious. Have I done something wrong?"

"Oh, my goodness, no," Hunter said. She took a long drink as she felt her burst of confidence fading. "You are almost too good to be true. I find myself falling deeper for you every day, but I need to share something with you before I let myself get head over heels for you. I'm not sure I can handle another heartbreak at this point in my life."

Michelle leaned forward and stroked Hunter's cheek. "You're trembling." She placed her beer on the table. "What's wrong?"

"Are you interested in a relationship with me?"

Michelle's mercury eyes searched Hunter's face. "You are the first person that makes me want to settle down as a family. From the first night we met, I knew deep in my heart you were the one. Everything that has happened since gives me confidence that we are meant to be together."

Hunter relaxed a bit, but she felt her body trembling with anxiety. "I don't want to have any secrets from you, and there is something that happened in my past that could surface one day, and I don't want you blindsided by not knowing the full story."

"I appreciate that."

"You are the first person I've told the entire story. Carson knows parts of it, but not the whole story."

Michelle's expression softened. "You can tell me anything."

Hunter took another sip of her tea. Her mouth felt suddenly dry. "May I have a refill first? I think I'll need it."

Michelle refilled her glass and returned to sit close to her.

Hunter took a deep breath and released it slowly. "I'm sure you know that Carson and I were a couple in college. We were rivals in high school, but we quickly became lovers when we met again in college, playing on the same team."

Michelle nodded. "Carson has told me that much."

"We were halfway into our freshman season and had a late practice one night. I missed a call from Lilly, my little sister. When I got her message, I thought it was too late to call. Carson and I had gone to dinner, and it was almost midnight when I checked my messages. Lilly was my world. I let her down when she needed me most. Not returning her call that night was the worst decision I ever made." Hunter took a drink. "The following day, my mom called and woke me in a panic. She had gone to Lilly's room to get her for breakfast, and Lilly had committed suicide."

"Oh my God. How old was she?"

"She would have been fifteen in a month. Carson held me while I cried and helped me pack to return home. She wanted to come with me, but I told her to stay with the team. I would let her know when the funeral would be held. When she finally relented, I climbed on my bike and drove home through a flood of tears." Hunter wiped tears from her cheek.

"I know this is hard. Do you need a break?"

Hunter shook her head. "I'm not sure I can finish if I stop."

"Okay," Michelle said.

"I didn't make it home before they removed Lilly to take her to the funeral home, so Mom took me to see her. She was so beautiful lying there. Like she was asleep. The funeral home staff had made an attempt to hide the rope burns on her neck, but they bled through the makeup. It was gut-wrenching to realize I would never talk or laugh with Lilly again. She was gone, and I had not answered her call. I had promised that I would always be there for her."

Michelle started to say something, and Hunter touched her lips. "Please let me finish."

Michelle nodded, and Hunter could see tears in her eyes.

"Dad was drunk off his ass when we returned home. Mom tried to console him while I curled up in a ball on Lilly's bed. When I reached for her pillow to smell her lavender scent, I felt a book under her pillow. I removed the pillow, and it was Lilly's journal. I couldn't keep myself from opening it and reading her entries. I was more confused when I read her last entry and flipped several pages back. What I read tore my heart from my chest."

Hunter took a drink and continued. "Since they were in diapers, Lilly's best friend was Jen. They did everything together. Lilly was sleeping over at Jen's one weekend and woke to go downstairs for a drink. Jen's older brother, Jay, was in the kitchen and was high on something. He took advantage of Lilly. Fuck it, he raped her," Hunter cried out. "He threatened that if she told anyone, he would let all her friends know she was a slut and begged him to fuck her. She left the house and walked home, creeping into her bedroom in the middle of the night. It was this shame that Lilly was dealing with, and when she couldn't bear it any longer, she took her life."

The timer on the stove sounded. Michelle picked up her tea glass. "I'll be right back." She entered the kitchen, pulled the lasagna pan from the oven, and refilled Hunter's tea.

"Thanks," Hunter said after taking a sip. She took another slow, deep breath and closed her eyes as she released it. "The rage I felt after reading that was indescribable. I honestly wanted to kill him, but instead, I bolted from the house and ran the short distance to their home. Jen opened the door, and I asked her where Jay was. She pointed upstairs, and I bolted up the stairs and burst through his door. He was sitting in a video chair playing a game. I looked to my right, and there was a baseball bat. I grabbed it and rushed him before he realized I was in his room. I unleashed a powerful swing and struck his left knee. I can still remember the crunch of breaking bones and the howl of pain he let out. Jen had chased me upstairs and stood in the doorway in shock when her parents rushed into the room.

"Her dad yelled out to me to put the bat down, but I wasn't done yet. Tears were rushing out of me as I pointed the bat at Jay. 'You tell them. You tell them what you did to Lilly, or I swear I will smash your head in.'

"When his dad demanded to know what I was talking about, Jay shrugged.

"He tried his best to lie. 'I don't know. She's gone crazy. She fucking broke my leg.'

"I lifted the bat to swing again, and he held up his arm to shield himself. 'Wait. Wait, he pleaded.'

"'Tell them,' I growled. 'Tell them what you did to Lilly.'

129

"My heart burst again while I listened to him answering so nonchalantly that he had been home high one night when Lilly was here for a sleepover. She came downstairs for a drink, and he couldn't help himself.

"Jay's dad roared at him. 'What do you mean you couldn't help yourself?'

"I saw the look of utter hatred when Jen cried out. 'You raped Lilly? You bastard, that's why she killed herself?'

"Their dad's face turned ashen. 'Son, is that true?'

"I dropped the bat, satisfied that the truth had come out. The son of a bitch wouldn't take a step for the rest of his life without the pain of the memory of what he did. Jen was in tears as I rushed past her. 'You can tell the cops I've gone home,' I told their dad and left the room. Somehow, I made it home and collapsed on our front porch. Later, Mom stepped outside and found me when the lights and sirens filled the neighborhood. 'What has happened?' she asked.

"I broke into tears again and told her what I had done between sobs. She was holding me in her arms, rocking me, when the police arrived and arrested me. 'Don't say a word until I get you a lawyer,' she warned when they cuffed me and placed me in the car."

Hunter paused before continuing.

"To skip ahead a bit, I was convicted of aggravated assault and sentenced to five years in prison. That's why I disappeared from basketball and broke up with Carson. I couldn't stand the thought of her seeing me in prison. She deserved more than I would ever be able to give her. I did my time and had my record expunged as part of my prerelease agreement, so my record is clean, but I fear the story may resurface one day. I won't start anything serious with you without you knowing that part of my history. It would be unbearable if it happened and you had no prior knowledge. I won't break your heart like that."

She hadn't noticed Michelle was crying.

"Oh, Hunter. I'm so sorry that happened."

The flood of tears Hunter was fighting broke through the dam, and Michelle pulled Hunter into her arms. She rocked her just as her mom had years ago. They ugly cried together until there was nothing left for either of them.

"Will you stay with me tonight? Or let me drive you home if you insist on leaving."

Hunter nodded her head. "I'm sorry I ruined your dinner."

"We can have it for lunch tomorrow. Come with me." Michelle held out her hand and led Hunter to her bedroom. She handed her shorts and a T-shirt to sleep in. "I'll be right back."

Hunter nodded and sat on the bed to change clothes.

†

Michelle pulled out her phone to text Carson.

Hunter is staying with me tonight.

Oh, you go, girl Carson responded.

It's not like that. We had an emotional talk tonight, and I didn't want Hunter to try to ride home. We'll see you at practice.

Is she okay?

She will be. I'll fill you in tomorrow.

Thank you, Michelle. She means a lot to me.

Me too. Goodnight.

Michelle stored the lasagna in the fridge and poured two glasses of tea to carry to the bedroom. She stopped in the doorway when she saw Hunter curled up on her side. She crept into the room and found her asleep. Michelle dressed for bed, turned off the lamp, and climbed in beside Hunter, wrapping her arms around her. Hunter moaned and pulled her closer.

Michelle held her and listened to Hunter's soft breathing as she considered the story Hunter had shared. *I probably would have killed the bastard.* She pushed the thought from her mind and allowed sleep to take her.

†

The sunlight streaming through the window woke Michelle. Hunter had turned to face her during the night and was still asleep. Michelle's kidneys screamed for relief, but she refused to leave the bed.

Michelle's movement on the bed caused Hunter to stir. Her eyes opened, and she found Michelle watching her closely.

"Good morning," she whispered.

"Good morning. I'll be right back, okay?"

Hunter nodded and watched Michelle leave the bed.

When she returned, Michelle let out a sigh of relief. "That's better."

Hunter smiled. "I peed a few hours ago. All that tea had me aching."

Michelle returned to the bed and lay on her side facing Hunter. "How do you feel this morning?"

"Relieved to have that weight off my chest. I had planned to talk to you this weekend, but the older man I picked up yesterday, Walter, filled me with encouragement and the confidence to talk to you."

"Walter, huh? Should I be jealous?" Michelle teased.

"I pulled into a small gas station on my ride for a drink, and he was sitting on a bench enjoying the sunshine. We talked about motorcycles, and I offered him a ride. He and his wife Betty owned the station, and she asked him to take me to the waterfall."

"So, you picked up a married man, and his wife sent him off with you?" Michelle's smile brightened the room.

"I promised her I'd bring him back. They have been married forever. He rode an Indian in his younger days and sold it when they started having kids. He was a joy to talk to, and I quickly realized offering him a ride was the right thing to do. Without knowing anything about me, we talked about letting go of the past and seeking happiness with someone you love."

"So, you gave him the ride of his life, and he gave you what? Courage?"

"Yeah. I think that's a good explanation."

"I know last night was hard for you, but thank you for trusting me enough to share your story. I can't begin to imagine surviving something like that."

"Carson hit the nail on the head. She told me I was trapped in heartbreak hell, and I needed to work through it because Lilly would want me to be happy and find love."

"Carson's a smart cookie," Michelle said. "Just don't tell her I told you."

"Carson loves you." Hunter took a deep breath. "I do, too."

"Wait. Will you say that again?"

"I said I love you, too."

"That's what I thought I heard. I thought love at first sight was a fairytale, but you've proved it isn't." Michelle ran her hand through Hunter's hair and locked eyes with her.

Hunter's tongue wet her lips, and Michelle smiled and leaned in to kiss her softly. "I've wanted to do that for days."

"I have dreamed of it," Hunter said. "Oh my God, I need to call Carson."

Michelle shook her head. "I texted her last night to let her know you were staying over."

"Thank you. I was in no shape to ride home last night."

"I wouldn't have let you," Michelle said. "I needed you here, so I knew you were okay. Call me selfish, but I wasn't ready to let you go."

"Are you ready to let me go this morning?" Hunter asked.

"If it were up to me, I'd never let you out of my sight again, but I will practice patience until you are ready."

"I was right last night when I said you were almost too good to be true," Hunter whispered.

"Oh, I have my flaws." Michelle grinned.

"Name one?" Hunter teased.

"I snore loudly when I'm tired."

"I know that already." Hunter smiled. "You stopped when I poked you, though."

"So, I wasn't dreaming you elbowed me?"

"Nope. It worked very well." Hunter laughed.

Michelle leaned forward to kiss Hunter again. "I love that sound."

"What? Of me laughing?"

Michelle nodded. "It warms my heart. There's nothing I want more than to make you, us, happy."

"I'd like that too," Hunter replied.

"Are you up for an early brunch? I'm starving."

"Yes. Then I need to go home to shower and dress. I don't need to show up to practice in the same clothes I wore yesterday. I'm sure someone would notice."

"You'd never live it down, but I can loan you a shirt. Jeans are jeans," Michelle said. "You can shower and dress while I warm up our food. Is a green polo different enough from the shirt you wore yesterday? Feel free to pick out anything from my closet that suits your fancy."

"Thanks, Michelle. I'm sure I can find something."

"Let me brush my teeth, and I'll get started on the food." Michelle climbed from the bed while Hunter snuggled back under the covers. When she returned to the room, she looked at Hunter. "Do you need to sleep some more?"

"No. It's just so comfortable. I'll get moving in a minute."

"I put a new toothbrush on the counter for you." Michelle picked up the untouched tea glasses and walked to the kitchen.

†

Hunter climbed from the bed and made it before stripping out of her clothes to shower. The water caressing her skin felt delightful as she bathed and washed her hair. Hunter dried and returned to the bedroom to dress. She chuckled and picked up her phone to send Carson a text.

Will you bring me two pairs of underwear to practice today? Good morning, by the way.

Good morning to you, too. Yes, to the underwear. Are you okay?

I am. I'll tell you all about it tonight. I promise.

Okay. I'll see you at practice.
Thanks for having my back, Carson.
Always.

Commando it is for now. Hunter slipped into her jeans, socks, and boots before walking to Michelle's closet. When she opened the door, she smiled at how well everything was organized and reached for the green polo Michelle had suggested. Hunter rolled her underwear inside the T-shirt. She would place them in her saddlebags when she left.

†

Michelle was setting the table when Hunter entered. "I'm going to take these to my bike. I'll be right back to help."

"Take your time. We've got another fifteen minutes before it's ready."

Hunter nodded, walked out into the morning heat, and tucked her clothing into a saddlebag. "It's going to be another scorcher today," she said as she returned inside.

"Welcome to Vegas," Michelle teased. "There will be a lot more of those."

"What can I do?"

"You can pour some tea. We can start on salads if you want. I have Ranch and Honey Mustard."

"Honey Mustard is good. Do you want me to pull out the salad and some dressing?"

"Sure. That dressing is good for me, too. You can fill our salad bowls while I get the bread ready to go in."

†

"That was another delicious meal. Thank you."

"No problem. I enjoy cooking when I have someone to share it with," Michelle replied.

"You can cook for me anytime."

"There's no way I can eat the rest of this, so I'll bring a dish and place it in the breakroom for you and Carson to eat if you're not sick of lasagna yet."

Hunter looked at Michelle. "That would be great. Thank you."

"Not to brag, but Carson loves my lasagna."

"I do, too." Hunter smiled. "Can I clean the dishes while you shower?"

"Just rinse them and place them in the dishwasher. Leave the food, and I'll assemble a salad and lasagna for you."

Hunter cleaned the kitchen while she waited for Michelle to shower and dress. She was seated on the couch when Michelle returned. Michelle sat beside her and grinned. "I feel better. How about you?"

"I definitely smell better," Hunter said. "I love your products. They remind me of you, so if you see me sniffing my arm today at practice, you'll know why."

Michelle broke out laughing. "You are too funny. Is it too early to ask you about spending the night Saturday night after our night on the town?"

"I would like that. It also gives Carson and Stacy some privacy. When you pick me up Saturday morning, I will have a bag packed if that's good with you."

"That's perfect," Michelle replied. She reached for Hunter and pulled her into a kiss. "I'll get the food together and meet you at practice."

"Thanks." Hunter leaned into another quick kiss before walking to the door. She stopped short of the door and turned back to Michelle. "Are we good?"

Michelle smiled. "Yes. We are good."

†

Hunter was pleased when she arrived at the training facility to see Carson's car in the lot. Carson sat behind the wheel and was talking on the phone. When she looked up, she motioned for Hunter and held out a small bag with underwear.

"I'll be inside in just a few."

Hunter held up the bag. "Thanks."

She was tying her shoes when Carson entered the locker room.

"Sorry, I was on the phone with Stacy. Are you okay?"

"No problem. Yeah, I'm good. I had a talk with Michelle last night about what happened with Lilly. She was worried about my emotional exhaustion and wouldn't let me drive home. It was nice to wake up beside someone again. Michelle is an incredible person."

"Yes, she is. So, what's next?"

"An overnight Saturday night after we have a night on the town with you and Stacy. We agreed to take things slow, but I feel better now that we have no secrets."

"That's great to hear. I think you two are adorable together."

"She's bringing salad and lasagna for us for tonight. She knows how much you like it. Michelle's putting it in the fridge in the breakroom for us, so don't forget."

"I won't. That woman can cook for me anytime."

"I hear that."

The door opened, and Michelle strolled into the locker room. "Hello, lovelies," she said with a grin. "Your dinner is in the breakroom. I hope you will enjoy it."

"Thank you. I'm sure we will," Carson said. "I'm going to start stretching. See you in a few."

"All good?" Michelle asked.

Hunter turned to straddle the bench and looked up at Michelle. "Perfect now."

"What's the plan for today?"

"What do you feel the least confident about?"

Michelle pulled her shirt over her head. "My three-point shot."

"Let's start with some midrange shots, and when you're warm, we can work on those. What are the keys?"

"Bend my knees and lift."

Hunter clapped. "You do listen to me."

"Of course. Why wouldn't I? You gave me a great analysis of my good and bad performance. I know you're working hard to expand my range."

"All-star team, here we come." Hunter smiled.

"I wouldn't go that far just yet."

"The season is still young. Play well, and you could make it. Fans love you."

"We'll see."

"Is it a bad goal?" Hunter asked.

"Not at all."

"Good, I'm going to start stretching." Hunter left the locker room and joined Carson and Coach in the gym.

"Hey, Hunter," Coach said.

"Good afternoon, Coach."

"What are you working on with Michelle today?"

"More midrange and some three-pointers. I want to build Michelle's confidence to try a few step backs and midrange shots for Friday's game."

"I can see a drastic improvement in her shots already. Keep pushing her."

"Yes, Coach." Hunter sat on the floor next to Carson and began stretching. When Coach walked off, Hunter looked at Carson. "I'm also encouraging her to attempt a three if the situation arises. I think it will catch the defense flat-footed. You should have a great shooting game, too."

"I hope you're right on that."

"I'd love to see you and Michelle make the All-Star team this year."

Carson chuckled. "There's nothing like lofty goals. I love it, though."

"Let's make it happen," Hunter said, stretching her legs. She jumped to her feet when Michelle entered and sat. "Let's get you loose." She stood behind Michelle and applied gentle pressure to her back as she reached for her toes.

†

Practice went well that day and Thursday. Hunter was proud of the improvement in Michelle's shooting. "I can't wait to watch you in action tomorrow," she told Michelle after Coach had ended practice.

"Are you planning on running today?"

"I need to get a few laps in," Hunter answered. "Do you need something?"

"Carson invited me for dinner tonight. She's ordering a bunch of pasta to do some carb loading. I'll stay and take you home if that's okay."

140

"Perfect," Hunter answered. "Get showered, and I promise I won't take long."

"There's no hurry, so run all you want."

Hunter nodded, took a ball from the rack, and jogged down the court as Michelle left. Today, she would vary her routine a bit. Instead of running laps around the court, she planned to take a three-point shot, rebound, and sprint down the court to take another shot. Hunter felt her endurance was improving and wanted to work on increasing speed in short bursts. It would give her a thorough workout in a much shorter time and be much more fun than wind sprints. She shot, retrieved the ball, and raced to the other end to repeat the drill.

†

Coach was leaning on the door frame watching Hunter when Michelle returned from the locker room. She looked over when Michelle stood beside her. "I've never seen someone work so hard on a practice team."

"This is so much more for Hunter. It's getting her foot back in the door for something more."

Hunter drained a three from the top of the key. "She's got one of the most natural shots I've ever seen. A heart of gold, too. You can see how much the game means to her during live-action. She's right there on the court with you."

"Could you support Hunter, Carson, and me on a three-on-three team when the new league starts?"

"I could. Suzy and I have talked about cosponsoring a team with our ownership group. I think the three of you would be perfect. A good salary and staying in shape without traveling to Europe for the off-season, too. It would be great exposure for Hunter. I think it's going to be a very popular league."

"Is there any hope for her to make a roster with us next year?" Michelle asked.

"The expansion of the league will pull from some experienced teams. We can only protect five to six players from the expansion, so we will have some open roster slots. No promises, but I'd love to have her in uniform. That's between us. I don't want to raise her hopes if it doesn't work out for us. With her work ethic, any team would be foolish to pass on giving her a shot. I'd rather have her on our side of the ball."

"My lips are sealed," Michelle said.

"Have a good night, and get plenty of rest tonight."

"See you tomorrow for pregame," Michelle said as Coach turned away. She walked inside and took a seat.

Hunter looked up at her and smiled. She drained a final shot and jogged to place the ball on the rack. Sweat dripped from her face onto her shirt. "I need to walk a little bit to cool down before I hit the shower."

"No problem." Michelle pulled out her phone and scrolled through the WNBA news while she waited.

CHAPTER ELEVEN

Friday morning, Hunter woke with excitement. The game was hours away, but she was ready to see how the team performed from floor level. The practice team would sit on the end of the bench after the game started, providing her an excellent view of the game. She would also listen to Coach during breaks and time-outs to gain an intimate knowledge of her coaching perspective. Maybe if Hunter couldn't earn a roster spot, she could try to get an assistant coaching job somewhere for more experience and remain a part of the game she loved.

When Carson emerged from her bedroom, Hunter was on her second cup of coffee. "Good morning, sunshine."

"I see you woke up bright and chipper this morning," Carson said as she walked to the coffee pot.

"I am excited about the game tonight and couldn't stay in bed any longer."

"You do realize we don't play until tonight, right?" Carson said, taking a seat beside Hunter.

Hunter nodded. "I may ride to the practice facility for a challenging workout to burn off some energy."

"That's probably not a bad idea." Carson smiled. "I don't ever remember you being this excited before."

"I've really missed the game, and even if this is the closest I ever come to playing again, I'll be happy. What time does Stacy arrive today?"

"I pick her up at two. We'll meet you back here to attend the pregame dinner at four."

"I get to go to those?"

"You are a part of the team, so yes, you do. Stacy can drop us, grab a bite, and meet us at the game."

"Where's the dinner?"

"At the arena. We have meals catered before each home game," Carson explained. "Then we relax in the players' lounge until it's time to dress and warm up for the game."

"That's exciting. Do you mind if I go to work out?"

"Not at all. It's preferable to you bouncing off the walls here," Carson teased.

"I'll be back before you need to leave to pick up Stacy. I'll dress and be ready when you return."

"Do you want some breakfast before you go?"

"I had some cereal. Do I need to cook something for you?"

"Go. I can handle breakfast. I cooked it before you arrived, remember?"

"Pop-tarts and frozen waffles don't count." Hunter chuckled.

Carson punched her in the arm. "Just go already."

Hunter stood and placed her cup in the sink. "I'll see you later."

"Be safe, and don't pull a muscle. We are going for breakfast after the game. Michelle's already been notified."

"Perfect," Hunter replied, grabbing her keys and walking out the door.

†

Hunter dropped shades over her eyes and rode the familiar route to the practice facility. A few cars were in the lot when she arrived, but Hunter walked straight into the locker room to change. She planned to do a few circuits on the weight machines and then run and shoot.

After increasing the weights in her workout, she finished two rounds before breaking to hydrate. She had worked up a nice sweat and burned off some of her over-abundant energy. She emptied her bladder, walked into the gym to pick up a ball, and started jogging down the court. The sprint and shoot had worked well for her so far, so she dribbled down the court, swerved to evade an imaginary defender, and then dropped a three. Rebound, run, and repeat.

Hunter was beginning to get winded when she saw Coach enter and heard her call her over.

"Why am I not surprised you are here?"

"I was bouncing off the walls, so I decided to come to work off some energy," Hunter said between gulps of water.

"Will you bottle some of your energy for me?" Coach teased. "Are you excited about the game tonight?"

"Very much so. I can hardly wait to see the team demolish Dallas," Hunter replied.

"They are still a viable opponent."

"The team is well prepared, and I think they will drop a hundred tonight."

"That's a lofty goal."

"I feel pretty confident they will. Their defense will cause some easy points off turnovers, and Carson will have a hot hand this week."

"How do you think Michelle will do?"

Hunter beamed. "She's going to be epic tonight."

"Epic, huh?"

"I hope some of her new moves will surprise you and, more importantly, catch Dallas off guard."

"The crowd loves her and gets excited when she plays well. You two seem to be hitting it off well together, too."

"What's not to love? She's got a heart of gold." Hunter smiled.

"That she does. I'm going to head home for a power nap. I'll see you for the pregame meal."

"See ya, Coach." Hunter sat and finished another cup of water. When she heard her stomach rumble, she walked to the locker room and called Carson. "I'm finally hungry. Have you had lunch? I can bring some sandwiches home. Fine, I'll shower, dress, and see you soon."

†

Carson was watching television when Hunter arrived with lunch. "I made a fresh pitcher of tea if you want some. How was your workout?"

"It was just what I needed. I feel much more relaxed now. Hungry, too. Let's eat."

"I hope the outfit on your bed was what you planned to wear tonight. I went ahead and pressed it for you."

146

"It was. Thank you," Hunter said. "How long has it been since you've seen Stacy?"

"Several weeks. I can't wait for her to arrive."

"When does she have to go back?"

"I'll drop her at the airport Tuesday morning. We will play them the following week after a flight to Dallas."

"We have Dallas, Seattle, and LA all coming up?"

"Yeah, this will be a long road stretch for us. After we finish in LA, we fly into New York. I hope you can sleep on a jet. It will be a long night."

"That seems like a crazy schedule."

Carson nodded. "Every team in the league has at least one week like that. Poor planning, if you ask me, but they try to cram as many games as possible before the playoffs."

"Where are the playoffs this year?"

"We are the host team this year, so we'd better make it."

"Do you have any doubts?"

"As long as everyone stays healthy, we've got a great shot at winning." Carson smiled. "We've been lucky no one has been injured this season."

"Hush now. Don't talk anything up," Hunter warned.

†

When Carson left to pick up Stacy, Hunter showered and dressed in her game-day outfit. She looked at her image in the mirror and smiled. "Not bad." After spritzing on cologne, she returned to the living room to wait for Carson to return. She was nervous about meeting Stacy and paced around the room until she realized she was pacing. Hunter sat on the couch and picked up her phone. She took a selfie and sent it to her mom.

All set for my first game night.

You look very professional.

Thanks, Mom. Do you have the game on television tonight?

I do, and I'll be looking for you. Tell Carson good luck from me.

I will. I'll call this weekend and give you our schedule for LA.

Good luck to you tonight, too. Love you.

Love you too, Mom.

Hunter looked at the clock. Michelle would probably still be at home.

Are you ready to play?

Basketball?

Yes, silly.

I'm stoked. Tonight is going to be great.

Yes, it is. See you at the dinner. I hear we're going for breakfast afterward.

Are you dressed already?

Yes, just waiting for Stacy and Carson to return.

Send me a selfie?

Trade you.

Deal.

Hunter sent the selfie she had sent to her mom.

When her phone pinged, she saw the photo from Michelle. *Holy shit, be still my heart.*

I love the new outfit on you. It's a great look.

I hear Carson arriving. I'll see you soon.

Yes, you will.

†

Carson walked inside with Stacy in tow, carrying a small bag.

"Ten guesses who you were talking to," she teased.

"Not talking. Just texting to see if Michelle was ready for the game tonight."

"Hi, Hunter. I'm Stacy."

"It's nice to meet you. I've heard a lot about you," Hunter said.

"Likewise. Carson talks about you every time we talk." Stacy smiled.

"I promise I've only shared the best with you both," Carson said.

Hunter smiled. "Do you believe that?" she asked Stacy.

"Not for a minute." Stacy laughed. "Let me toss my bag in the bedroom. I'm starved."

Hunter watched her walk down the hall. "She's cute," she whispered to Carson.

"She said the same thing when I showed her your picture." Carson laughed. "You look nice, by the way. You smell good, too. I hope it doesn't distract Michelle."

"Naw, she's a professional. She'll stay focused," Hunter said.

Stacy returned and approached Hunter empty-handed. "Now for a proper welcome." She pulled Hunter into a hug. "Welcome to Vegas. I hear you're loving it so far."

"I am," Hunter said. "I appreciate being able to share your home for a while."

"Are you kidding? Carson says you keep her fed and laughing. Being so far apart sucks, so I'm glad you're here to keep her company."

"It's been great catching up and meeting some new people."

"One player in particular." Stacy smiled.

"I might have let it slip that you and Michelle have spent much time together." Carson shrugged when Hunter blushed.

"She's done a great job playing Cupid," Hunter said.

"A girl can do much worse than Michelle. She's got a heart of gold," Stacy said.

"Yeah, she does," Hunter agreed.

"Ready to hit the road?" Carson asked.

"I'm right behind you," Hunter answered.

†

When they arrived at the arena, Hunter pulled out her ID badge. "The press makes a big deal of the team's arrival, so I will enter first."

"Like hell you will. You're going in with me," Carson said. She leaned over to kiss Stacy. "We'll see you after the game."

"Good luck. Kick some ass tonight, baby," Stacy said.

Hunter pulled Carson's door open, and they walked to the player's entrance. They were almost there when they heard Michelle.

"Wait up a second," she called to them. "I need to enter with the two best-looking women in the arena."

"That should be my line. You two look great," Hunter said.

"Let's go strut our stuff." Carson laughed and held out her arms for Hunter and Michelle.

†

When they started down the hallway, camera flash units went crazy. The photographers called for them to stop so they could take more shots. Hunter could feel her anxiety increase with each snap of the shutter. She let go of Carson's arm and walked ahead of them.

Carson frowned when she caught up with Hunter. "Are you okay?"

Hunter nodded. "A bit of anxiety with all the cameras. I guess I'm paranoid someone will recognize me."

"The two people who matter the most know, so don't worry." Carson smiled at her. "Enjoy your first night." She grabbed her arm and dragged her forward.

The meal was a feast, and Hunter worried she would be sluggish when she hit the court. She shouldn't have worried. As soon as she dressed in the game warm-up gear, her excitement returned, and she was ready for anything. The black pants and coat fit her nicely, and the form-fitting silver warm-up shirt was comfortable. Hunter smiled at Carson and Michelle in the black and silver uniforms before walking to the tunnel. She stopped at the entrance to the court and took in the arena from a player's point of view. Fans were already coming in, and her eyes landed on Stacy sitting behind the bench. She thought of walking over to her until Michelle walked beside her.

"Will you help me stretch?"

"You know I will. What's your mantra for tonight?"

"Kiss the sweet spot," Michelle said, smiling.

"That's right. You are going to shine tonight."

†

The team didn't take long to jump to a lead, and their defensive scheme worked perfectly. Carson trapped the guard, stole the ball, and found Michelle racing down the court alone for a fast break. *Dunk it.*

Hunter watched Michelle take flight and slam the ball home. The packed arena erupted, and Michelle pointed to Coach, who gave her a thumbs-up sign. They were up by twelve when the first quarter ended. Carson was on fire from behind the arc, and Michelle dominated down low. Hunter laughed when Carson passed a ball into Michelle and yelled, "Kiss it."

Hunter smiled when Michelle performed the perfect step-back shot from ten feet to end the quarter. "Yes," Hunter cheered from the bench.

"Was that a new play call?" Coach teased when they sat on the bench.

"Yes, Coach, it was," Carson said, shooting a wink at Hunter.

"I like it, and the result was beautiful," Coach replied. "You've got a good lead but can't let off the gas. Their guards can heat up at any time. Let's double the lead by half-time."

When they broke the huddle, the players returned to the court.

"Kiss it? Your idea, I suppose?"

"Guilty," Hunter replied. "I told Michelle to kiss it off the sweet spot, meaning to bank that step back. It's kind of stuck."

Coach shook her head and laughed. "I like it. Any other new play calls I need to know about?"

"Not yet," Hunter replied.

†

At halftime, the players rushed to the locker room. Coach placed an arm around Hunter's shoulder. "You might get your hundred points tonight."

"I know we will." Hunter smiled. "I can feel it."

Dallas made a run in the third quarter, and when they pulled within ten with two minutes in the quarter, Coach called, "Time out."

The players huddled around her. "Did we forget how to play defense all of a sudden? Don't let them come back on you. Carson and Simone, shut their guards down. Box out and keep them off the boards."

"Yes, Coach," they answered in unison.

When play resumed, Michelle had another opportunity to dunk on a fast break after a great defensive play.

"That's more like it," Coach called out.

When there were two minutes left in the game, Hunter looked up to the scoreboard to see they had scored ninety-seven points. *Almost there.* Michelle moved away from the basket to the corner, and Hunter watched as the ball was passed around the arc to Michelle. Her defender hadn't come out, and she was wide open. *Bend and lift.* She jumped up from the bench and nearly came unglued when Michelle dropped her first three-point shot so perfectly that the nylon barely moved. She lifted her hand with three fingers in the air and jogged down the court.

Hunter laughed and pointed at the scoreboard when Coach looked her way. The final score was one hundred and five after several made free throws. After the team celebrated on the court, Coach walked over to her.

"Good thing we didn't bet."

"They played fantastic tonight," Hunter said. "Congratulations."

"Thank you for all your hard work, especially with Michelle. Her versatility is wide open now."

"She just needed to believe she could. I think you will see a different player moving forward. She's a hard worker."

†

Coach congratulated the team in the locker room on a well-played game. "Tonight, you played well as a team and perfectly implemented our game plan. It's a tough decision to award a game ball because so many of you played well, but tonight's ball goes to the player who hit her first-ever three-point shot. Congratulations, Michelle." Coach tossed her the ball, and the team erupted in applause. Michelle caught the ball, and her eyes were shining.

"Thanks, Coach and Hunter, for encouraging me this week."

Coach nodded. "Hit the showers, and I'll see you on Monday. Rest and enjoy your weekend. We've got a tough stretch over the next few weeks."

†

"Will you ride with me?" Michelle asked Hunter.

"I hoped you would ask. I'll let Carson know," Hunter replied.

"I'll be ready in a few minutes."

Hunter rushed to catch up with Carson. "I'm going to wait and ride with Michelle."

"We'll go ahead and get a booth," Carson said as she reached for Stacy's hand.

"We won't be far behind you," Hunter said. She returned to the locker room, and Michelle was slipping into her shoes. "They will go ahead and get us a booth."

Michelle picked up her game ball and offered it to Hunter. "I want you to have this."

Hunter shook her head. "Thanks, but I'll accept the next one. This one is all yours." She picked up a black marker and wrote on the ball in large letters. *MY FIRST THREE POINT SHOT.* Hunter added the date and handed it back to Michelle. "For your trophy case. I'm proud of how you played tonight."

Michelle took the ball and tucked it under her arm. "Thank you. It felt great."

"Good. Now let's go eat. I worked up an appetite," Hunter said.

†

They were eating when Stacy stopped and asked, "What was the 'kiss it' all about?"

"Coach asked, too, and when I told her, she loved it," Hunter said.

"Hunter has been working with me on my shooting, and when she was showing me the step back, she told me to kiss it off the sweet spot to bank the shot, so 'kiss it' has kind of stuck."

Stacy broke out laughing. "That's hilarious and brilliant."

"My coach from junior high taught me that. Of course, when I told Michelle the first time, she broke out laughing, thinking it was sexual innuendo. But it makes her relax and smile, so it's a win-win."

"I could hear you thinking *bend and lift* when I took my three, too," Michelle admitted. "It worked."

"Maybe I need to steal Hunter for a week," Stacy teased,

"Sorry, love, she belongs to Vegas," Carson said.

"I am so glad Coach gave us the weekend off," Michelle said. "What time can I pick you up in the morning?" she asked Hunter.

"Considering it's almost midnight, is nine too early for you?"

"Nine is perfect."

Carson looked at Stacy. "These two are exploring this weekend, and Hunter is spending the night at Michelle's to give us some time together."

"That's not necessary," Stacy said, "but thank you."

"We'll still meet you for dinner and a casino night tomorrow. I hear there's sushi in our future," Michelle told Stacy.

"I'm always up for that." Stacy smiled.

"Let's roll," Carson said.

"May I drop you home?" Michelle asked Hunter.

"Yes, please. I may or may not see you two in the morning. I know you like to sleep in, so we'll see you at six tomorrow night."

†

Michelle parked in the driveway when they returned to the condo. She turned to Hunter and kissed her. "I've wanted to do that all day."

"Again," Hunter said.

"Do you have your bag packed already?" Michelle asked.

"Yes, I do."

"Go get it and come home with me."

"I'll be right back," Hunter said, leaning over to kiss Michelle.

"Hurry."

The condo was quiet when Hunter slipped inside. She walked quickly to her room to collect her bag and rushed back through the front door. Hunter placed her bag in the back seat and climbed inside.

"Welcome back."

†

Michelle placed Hunter's bag on the couch and turned to pull her into a kiss. "Dance with me?"

Hunter nodded and melted into Michelle's arms.

"Alexa, play my smooth groove playlist," Michelle said.

Hunter and Michelle moved together while kissing deeply when the music started playing. Their bodies locked together as they became lost in the sensual music. Hunter buried her hands in Michelle's hair and moaned deeply into her mouth.

"I couldn't wait to let my fingers run through your hair. It's just as soft as I dreamed it would be," Hunter whispered into Michelle's ear.

"It's an incredible turn-on for me, so take your time," Michelle answered. "It feels so good."

When Hunter's hands moved down Michelle's back to untuck her shirt and allow her hands to roam over bare skin, Michelle broke the kiss. "Should we move this to the bedroom?"

"Yes, please," Hunter replied.

Michelle entwined their fingers and led Hunter down the hall. When they entered the bedroom, she began unbuttoning Hunter's shirt.

Hunter could see Michelle's fingers trembling as she manipulated the buttons. She placed her hands on Michelle's and looked into her eyes. "Let me help."

Michelle nodded and removed her shirt and sports bra while Hunter opened her shirt. She let the shirt fall to the floor and opened the front enclosure of her bra. Michelle stepped forward, guiding the straps down Hunter's arms, her hands caressing the smooth, taut muscles on Hunter's arms.

When Michelle looked into Hunter's eyes and smiled, Hunter could read the passion ignited in them. She pulled Michelle close, and when their skin touched, she gasped. It seemed forever since she had been skin-on-skin with Carson, and Michelle's body was so different. Her skin was smooth and supple, but the definition of the muscles in her torso cried out for Hunter's fingers to stroke their firmness.

"I love the way you feel under my fingertips."

"Your touch sets me on fire," Michelle breathed against Hunter's neck.

"I'm ready to feel all of you," Hunter said as her hands touched Michelle's belt.

"Are you sure?"

"Positive," Hunter answered. "I need you."

†

Michelle's heart was hammering in her chest as Hunter's hands opened her belt and pants. When Hunter's hands slipped inside and cupped her ass, she thought she would explode from the intense pleasure coursing through her veins. She kicked off her loafers as Hunter's hands guided the pants down her body. Her eyes glowed as Hunter removed the remainder of her clothes and stretched out on the bed. She reached up for Michelle.

"Come lay beside me."

Michelle lay on her back and watched Hunter's hand as she traced upward from her hipbone, across her abs, and to her right breast. She felt her body quivering under Hunter's touch.

"You have such a beautiful body," Hunter said as she continued her exploration.

"Your touch is electric," Michelle said as her nipples ached to be touched. "I need more."

When Hunter rolled on top of Michelle, she reached to guide her head down for a kiss. "We fit perfectly together."

Hunter rolled her hips into Michelle, causing her to moan. "I'd have to agree." She smiled and kissed Michelle.

†

The following two hours passed in a blur of touches and kisses as Michelle and Hunter made love for the first time. They were entwined and breathing hard when Michelle looked into Hunter's eyes from above. She frowned when she saw a tear trickle down Hunter's cheek and was confused.

She wiped away the tears. "Are you okay?"

"Things couldn't be more perfect than they are now," Hunter said. "I never dreamed I would feel this way again, but every breath is special with you. I'm afraid to close my eyes, fearing I will wake up and all of this has been a dream."

"You are a dream come true, but we are very real. Every inch of my body is trembling from our lovemaking. I've never felt anything like it before," Michelle said.

She rolled onto her side with a leg draped over Hunter. Her fingers trailed down Hunter's face. "I feel like I've looked for you all my life."

Hunter smiled as she buried her hand in Michelle's hair. "Isn't it odd how we've come together?"

"It just reinforces that we were meant to be. I am so happy you came to Vegas."

They cuddled until the ache in Michelle's bladder became too much. "Will you share a glass of tea with me? After I release some?" She grinned.

"I'll get one while you warm the toilet seat," Hunter replied.

†

Hunter was curled around Michelle's body when she woke hours later. She carefully moved from the bed and pulled on an oversized T-shirt before walking to the kitchen. Hunter looked at the coffee pot and was pleased it was already prepared, so she turned it on and walked to the fridge.

She removed a carton of eggs, shredded cheese, and a bowl of fruit chunks. She was cooking scrambled eggs when she felt Michelle's long arms around her waist. Michelle kissed her neck and sighed.

"Oh, no, you don't," Hunter said, waving her spatula. "We are having breakfast in bed this morning."

"Do you mean seconds?" Michelle teased.

"Well, yes. Pour us some coffee and go back to bed. I'll be there in a few minutes."

Michelle nibbled her ear. "Yes, ma'am," she replied and poured their coffee. When Hunter arrived, she was sitting in bed, propped against the headboard. Hunter sat on the bed before her and offered her a bite of eggs.

"Those are good," Michelle replied as Hunter took a bite and offered Michelle some melon. "I could get used to this treatment."

"I hope you will," Hunter replied.

"I will cook tomorrow." Michelle smiled. "Are you still up for some exploring today?"

"Very much so. I'll clean up from breakfast, and then we can shower."

Michelle shook her head. "We can clean up from breakfast."

CHAPTER TWELVE

After sharing a kiss-filled leisurely shower, Michelle turned to Hunter. "We'd better dress quickly before we fall back into bed."

"I agree. However, I would never pass on a day spent with you anywhere."

"You are so good for my ego," Michelle teased.

"I mean every word of it. Even when we've been apart, I am eager to be back with you."

Michelle nodded. "I know that feeling. Is it too soon to discuss you moving in here?"

Hunter hesitated. "Are you sure you are ready for that?"

Michelle took her hand. "I've never been more sure of anything. Please consider it, but if you feel it's too soon, I'll wait until you're ready."

Hunter shook her head. "I'm ready. I just don't want you to feel rushed."

"We can move your stuff Monday after practice if you want."

"Let me discuss it with Carson. Stacy leaves Tuesday, and then we head out on the road. Maybe we just wait until we get back from the trip from hell?"

"That would probably make more sense and not impede their time together," Michelle agreed.

"Let's do that then. Speaking of the road. What are the hotel sleeping arrangements like?" Hunter asked.

"Carson and I usually room together," Michelle said. "There won't be time for anything but sleeping, so maybe Carson wouldn't mind sharing."

"We'll see how that goes." Hunter tied her hiking boots. "Ready?"

"Let's pack a cooler of drinks. We can eat lunch out somewhere before returning home."

"That works for me," Hunter said, reaching for Michelle's hand.

†

"Will you show me the waterfall Walter took you to?" Michelle asked.

"I'd love to," Hunter replied and gave her directions.

When they drove by the store, Hunter frowned when she didn't see Walter sitting in the sun. Time permitting, they would stop to check on him if they returned this way. Hunter pointed to the turn, and several minutes later, they arrived at the falls.

"I would never have guessed these were here," Michelle said. "I haven't driven out this way much to explore. They are beautiful. Do you want to go get wet?"

Hunter jumped out of the Jeep. "Let's do it." She reached for Michelle's hand, and they walked down the trail to the falls.

"Wait," Michelle said and rushed to the back of the Jeep for towels. She tucked them under her arm and took Hunter's hand.

Hunter laughed when they reached a large boulder, and she began stripping out of her clothes.

"We're going skinny-dipping?" Michelle asked.

"Yes, love, we are." Hunter smiled.

Hunter entered the cool water first and reached for Michelle's hand to lead her under the water flow. The cascading water was relaxing as it pelted down their bodies, and Hunter moved them one step beyond the flow and kissed Michelle.

"Isn't this beautiful?" Hunter asked, reaching her hand beneath the water.

Michelle nodded. "Not as beautiful as you." They kissed until they were breathless.

"I think we should dry off and get dressed if we're going to see anything else today," Michelle said, reaching for Hunter's hand. "Thank you for sharing this with me."

"It was my pleasure," Hunter replied.

Hunter placed the towels in the back and pulled out two drinks before climbing inside the Jeep. She handed one to Michelle. "Drink up. We sure don't need to get dehydrated."

"That's right." Michelle opened the bottle and took a long drink. "Are you ready to continue exploring?"

"Let's go farther down the road and see what we can find. We might see some sheep or other wildlife."

A half-hour later, Michelle pulled off the road onto a trail and cut across the desert. She headed for a large outcropping of rocks, hoping to find sheep. When she pulled close, she turned to Hunter. "I think it's just too danged hot for anything to be out right now."

"Not quite." Hunter pointed toward movement as a large ram rushed across a ridge and disappeared into the shade of a cave. "But it is hot. Let's head back home and see if we can grab some lunch."

†

Hunter smiled when they approached the small store, and she saw Walter sitting out front. "Do you mind stopping for a little while?"

"Not at all," Michelle said, pulling into the lot.

Hunter followed Michelle out of the Jeep and reached for her hand as they walked toward Walter. He looked up to see them approach and broke into a smile.

"Welcome back, Hunter. I see you brought company this time."

"Hey, Walter, this is my girlfriend, Michelle."

Michelle's smile was almost as bright as Walter's when Hunter introduced her as her girlfriend.

"Nice to meet you. You sure are a tall drink of water." Walter smiled.

Michelle smiled. "I hear that often."

Betty opened the door and brought Walter a hot dog for lunch. "Hey, Hunter. If you two are hungry, I've got a fresh batch of hotdogs."

"Do you like hotdogs?" Hunter asked Michelle.

"Love them," Michelle answered.

"Betty, this is my girlfriend, Michelle," Hunter repeated.

"Nice to meet you both," Michelle said.

"Come inside, and you can bring out hotdogs," Betty told Michelle. "Watch your head coming through the door," she teased.

Hunter settled in beside Walter. "How are you doing?"

"I'm blessed to be waking up every day. It looks like you are happy," he said.

"I took your advice and let go of the past. Michelle makes me happy, and I realized I deserved happiness."

"That sounds like a great decision. You are much prettier with a smile," Walter said.

"I took her to the waterfall you shared with me, and we went skinny-dipping."

"No, you didn't," Walter said.

"Just ask Michelle. I'm sure the blush on her face will confirm my claim."

Michelle returned carrying a tray with four hotdogs, and Betty followed her with two sodas.

Walter winked at Hunter and looked at Michelle. "I heard you two went skinny-dipping."

Michelle's face turned scarlet. "Um, yes, sir, we did."

"Don't let him tease you. We did it all the time when we were younger."

"That's how we ended up with six kids." Walter chuckled. His eyes grew wide. "I know where I've seen you before. Don't you play basketball for Vegas?" he asked Michelle.

Michelle smiled. "Yes, sir, I do. That's where we met."

Walter turned to Hunter. "Do you play, too?"

"I'm just on the practice team," Hunter replied.

Michelle sat next to Hunter. "For now. Did you see me hit that three-pointer the other night?"

"Right near the end of the game," Walter said.

Michelle nodded. "Hunter taught me that."

He smiled at Hunter. "I'd say you taught her well."

Hunter grinned. "She's a good student. These dogs are great, Betty."

"There's more if you're still hungry. I'm going back inside where it's semi-cool," Betty announced. "Let me know if you need anything else. It was nice to meet you, Michelle."

"Likewise, Betty. Thanks for a great lunch."

"Thanks for the business." Betty smiled.

"It will be two weeks before we play at home again, but would you and Betty come to a game if I bring you tickets?" Michelle asked.

"If you have a Sunday game. We close the store on Sundays."

"I will check the schedule and let you know. I know we've got some Sunday games on the schedule."

"I'd like that. We don't get to town often anymore. Especially at night since neither of us sees well enough to drive."

"That's perfect then. Our Sunday games are usually in the afternoon," Michelle answered.

After they ate, Hunter looked at Michelle. "I think we should head home. We are meeting friends for dinner tonight."

"Thanks for stopping in today, and keep that smile on your face."

"I will," Hunter said. "Let me take the tray back to Betty."

"Go ahead. I'll take it inside. Thanks for sharing lunch with me."

"We'll see you once we return from our road trip," Hunter promised.

"Drive safe. You're carrying precious cargo," Walter told Michelle.

"Yes, sir, I am." Michelle smiled at him and reached for Hunter.

†

"We've got two hours before we need to head into town. What would you like to do?" Michelle asked when they returned home.

"I'd like to snuggle with you," Hunter replied. "We won't be out late tonight, right?"

"Not unless one of us gets on a hot streak," Michelle chuckled.

"I'd rather get lucky with you any night." Hunter laughed. "Oh boy, that was cheesy, wasn't it?"

"Yeah, a bit, but sweet," Michelle said. "Even if we get home late, we don't have to wake early in the morning."

"That's true," Hunter said, closing the door behind them.

They stripped out of their clothes and stretched out on the bed. Hunter let her fingers trace the lines on Michelle's abs. "I had fun with you today."

"I did, too. That was the first time I've ever been skinny-dipping."

"What was it like for you growing up?"

"We traveled a lot from church to church until I was ten, and Dad settled on a church in Oregon. My childhood was relatively dull until I started playing basketball and found my first true love. I was over six feet entering high school, so I towered over everyone we played. It wasn't long before coaches began approaching me to play college ball. Dad was none too pleased, but he couldn't support a family and a college student on his salary, so he finally relented."

"Were you worried he would prevent you from playing?"

"For a time, yes. It was one of the few times my mom stood up to him."

"I'm glad she did."

"Me too. College was the best time of my life until now. I met my first girlfriend, which turned into the beginning of the end with my dad. He forbade anyone in my family to communicate with a deviant daughter. Mom would call me occasionally to apologize, but my dad held steadfast. The last time I talked to her was right before I graduated and was drafted by Vegas. She called to congratulate me, which was bittersweet."

"I'm fortunate my family supported my lifestyle," Hunter said. "It makes me sad to hear you didn't experience that kind of love, especially from a man of faith."

"Dad refused to allow his parishioners to know about me once I came out to them. It was like I never existed. My basketball family is all I have."

"I can't wait for Mom and Jim to meet you. Mom will fall in love with you immediately," Hunter said.

"I'm sure I'll enjoy meeting them. Do they plan to come to the LA game?"

"It's a long trip, but Mom assured me they'll be there."

"Tell her I'll make sure comped tickets are at the box office for them."

"That's sweet of you. Thank you."

"We typically get comped tickets, but I don't have family to share them with."

"I'm thankful I have the best seat in the house," Hunter said.

"It's great to have you on the bench, but I look forward to the day we are on the floor together."

"Do you really believe that will happen one day?"

"I do," Michelle answered. "You are too talented to be wasted on a practice team."

Hunter rolled onto her back. "We would be unstoppable."

"Yes, we would." Michelle rolled onto her side to kiss Hunter. "Coach said she would support us playing three on three next year if that's what we wanted after the season ends. We would have to move to Miami for the league, but I know it would be fun."

"How long would we be in Miami?"

"Three to four months. The season is only eight weeks, but we must train before it starts. The game is very different from full-court basketball, but I think it would benefit all three of us to play."

"How so?" Hunter asked.

"It's a much faster game. The league will play a compressed full court, unlike the half-court FIBA games. The shot clock and scoring are still being discussed. In the International three on three, the shot clock is only twelve seconds, so we will learn to make decisions faster and shoot quicker. Two-point shots are only worth one point, and threes are good for two. The game is played for four quarters. Teams only have five players to allow for subs due to the fast, intense play. No coaching during the game, so players are the coaches on the court. There are still rules and details to be worked out, but I know we can adapt."

"Who would we want for a fourth and fifth player?"

"Stacy would be our ideal fourth if she's interested. We probably need another big."

Hunter smiled. "We could have so much fun together. During breaks, we could travel to the Caribbean for some relaxation. Or even to Key West."

"We could take a month or so off at the end of the season and then start working out here a few days a week to learn the game. That should give us time to gel as a team and learn each other's strengths and weaknesses."

"You've been giving this much thought, haven't you?"

"Yes, I have," Michelle admitted. "I think it's perfect for us. I've never wanted to go overseas to play."

"I can understand that. I know the money is good, but if there is another option in the US, that will make it much better," Hunter said.

"That it will. Are you ready to prepare for a night on the town?"

"Yeah. I need to hit an ATM somewhere for casino cash," Hunter replied.

"Will you allow me to treat you tonight?"

Hunter cocked her head. "There's no need for that."

"No, but I would love to do it for you." Michelle gave her a charming smile.

Hunter found it hard to resist. "Fine, you can pay for our gambling, but I insist dinner is on me."

Michelle raised her hands in surrender. "I have no problem with that."

†

They shared a delicious meal of sushi and hibachi, and after an hour, Carson and Stacy decided to head home. After saying their goodbyes, Michelle looked at Hunter. "We both seem to be on a hot streak. Do you mind staying a bit longer?"

"Not at all," Hunter replied, pushing the button for her next spin.

Michelle was up considerably when her machine went cold, and she stopped playing. Hunter continued to hit minor jackpots, so Michelle watched her play. Hunter was like a kid at Christmas, celebrating each new win with a clap and an excited smile at Michelle. *So beautiful to watch.* When lights flashed and a siren wailed, Michelle returned to reality. Hunter had hit the jackpot.

"What's happening?" Hunter cried out to her. "Did I break it?"

"I sure hope so," Michelle teased. "You hit a major jackpot. Watch the number growing here to see how much you just won," she said, pointing to the payout line.

Hunter's eyes grew wide as the amount continued to climb. She looked at Michelle in disbelief when the balance stopped at seven hundred dollars. "Are you freaking kidding me?"

"No, honey. You just won seven hundred dollars on top of your three-hundred-dollar balance," an attendant said. "Congratulations. Do you want to cash out or continue playing after I reset the machine?"

Hunter smiled at Michelle. "Cash out. Let's go home."

"Good decision," Michelle said.

"Follow me then," the woman said, leading Hunter to the payout office.

Hunter placed her winnings in her wallet and tucked it into her front pocket. She reached for Michelle's hand. "Let's get out of here."

The valet brought the Jeep around, and after tipping the driver, Michelle climbed inside to take them home. As she reached the exit, Hunter asked. "Is the frozen yogurt place open this late?"

"Honey, this is Vegas. It's always open." Michelle chuckled.

"May I treat you to frozen yogurt, then?"

"I can't refuse such a sweet offer."

†

Hunter finished brushing her teeth and stretched out beside Michelle. "Thank you for such a beautiful day. I had so much fun with you."

"I hope it's the first of many we will share," Michelle said.

Hunter leaned down to kiss Michelle, and they made love until they were content to hold each other.

"What's the plan for tomorrow?"

"I'm cooking you breakfast in bed in the morning. Have you ever been to the Grand Canyon? The West Rim is less than one hundred and fifty miles from us, and we can make it a day trip."

"Do you like egg salad?" Hunter asked.

"I love it."

"You have plenty of eggs. Why don't I make a bowl to stick in the cooler with more drinks? We can stop for a loaf of bread and chips along the way and find a nice spot to picnic."

"So, no breakfast in bed?" Michelle frowned.

"We can do that tomorrow."

Michelle smiled. "I won't forget. We will have plenty of time to enjoy it tomorrow and not feel rushed."

†

Michelle cooked breakfast while Hunter made the egg salad and put it away to chill while they showered and dressed. Hunter was surprised they were loaded and on the road by nine.

"On the road again," Hunter sang as they pulled out of the drive.

"Is that a hint you want some music?"

Hunter took Michelle's hand. "No. I'm just thankful for another adventure with you."

Michelle drove for an hour before pulling into a store for gas and supplies. "I'll grab bread and chips while you fill up. Any special requests?"

"Sour cream, onion potato chips, and something sweet to snack on now."

"Do you want a cold soda or water?"

"I could drink a Dew," Michelle answered.

"Be right back." Hunter entered the store and found a fresh loaf of bread, chips, and drinks. She studied the candy aisle and decided on red Twizzlers and Swedish fish." When she returned to the Jeep, Michelle was waiting for her. "I hope you didn't want chocolate."

"I can live without it," Michelle said. "What did you get?"

"You have two choices." She reached into the bag and pulled out the candies.

"Oh, damn. I like both." Michelle smiled. "The Twizzlers would probably be easier to eat and drive."

Hunter opened the bag and handed her a string after she pulled onto the road. She opened the Swedish fish for herself and slowly chewed. Michelle looked over and saw the smile on her face.

"Damn, those look good."

Hunter reached into her bag and placed a small candy into her mouth. "Oh, yeah. Those are good."

They alternated candies until they drove close enough that they could begin seeing the massive depression in the ground. "Welcome to the Grand Canyon."

"Wow," Hunter replied with a Twizzlers hanging out of her mouth. "I knew it would be big, but this is massive."

"It's just the beginning. We'll be at the West Rim in a few minutes."

Hunter stared at the layers of colored rock as they rode. "The colors are so beautiful."

"Yes, they are," Michelle said. "They get better."

Michelle put on her blinker and turned into a parking lot. "It's a short walk to the picnic area, but I promise the view is worth the hike. Grab the bread and chips, and I'll bring the cooler."

Hunter carried the bag in one hand and filled the other with Michelle's hand. She loved the feel of their fingers entwined as they hiked to the picnic tables. Hunter was surprised when they found an empty one close to the rim. She placed the bag on the table, pulled out her phone, and took pictures. She tried to capture every angle, and the depth took her breath away when she looked down. "Ginormous is an understatement. It goes on forever." She turned back to find Michelle taking a picture of her.

"Beautiful, isn't it?" Michelle walked over to her. She slipped her arms around Hunter's waist and rested her chin on her shoulder. "Mother Nature graced us with this beauty. I'd like to show you from the air one day soon."

"From the air?"

"Yes. There's a helicopter company that gives tours from the air. They stay booked months ahead, but we can plan for something after the season ends."

"I bet that would be stunning."

"It is. That was one of my first solo explorations in Vegas."

"Do you do much travel?"

"I haven't, but primarily because I didn't have anyone to share the experiences with." Michelle smiled. "I hope that has changed for my future."

Hunter returned her smile. "My middle name is 'Go,'" she teased. "I haven't seen much of the Pacific Northwest, and I'd love to see Alaska and Canada."

"That's doable." Michelle smiled. "I love the PNW. I haven't seen Alaska or Canada, but I would love to go with you."

Hunter leaned in to kiss her. "I guess we've got some planning to do."

"If we make it to the finals in mid-October, that will only give us a few weeks to travel if we plan to join the Unrivaled League."

Hunter turned in her arms. "Not if. When you make the finals. I want to see a new ring on your finger."

"You will get one, too," Michelle said. "Everyone on the team does. Maybe not as big, but just as nice."

"Size doesn't matter. I just want to help the team win," Hunter replied.

"I do, too. I think we've got a good shot."

"One game at a time," Hunter said. She turned back around to stare at the enormity of the canyon.

They gazed out at the canyon for several minutes and watched a hawk ride the thermals through the canyon. "He's got a great view," Michelle said, pointing him out to Hunter.

"Are you getting hungry?" Hunter asked.

"My mouth has been watering all morning thinking about egg salad."

"Will you take a selfie of us first? I'd like to send one to Mom," Hunter said.

"Sure," Michelle said, taking Hunter's phone.

"I want your arm around me, please."

"Are you sure? Would your mom be okay with that?"

Hunter laughed as Michelle took the first photo. "Mom knows I'm head over heels for you."

Michelle took several more photos. "Head over heels, huh?"

Hunter took a deep breath. "I love you, Michelle."

Michelle's smile broadened. "I love you, too. I didn't want to scare you off by saying it too soon."

"You don't have to say it. I feel it in everything we do together," Hunter said. "We were made to be together."

Michelle kissed her cheek. "Yes, we were." She handed Hunter the phone. "You better check those. I think my eyes were closed on one of them."

"They are perfect," Hunter said. "Which do you like best?"

"The first one with you laughing. It shows you being happy."

Hunter sent it to her mom. "Let's make some sandwiches."

†

Hunter relaxed into Michelle's arm as they enjoyed the view before deciding to start for home. "Any idea what we are eating for dinner?" Michelle asked.

"We practice tomorrow, so we need to do some carb loading. Can I treat you to some Italian?" Hunter asked.

"Take home or eat in?"

"Your choice. It doesn't matter to me."

"Would it be selfish of me to ask for take home? I don't want to share you with anyone tonight."

"That's fine with me."

"When we get closer, I'll place an order to go," Michelle said.

"Perfect." Hunter reached for Michelle's hand and stared out the window as they rode.

†

Michelle ordered a pasta feast, and after storing the leftovers, they curled up on the couch. "Would you mind watching basketball? New York and Connecticut play tonight."

"That's fine with me," Hunter said, laying her head on Michelle's arm. "We play New York to end the road trip, right?"

"Yes, and both teams will be playing hard to make the playoffs," Michelle said. "We barely beat Connecticut earlier this year."

During the first quarter break, Michelle kissed Hunter's cheek and chuckled. "Do you play every game you watch?"

"What do you mean?"

"You move with every cut and pass. Do you not know that?"

"I do now," Hunter said. "I've always wondered why people didn't want to sit beside me when we watched games."

"You are very active. I love it, though. What's your analysis so far?"

"New York's bigs are strong and tall. They will be challenging for us. The guards appear streakish, but if they get hot, they have great shooters. We can beat them in transition if we play fast. They don't have the speed we do." Hunter stood and walked to the kitchen to refill their tea glasses. "You'll have to use your muscle to get to the basket. They will collapse inside on defense, but your midrange and threes will force them to come out on you. They are big but not as quick."

"So, we trap to get turnovers and beat them on the fast break?" Michelle asked.

Hunter nodded. "If we let them get into their half-court offense, they will win the paint."

"It's a close game, so let's see how they are defended, especially in the second half. They have starters who they rest in the third for a final push in the fourth quarter. The younger players aren't as talented, so we can push hard to get a lead or extend a lead."

"Coach is going to love your analysis."

Hunter shrugged. "I had five years to watch teams play. I have a knack for picking up on some things."

"You are totally spot on," Michelle said.

As the game came near the end, Hunter sat up. "Watch the Connecticut guards. They will use their bigs to screen and bust a couple of threes while New York continues to work it inside. They can't exchange twos for threes and win. And then there's that," Hunter said. "Their player was stripped, and they were too slow to get down on defense. That's a recipe for an easy layup or wide-open three. Boom! Another three."

New York was down by two with thirty seconds left. They called time out to advance the ball to half-court. "What would you do here, Coach?"

Hunter laughed. "Three options. Inbound for a quick three with time to rebound a miss is one. If that's not open, go inside and hope for a tie or a plus one to win. Option three is to spread the court and see if one of the power forwards can drop a three or find an open guard."

"What would you do?"

"I'd always go for the win, so I'd go with a three-option for the win. It's not always the preferred call, but if you're going to play, play for the win. I don't think New York has enough gas in their tanks for overtime. Thirty seconds is plenty of time for them to find the best shot. If they hit, they have to play defense if there are more than a few seconds left."

They watched New York inbound the ball when play resumed, but the guard wasn't open for the shot. She passed the ball to the big at the top of the key and cut through the lane to the opposite side of the court. The big faked a shot and threw a no-look pass to the shooting guard, who stepped aside from the defender flying out to intercept her shot and let the ball go."

They watched the ball hit the backboard, bounce once off the rim, and drop inside.

"Kiss it," Michelle yelled.

"Exactly," Hunter died laughing.

With two seconds left, another time-out was called to advance the ball. It would take a great inbound and a Hail Mary for New York to lose, but anything was possible. They watched as Connecticut inbounded the ball but didn't get a shot off in time. New York had come out with the win.

"That was too close," Michelle said.

"Always better to have a larger lead at the end of the game. Players are getting much better on half-court shots." Hunter looked at Michelle. "Hopefully, the LA game will go well, and Coach can rest the starters for the fourth quarter."

"Flying that night will give us a full day of rest once we land. We will have a shoot-around before the game, but should be rested and ready to go," Michelle said.

"If you win these next four games, that will give us a nice lead going into the All-Star break, won't it?"

"Yes, but it will be a tough stretch. Seattle is always hard to beat at home."

"Even three out of four would be good."

"It would be excellent."

†

Michelle turned off the television and pulled Hunter to her feet. "It's time to 'kiss it,'" she teased.

"Let's go practice your moves." Hunter chuckled. She knew Michelle didn't need practice, but she enjoyed the benefit of Michelle's mouth and hands on her body. It hadn't taken Michelle long to discover exactly what she wanted most, and she proved to be an excellent lover.

Hunter curled into Michelle's body when they were exhausted. "I love loving you," she whispered to Michelle.

Michelle lifted Hunter's chin to look into her eyes. "I love every ounce of you with every ounce of me."

†

Hunter slept soundly after their long day and didn't stir when Michelle woke the next morning and left the bed to cook breakfast. She hadn't realized the morning had arrived until Michelle kissed her awake, handing her a plate filled with strawberry-filled crepes covered in Cool Whip.

"Oh, my goodness. These are too pretty to eat."

"Pretty or not, eat up," Michelle said, sipping her coffee. "I'll be right back. Do you need anything?"

Hunter's mouth was full, so she nodded and pointed to her mouth. "Another kiss," she said after swallowing.

Michelle leaned down, licked the cream from her lips, and softly kissed her. "Mmm, tasty."

"Hurry back."

When Michelle returned carrying her plate and phone, she was smiling. "Carson wants to know if we've come up for air yet."

Hunter nearly choked on her breakfast. "We've had a busy weekend."

"They want us to come for beer and pizza tonight."

"Will you stay with me tonight?" Hunter asked.

"Just try to make me leave," Michelle answered. "I'll pack a bag. You can leave your clothes here, and I'll wash them with mine."

"You cook and do laundry?" Hunter teased.

Michelle looked shocked. "I'll have you know I am very domesticated."

"You, my love, are perfect."

"Will you need that game-day outfit for the road trip?"

"Yes, since we'll be gone for so long."

"I'll bring it to you at practice Tuesday so you can pack it. Do you need a suitcase?"

"Oh, shit. I didn't think of that."

"No worries. I have plenty. I'll bring you a large roller and a smaller hygiene bag."

"Thank you. Did you respond to Carson?"

"I did. I told her we would be delighted to join them." Michelle smiled.

"I could put a load of laundry in before we shower if that helps."

"I'll come home Tuesday morning and get it done before practice. We can take the luggage tonight, though. I hope you will pack some of your new jeans," Michelle said.

"If you will."

"They are perfect for the days between games. I usually fly in athletic wear, pants, and a shirt for comfort."

"I probably need to pick up some of those."

"We can go today after practice. There's a good Nike outlet close to where we shopped."

"I can use some of my gambling winnings." Hunter smiled.

CHAPTER THIRTEEN

Dallas was a blowout, and the starters rested the entire fourth quarter. When the jet landed in Seattle, Stacy was there with flowers for Carson, and they were able to spend the night together. Hunter and Michelle took advantage of the privacy for some loving of their own.

Michelle woke well-rested and led Hunter to the lobby to impress her with her waffle-making skills. Hunter filled plates with scrambled eggs and fruit while Michelle cooked waffles. When Michelle placed the waffles on the table, she offered Hunter syrup. Hunter shook her head and walked to the counter for peanut butter.

"Seriously?" Michelle asked.

"Don't knock it until you've tried it," Hunter said, spreading peanut butter across the waffle and cutting an offering for Michelle. She smiled when Michelle's eyes grew wide after tasting the waffle.

"Damn, that's good."

"The protein is much better than that sugary syrup," Hunter teased.

"Is there more peanut butter?" Michelle asked.

"You work on this one, and I'll get more," Hunter said, passing her plate to Michelle.

"How did you come up with this?"

"The sugar always left me sluggish, so Mom suggested peanut butter. Don't worry. I still use syrup on pancakes. Just not a lot."

"Smart move."

"You can tell her when you meet her in a few days."

Michelle nodded. "I'm excited and nervous to meet her."

"Why are you nervous?"

"I'm afraid she won't like me."

Hunter broke out laughing. "Mom is going to love you. Relax."

"I hope you're right."

"Of course I am."

Hunter watched Coach walk in for breakfast. She looked at Michelle. "I really should talk to her before we get to LA."

"We stay one more night before we fly to LA tomorrow."

"I'll ask her if we can talk after we return tonight."

"Do you want me there for support?"

"You will be," Hunter said. "Right here." She pointed at her heart. "It would be harder if you were there, but thank you."

"I'm all about what you need, baby." Michelle smiled.

"I know, and that means the world to me."

"I'll be right back." Hunter walked over to the table where Coach was sitting. "Good morning, Coach. Mind if I join you for a minute?"

"Grab us a juice and sit down."

Hunter walked over to pour two glasses of apple juice and returned to the table. She placed one in front of Coach and sat.

"So, what's on your mind?" Coach asked.

"I need some time tonight when we get back to the hotel. Can you spare me a few minutes?"

"You can have all night if you need it. What's up, Hunter?"

"I need to share something with you before we arrive in LA. I've waited until the last minute, but this conversation isn't easy."

Coach calmly looked at her watch. "We have five hours before we leave for the shoot-around. Can we do it now? I'll be worried all game long if I don't know what's on your mind. I'd rather not be distracted."

"I didn't think of that, Coach. Of course, you're right. You need to focus on the game."

"You do, too, and something is weighing on your mind, so let's go ahead and talk."

Hunter took a sip of juice. "Not here, please, Coach."

"Can you meet me in my room in thirty minutes? It won't take me long to finish breakfast." She gave Hunter the number.

"Yes, ma'am. Thanks, Coach."

Coach looked up from her meal. Her blue eyes were sparkling. "Relax. You can't tell me anything that will make me feel differently about you."

"Thanks, Coach. I'll see you then."

†

"Are you okay? You look pale," Michelle said.

"Coach wants to talk this morning. I'm supposed to meet her in half an hour. I need to go."

Hunter left Michelle sitting at the table and rushed back to their room. Hunter barely reached the bathroom before her revolting stomach purged her breakfast.

"Fuck," Hunter said as she rinsed her face and mouth after flushing. Hunter brushed her teeth and was sitting on the tub with her face in her hands when Michelle returned and rushed to the bathroom.

Michelle rushed to Hunter and knelt. She wrapped her arms around her. "Everything is going to be fine."

Hunter broke into tears and melted into Michelle's body.

Michelle smoothed her damp hair away from her face. "I know you've been dreading this conversation, but it's almost over. Coach will listen closely. I'm sure she will understand your story."

"I can't tell her everything like I did you. I'm not sure I have that in me again."

Michelle lifted her face. "She doesn't need all the details, just the threat of someone recognizing you." Michelle kissed her lips and forehead. "You will feel better once it's done. Nobody else matters." Michelle stood, walked into the room, and returned with ginger ale. "This will settle your stomach."

Hunter took a tentative sip. "Thanks."

Michelle picked up her hairbrush and brushed Hunter's hair. "There. All gorgeous again. One more thing." She dug through her kit and pulled out eye drops. "Tilt your head back. These will help."

"That does feel better. Thank you."

"I'm here for you and only you," Michelle said. "I love you."

"I love you, too."

"Take that ginger ale, and don't keep Coach waiting. I'll relax until you get back. Then we can shower and dress for lunch and the game."

Hunter stood and nodded.

†

Hunter's legs felt like concrete when she left the room. She was glad when none of the team was in the hallway as she walked to Coach's room and knocked.

Coach opened the door and welcomed Hunter inside. "Let's sit on the couch."

"Thanks, Coach. I should have talked to you sooner, but I didn't."

"You're here now. That's all that matters. Take your time and tell me what's on your mind."

Hunter took a sip of the ginger ale and a deep breath. She looked up to find Coach watching her carefully. "I need to tell you why I disappeared from playing basketball." She took another sip. "When we were halfway into the season, I received a frantic call from my mother. My baby sister, Lilly, had committed suicide at fourteen. Lilly was my world. I let her down when she needed me most. I missed a call from her the night before and didn't get her voicemail in time to call back. I put off returning the call until the next day, and it was too late. When I returned home, I found her journal. I read it and discovered what had led her to make such a desperate decision." Hunter felt tears running down her face.

"I'm sorry, Hunter. I know this is hard."

"That's not all, Coach. When I read that she had been raped, I lost my shit. Her best friend's older brother was the rapist. I ran to their house and took a baseball bat to him in his room. I didn't kill him, but I wanted him to remember what he did to Lilly with every step he took. I made him confess his actions to his parents. God, how I wanted to smash his head in, but I didn't. I walked home and waited for the police to arrive. I didn't want the rape to tarnish anyone's memory of Lilly, so it never came out in court. There was no sense in ruining another family any further than I had. I did speak to the judge in his quarters to explain my actions, and while he was sympathetic, he still had to sentence me for aggravated assault. He was lenient, and I spent five years in Chowchilla. My record was expunged as part of my prerelease agreement when I was released a few months ago. I didn't want to take a chance of returning to California and possibly being recognized without you knowing about my past. You've done so much for me. I would never want you to be blindsided by anything."

When Hunter looked up, she saw Coach was crying.

"I am thankful that you shared this. I have always wondered what happened but never researched why you disappeared. I would probably have bashed his head in, consequences be damned."

"I was close until I saw the horror on Jen's face when her brother admitted what he had done. I couldn't hurt her any more than he had."

Coach wiped away her tears. "I would be surprised if this ever surfaced again, but I understand your apprehension. I assume Carson knows."

"Yes, we were lovers then, but she doesn't know all the details. I refused to let her visit the prison. I figured my life was ruined, and I didn't want to drag her down with me.

189

Coming to Vegas to reconnect with Carson has been one of my best decisions."

"Michelle?" Coach questioned. "I've noticed there is love between you."

"She knows all the details. I could not become serious with her while hiding this secret. I wanted her to know everything that I did and why."

"No wonder those two love you so much." Coach smiled. "You are a great person, Hunter. Life dealt you and Lilly a crappy hand, but you've paid the price, and now it's time to move forward."

"Thanks, Coach. I love them, too. Michelle is better than I ever dreamed I deserved."

"She's a beautiful person, too, and has had more than her share of heartache with her family situation. You are good for each other, and it's obvious how much you're in love. I swear her feet don't touch the ground when you walk into a room," she teased.

"Will this affect my position on the practice team?"

"Hell, no. You're the first player to push them so hard that they want to improve. I can't even get that out of some of them. Even if you never play professionally, you've got great potential as a coach. I would welcome you on my staff any day. You have such vision for the game, and I'll do everything I can to help you get a roster spot if that's still your dream."

"It is, Coach. I'd like to see if I'm good enough."

"I can answer that for you. You are more than good enough. You could start on any team in the league. We just need to get you exposed, and I pray I can find a way to keep you in Vegas. You three would be unstoppable. You realize we haven't lost a game since you started. You're our lucky charm."

"Don't jinx us, Coach." Hunter smiled for the first time since she entered the room.

"I hope your mind is at ease now that you've shared with me. Go relax with Michelle, and I'll see you on the bus when we go for lunch."

They stood, and Coach reached out to hug Hunter. "Thank you."

"Thanks, Coach." Hunter left the room and rushed back to Michelle.

†

Michelle rushed to the door when Hunter returned. She pulled her into a tight embrace. "How'd it go?"

Hunter stepped back. "Good. It feels great to have that off my chest. Coach took it all in stride."

"Excellent. We have a few hours before we need to leave for lunch. Come snuggle with me."

Hunter allowed Michelle to lead her back to the bed and curled into her arms.

Michelle set an alarm on her watch in case they drifted asleep. She stroked Hunter's hair and back, and the emotional exhaustion Hunter had experienced allowed her to fall asleep in Michelle's arms. Two hours later, the alarm woke them.

"Time to shower and dress, gorgeous," Michelle said. She kissed her and started undressing.

"I'll never get tired of seeing that," Hunter said.

"What?"

"That gorgeous body of yours." Hunter smiled.

191

"Even when we're old and gray with wrinkles and love handles?"

"Even then." Hunter stripped out of her clothes and followed Michelle into the shower.

†

It was interesting to see Carson and Stacy play on opposing teams, but they were true professionals. The game was close at the half, but Michelle came alive in the second half, scoring twenty points, and allowing them to pull ahead of Seattle. Hunter was proud when Michelle nailed two three-point shots late in the fourth quarter. She also put the game away on a fast break after a steal when Carson found her racing down the court, and she slammed home a dunk. With seconds left in the game, Stacy hit a three, putting Seattle within four points, but Vegas pulled off a hard-fought win.

Stacy and Carson spent a final night together after the game. Stacy left the following day, promising to see them at the All-Star game.

When they boarded the jet, Hunter turned to Michelle. "Two down and two more to go."

The flight to LA was barely long enough to get a nap. They checked into the hotel, and Coach instructed everyone to meet at six for dinner. Afterward, they would have a night's rest before the game on Sunday.

†

When they arrived at the arena in LA, Hunter was excited to see her mom. She was sad it would only be a short visit since they would fly to New York after the game. Hunter dressed quickly and rushed out to the court. It didn't take long for her to find her mom and Jim in the stands. She climbed the rail and hugged them.

"It's so good to see you."

"You look amazing," Elizabeth said.

"Happy, too," Jim added.

"I've not felt this good in a long time."

"I see why," her mom said. "She's even more adorable in person." She nodded to Michelle, who walked toward them.

"Mom and Jim, this is Michelle," Hunter said when she arrived.

"It's good to finally meet you. We've heard so much about you."

"Likewise," Michelle replied. "Hunter talks about you both often. I hope you are planning to come visit Vegas soon."

"We are when you get a break soon. Jim and I plan to ride over to retrieve the bike trailer and will stay a few days if it fits into your schedules."

"We'll make sure it fits," Michelle said. She looked at Hunter. "I need to start stretching."

"I'll be right there."

"Take your time," Michelle said. "Will we see you for a few after the game?"

"Yes. We understand the team is flying to New York, but we'll say goodbye. Thanks for the tickets, too."

"Tickets have been sold out for months. We were about to rob a bank to pay a scalper until Hunter said you were reserving tickets for us," Jim said.

"My pleasure."

"Good luck," Elizabeth said.

She hugged Hunter. "I'm so pleased you two are so happy. You make a beautiful couple."

"Thanks, Mom. Sorry, I haven't been able to return the trailer," Hunter told Jim.

"Are you kidding? I've been dying to take your mom to Vegas. Thank you for taking good care of it for me."

When the rest of the team arrived to start stretching, Hunter was torn between helping or spending a few more minutes with her mom. Coach walked out, smiled at Hunter, and then nodded.

"Go. We'll see you after the game. Good luck."

"Thanks, Mom. Love you."

"Love you, too."

†

Hunter jogged over to assist Michelle with stretching. Coach joined them. "Parents?" she asked.

"Mom and her boyfriend," Hunter answered.

"I can stretch her out if you want to spend more time with them," Coach offered.

Hunter shook her head. "Thanks, Coach. They are coming to Vegas when we have a break in a few weeks."

After warming up, the team returned to the locker room for a final meeting.

"Okay, ladies. Game three of this road trip is yours for the taking. You've played well so far, so keep playing like you have been, and we will kick some LA butt. Let's do this."

The players remained in the tunnel for introductions while Hunter and Coach walked to the bench. "Will they hang a hundred tonight?" Coach asked.

"If you rest the starters for the fourth, it might be close with the second string."

"You think we will have that big of a lead?"

Hunter nodded. "Yes, Coach, I do. The ladies are firing on all cylinders right now. New York will be a hard game, and they must be rested if possible."

Coach smiled and showed her notepad to Hunter.

Hunter laughed when she read "Pull starters in the fourth," written in big letters.

"Great minds," Coach said.

†

Vegas entered the locker room with a twenty-two-point lead. "The second half is about preserving energy for the New York game and not chasing stats. I will start substituting players in the second half to give the starters a rest. You've played a great game, and it's time to share some game time with the reserves. Make the most of your minutes, ladies. Take us home."

Michelle sat next to Hunter as they watched the game. "Not a bad night for you," Hunter teased. "Twenty points, eight rebounds, and four assists in the first half is wonderful."

Michelle looked at Hunter. "I know I need to conserve energy, but damn, I hate riding the pine."

"The reserves need the playing time, and besides, you get to sit with me for a change," Hunter said.

"There is that," Michelle said.

195

Carson was the last starter to come out of the game. The crowd gave her a standing ovation when she exited the game. She was, after all, a Cali girl.

Hunter looked back at her mom and Jim, who seemed to enjoy the game. Just one person was missing. Lilly would be cheering at the top of her lungs. That thought brought tears to her eyes, and Hunter turned away before Michelle noticed.

They won by eighteen, and Hunter rushed back to her mom after the game. Hunter and Carson were being swamped by young fans for autographs. Carson looked up and waved at Elizabeth.

Elizabeth waved back. "Tell her hello for me."

"That was a great game," Jim said. "Even the reserves were impressive."

"We are conserving energy for the New York game. That will be a tough one," Hunter explained.

"Tuesday night, right?" Elizabeth asked.

Hunter nodded. "If we win that, it will give us a seven-game lead going into the All-Star break."

"Where is the game this year?" Jim asked.

"Phoenix," Hunter answered.

"Are any of the team playing?" Elizabeth asked.

"Michelle and Carson have both been invited."

"You'll definitely be there then?" Elizabeth smiled.

"Yes, I plan on it."

Jim looked at Elizabeth. "Road trip?" he asked.

"That sounds perfect. I won't be on the floor, so we can visit more," Hunter said.

"We will be there," Jim promised.

"You need to go, don't you?" Elizabeth asked.

"I probably should," Hunter said. She hugged both of them. "Thanks for coming tonight. I wish Lilly could have been here."

"She would have been yelling at the top of her lungs."

Hunter chuckled. "Yeah, she would have. See you soon. Love you both."

"Have a safe trip, and say goodbye to the girls," Elizabeth said.

"I'll call from New York," Hunter said, jumping over the railing.

The crowd of fans was thinning out. Hunter stopped to tell Michelle she was going to shower.

"I'll be right behind you," she said, handing a signed program back to a young girl.

†

Michelle stepped into Hunter's shower stall for a quick kiss before stepping under the flowing water. Hunter had dressed in a warm-up suit and was packing her bag when Michelle and Carson entered. She carried her game gear and their uniforms to Sandy.

"Do you need some help?"

"Thanks, Hunter, but we've got this." Sandy smiled.

Hunter waited for Carson and Michelle, then picked up her bag and followed them to the bus for the ride to the airport. Sandy and her crew were storing game gear when they entered the bus and placed their bags in the overhead bin.

"New York, here we come," Michelle said as she sat beside Hunter. "I hope we have a good meal on the jet. I'm hungry."

197

"I think it's steak tonight," Carson said.

"That's always a winner for me," Michelle said.

†

After a great meal, the team settled in for some sleep. Hunter fell asleep with her head on Michelle's shoulder. Carson snapped a quick photo of them and then curled up in a blanket.

Hunter's bladder woke her midflight, and she stood and walked to the restroom. When she returned, she noticed Coach was still awake reviewing the game film. Hunter slipped into the seat beside her.

"You can't sleep, Coach?" Hunter asked.

"I'll catch a nap soon. I wanted to watch a bit more film. Did your family enjoy the game?"

"Yeah, they did. I just wished Lilly could have been there. You would have heard her over everyone else in the crowd."

Coach looked up at Hunter. "She was there. You just couldn't see her. She would be very proud of you."

"Thanks, Coach. I think she would be, too."

"Go snuggle into that woman of yours and get some sleep. We still have hours to fly. Damn the league for scheduling like this," Coach growled.

"Goodnight, Coach."

"Goodnight, Hunter."

CHAPTER FOURTEEN

Hunter's ears popped as the jet descended into New York, startling her. Michelle smiled and reached for her hand. "It's okay. We are about to land."

Hunter squinted to look out the window where the sun began cresting the horizon. "What time is it?" she asked.

"Our time or local time?" Michelle grinned.

"Let's start with local," Hunter replied.

"Six-thirty, I think. Time zones have always confused me." She checked her watch. "Four-thirty at home. I think."

"Did you sleep much?"

Michelle nodded. "I haven't been awake long."

Hunter sat up and stretched. "What's the plan for today?"

"Breakfast on the way to the hotel and then a relaxing day. I think some of the players plan to lounge around the indoor pool."

"I hope they have a hot tub by the pool or a whirlpool tub in the room. I could use a good soak."

"That sounds nice. I think Coach wants to meet before dinner to discuss the game plan for tomorrow's game. She's booked a conference room for us."

"Have you ever been to New York?"

"Only once for a game. It was a quick trip. How about you?"

Hunter shook her head. "I haven't been beyond the Mississippi River before."

"Such a sheltered life," Michelle said and then grimaced when she realized what she had said. "Sorry. Growing up a pastor's kid, we moved a lot when I was younger."

Hunter leaned over and kissed her. "Nothing to be sorry about. We never ventured far from California."

The jet touched down, and they taxied to a private gate within minutes. Michelle looked out the window and turned back to Hunter.

"Our chariot awaits. I hope he drives better than New York cab drivers. I hear that can be a harrowing experience."

Hunter stood and removed their small bags from the bin before walking to the front of the jet. She stepped out to find a crew unloading their luggage and transferring it to the waiting bus. "I'm glad we don't have to drag all that through an airport. Especially one this size."

"Me, too." Michelle stepped off the bottom step and stretched. "It feels good to be on solid ground again."

†

Breakfast was terrific, but the city had sprung to life while they were in the restaurant. Traffic filled the streets, and the sidewalks were packed with pedestrians.

"Busy place," Hunter said as she looked out the window.

Fortunately, the hotel wasn't far away, and they were surprised when a crowd of fans were at the front door waiting for their arrival.

"This is a nice reception," Michelle said.

"I'll get our room key when Coach gets us checked in. I'm pretty sure you will be busy signing autographs. I'll wait for you inside."

"I hope I won't be long." Michelle smiled.

"No rush. I'll be kicked back watching."

Carson smiled at Michelle. "Better get your writing hand warmed up."

Michelle flexed her fingers. "All set." She grinned.

"I'll get our room key and wait for you inside," Hunter told Carson. She followed Coach inside.

"Nice reception for New Yorkers," Coach said.

"Yeah, it is. I will get our key and wait for Michelle and Carson in the lobby if that's okay."

"That's fine. I've ordered a late lunch service at two. Then we will meet to discuss the game plan and spend the rest of the day relaxing until we go to dinner tonight."

Hunter took a key from Coach and walked over to sit in a comfortable chair. She watched cart after cart of luggage pass through the lobby as the crowd outside grew. *This may take a while.* She smiled as she watched Michelle sign a young girl's T-shirt. *At least I have a nice view.*

When the crowd thinned, Michelle and Carson entered the hotel. "That was fun," she heard Michelle tell Carson.

Michelle smiled when she saw Hunter approach. "There you are. I'm ready to stretch out for a bit."

"Your room awaits, Madame," Hunter replied and bowed.

"I hope our luggage has made it. I'm in serious need of a toothbrush," Carson said.

"It's supposed to be waiting for us in our rooms," Hunter informed them. "Cross your fingers."

†

They were only missing Carson's game bag, and a knock on the door a few minutes later revealed Sandy holding the bag. "I do believe this is yours," she said, handing the bag to Carson.

"Thanks, Sandy." Carson tossed the bag on the bed and walked over to Hunter and Michelle, looking out the window.

"I thought Vegas was bad. No way I could live in this rat race," Michelle said.

Carson nodded. "I agree. Nice place to visit, but I wouldn't want to live here."

Hunter walked into the bathroom. "Aha, a whirlpool tub."

"There's also a hot tub by the pool, according to the map," Carson added. "Are you two up for a soak?"

Hunter shrugged. "I don't have a swimsuit, but I guess shorts and a T will work."

"What? No skinny-dipping for you?" Michelle teased.

"Um, not today." Hunter chuckled and punched Michelle's arm.

"Did I miss something?" Carson asked.

Michelle smiled. "We went skinny-dipping at a waterfall in the desert while exploring."

"Uh huh." Carson grinned. "No suit for me either."

"Am I the only one who packed a suit?" Michelle asked.

"Please tell me it's a bikini?" Hunter said.

Michelle grinned. "Not quite. A bikini top and boi shorts for bottoms."

Hunter wiggled her eyebrows. "That's still some serious skin showing. I can deal with that."

†

Hunter lifted her hand. "I'm starting to prune. I'm going to shower and lay down until it's time for lunch."

"That's not a bad idea," Michelle agreed.

"Go ahead, I'll come up in a little while," Carson said.

Hunter handed Michelle a towel. "That felt good. I'm super relaxed now."

"We may need to get one for the house," Michelle said.

Hunter nodded. "That's not a bad idea. I know we can use the equipment at the practice facility, but it would be nice to have one at home."

Michelle smiled brightly. "I'm happy you consider it home."

"Wherever you are is home to me," Hunter said.

Michelle chuckled. "That's a perfect answer." She reached for Hunter. "Let's go shower."

†

The meeting with Coach went well as they discussed their game plan.

"Their shooting guard is banged up and won't be at one hundred percent. We should take advantage of that on both ends of the court."

Carson nodded. "Whoever she is assigned to defend should have a great day."

Coach smiled at Carson. "She's normally assigned to the opposition's point guard, but she has trouble keeping up with her on a good day." Then she turned her attention to Carly. "That should give you opportunities to drive and make good shots."

"Got it," Carly said.

When Coach called the meeting to an end, she instructed. "Meet in the lobby at six-thirty to go to dinner. Be in bed no later than eleven. Breakfast by ten, and we'll ride to the arena at eleven. Eat a hearty breakfast, and we'll find some New York pizza after the game."

"That sounds delicious," Michelle said. "We can't visit New York without eating a slice or six."

Coach laughed. "I don't even think you can eat six."

"Probably not, but it sounded good." Michelle grinned.

"I promise you won't go hungry. See you in the lobby."

†

"What are we wearing to dinner tonight?" Carson asked.

"Jeans," Michelle said.

"Yep, me, too," Hunter added.

"I'll press them for you if you'd like," Carson offered.

"I think Atlanta and Chicago are playing this afternoon," Michelle said as she picked up the remote.

"We play Atlanta at home next week, right?" Hunter asked.

"Yep, Wednesday night before we fly to Chicago on Friday," Carson answered. "Give me your game day outfits, too. We might as well get them ready."

"Nervous energy?" Michelle asked.

"Yeah. We're on a six-game win streak, and I don't want it to end here."

"Then we play our asses off tomorrow," Michelle said. She opened a bottle of water and handed one to Hunter.

"Play like you have been, and you won't have an issue," Hunter said. "Even Coach Jr. has confidence we will win."

"I love your vote of confidence," Michelle said.

Hunter laughed as the teams were announced for the game. "Chicago looks huge compared to Atlanta."

"They have some tall post players, but they are young and still learning," Michelle said.

"Their guards are mean girls," Carson said. "They don't hesitate if a cheap shot presents itself. Unfortunately, the referees tend to let the games get more physical than necessary."

"Yeah, I remember one of them sent you flying across the floor the first game I attended."

"She did. I think she got Michelle's message loud and clear when she smashed her in the face during a blocked shot."

"Hopefully, she will have a long memory and not try any shit when we play them in Chicago. I won't hesitate to give her seconds, but you must watch out for her," Michelle warned. "I think players like that should be banned for hurting people intentionally."

"I couldn't agree more. If she accumulates a few more technicals, she'll be suspended by the league. That's a big if," Carson added. "She's damned sneaky at times."

"Playing physically to establish territory during a game is part of the game, but shots after the play is over are uncalled for," Carson said.

Carson smiled. "No more Hulk mode from you."

"I'll make it a point to legally show my wrath if she pulls any stunts," Michelle warned.

"Don't stoop to her level, but please protect yourselves." Hunter reached for Michelle's hand.

Michelle's tone softened when Hunter reached for her hand. "Yes, love." She leaned over and kissed Hunter.

"You two are too cute together," Carson noted teasingly from behind the ironing board.

"The lady makes a great point," Michelle said, placing an arm around Hunter's shoulder.

†

At breakfast, the waitress's eyes grew wide when she took Michelle's order. "Two waffles, ham steak, and four scrambled eggs?" she repeated.

"Yes, please," Michelle answered.

She smiled and looked at Hunter. "For you?"

"Cut that order in half with a glass of apple juice, please," Hunter answered.

"Yes, juice too, please," Michelle added.

The waitress placed a syrup container on the table when she delivered the food.

"Do you have peanut butter?" Michelle asked.

"Smooth or crunchy?" she teased.

"Smooth, please," Hunter answered.

The waitress chuckled. "I'll be right back."

"I've got you hooked, huh?" Hunter teased.

"In more ways than one." Michelle smiled.

†

By the middle of the fourth quarter, they had built a fifteen-point lead over New York. New York hit several shots as they made a final push, cutting the lead to eight. With only four minutes left in the game, Carly drove the ball to the basket and stepped on another player's foot when she landed. Carly collapsed on the court, clutching her right knee.

The medical staff rushed out onto the court to attend to her injury. Mary, the lead athletic trainer, looked at Coach and shook her head.

Coach looked at one of the reserve guards. "Get warm." Coach walked onto the court, and Hunter watched a stretcher roll onto the floor. Coach comforted Carly and walked back to the team.

"Huddle up," she barked. "Carly has blown her ACL and will be heading to the hospital for emergency treatment with Coach Warren." She looked up at the clock. "We only have four minutes to go for the win." She looked at Alisha, the reserve guard. "I know you aren't warm, but protect the ball. If we play smart, we can run the clock down and preserve the win. No quick shots unless you are open under the basket. Defend the three-point shots."

Hunter watched the team jog onto the court and watched the clock tick slowly. She watched Coach's face tense when Carson got trapped, and her only option was to pass to

Alisha. Hunter heard her growl when Alisha threw up an airball with twelve seconds left on the shot clock.

"Slow it down," she yelled out to Carson.

New York drained a three when Alisha failed to contest the shot to pull them within two points with ten seconds.

Coach yelled to the ref. "Time out."

When the players huddled around her, Coach looked at Carson. "There's only ten seconds left. They will go for a steal on the inbound pass, and if that isn't successful, they will foul. I don't want that ball to leave your hands unless it goes to Michelle. Understood? Michelle, you inbound the ball to Carson and stay close for an outlet."

"Got it," Michelle said.

Hunter held her breath as Michelle passed the ball to Carson, who was trapped immediately and barely got the ball back to Michelle, who was fouled immediately.

"Two shots," the ref called.

Coach saw there were only three seconds on the clock. "Drain the first one and miss the second. Rebound it if we can to finish the game. They won't have time to get a shot off if they gain possession."

Michelle stepped to the line and calmly drained the first shot. Between shots, she positioned Carson on the right side of the lane. Hunter watched as Michelle missed the shot to the right, and the rebound ricocheted to Carson, who covered the ball to protect it as the game timer ended. Coach cheered and looked at Hunter.

"That's why I have gray hairs." She laughed and walked down the court to shake hands with the New York coach and team.

In the locker room, Coach addressed the team. "That was a close one, but you pulled it off. I'm going to the hospital to check on Carly. Coach Watson has instructions to take you for pizza and ensure you get all you want."

Carson looked at Coach. "Could we come to the hospital with you?"

"The last thing the emergency department needs is this motley crew filling up their waiting area," Coach replied. "I will make sure Carly knows she is in your prayers. Eat a great meal, and I'll update you when we return."

"Can we compromise?" Carson asked. "It will take an hour at least to shower and dress. I think we have fans waiting for autographs, too. We leave here, order pizzas for delivery, and eat together when you return from the hospital. Preferably with Carly."

Coach smiled at Carson. "The captain has spoken. Is everyone good with this plan?"

"Yes, Coach," came the chorus of responses.

Coach pulled her wallet out and handed a credit card to Coach Watson. "You better call in an order for delivery around six to give them time to coordinate that many pizzas. Book the conference room and order drinks to cover everyone. That should give us time to bring Carly back to the hotel."

"Thanks, Coach," Carson said.

"I'll see you all soon." Coach turned to leave the locker room with tears in her eyes.

Hunter stood to walk out with her. "What are you doing?"

"I'm going to find out who has the best pizza," Hunter replied.

The team laughed. "Good idea. Get the down low from a true New Yorker," Carson said.

Hunter left the locker room and watched Coach as she walked out to hail a cab before she approached one of the policemen working security. "Excuse me. Officer."

"What can I help you with?" He saw she was wearing her team jacket.

"Can you tell me who has the best pizza in town and can deliver a lot of pizza to a hungry bunch of women?"

"That's easy." He smiled. "Lombardi's is the best. They should be able to accommodate an order of your size if you get them a couple hours' notice. We order for the Precinct all the time."

"Thank you," Hunter said.

"You're welcome. Tell them that Joe Roger recommended you when you order. I don't know if you'll get a discount, but I'll get a free pie out of it." He chuckled.

"You got it," Hunter said. "Thanks again."

He nodded and tipped his hat to Hunter.

Hunter returned to the locker room and shared the information with Coach Watson. "I've got this. Hit the shower," she said.

†

As expected, there was a large crowd waiting for the team when they emerged from the locker room, and the team signed autographs for thirty minutes while the bus was loaded with equipment and bags.

When they returned to the hotel, Coach Watson made arrangements for the conference room, notified the hotel of the large pizza delivery, and ordered drinks for the team. Hunter, Michelle, and Carson returned to their room.

"That sucks about Carly," Carson said. "She will be out for the rest of the season after surgery."

"That was such an odd injury," Michelle said.

"Coach may have you work with Alisha to sharpen her skills when we get home. We can't continue to win without a stronger performance from her," Carson said. "I thought Coach would explode when she threw up that airball."

"That was not a veteran decision," Michelle said.

"I don't mind working with her. Michelle is doing well," Hunter said.

"You can't just abandon me, Coach Jr.," Michelle complained.

"You know I won't, but you may need to work out with me after practice."

"That's not a problem." Michelle smiled.

"I'll do whatever I can to help, too," Carson said.

†

Carly was sitting in a recliner when they returned to the conference room for dinner. She was in obvious pain but opted to eat with the team instead of in her room.

"What's the diagnosis?" Carson asked.

"Surgery when we return to Vegas and months of rehab. Hurts like a bitch," Carly said.

"I'm sorry. You know we will do anything to help with rehab," Carson said.

"Thanks, guys. I'll be your biggest cheerleader for the rest of the season."

"Your guy was spot on with this pizza recommendation," Michelle told Hunter.

"You can always count on the local police to know the best places to eat." Hunter grinned.

"That's true," Carson said and reached for another piece.

Hunter placed a plate in front of Coach as her phone rang. "Guard my pizza," Coach said and walked out to take the call.

Hunter ate the pizza and served Coach a fresh plate when she returned smiling.

"Thanks, Hunter."

†

When they landed in Vegas, Coach told the team, "Tomorrow, we will have a short shoot-around since we play again Wednesday. I want a team meeting before, so please come to the theater at one."

"It's good to be home," Michelle said as they entered the house.

"Let's empty these bags, and I'll start some laundry," Hunter said.

"Laundry can wait." Michelle pulled Hunter into her arms for a kiss. "I need some you time."

"I do like the sound of that," Hunter replied, dropping her bags beside Michelle's. She reached for Michelle's hand, and they walked into their bedroom.

Their travel clothes were tossed into a pile as they moved to the bed. Michelle pressed their bodies together. "I've missed this."

Hunter nodded. "Snuggling is nice, but skin-to-skin is beautiful."

"I don't think we'll have another extended road trip like that for a while," Michelle said.

"Hallelujah," Hunter said. "The shower sex was great, but there's nothing like having a big bed to share in private."

"Do I need to have a chat with Carson?" Michelle asked.

"Not at all. The anticipation makes this more enjoyable," Hunter said, taking one of Michelle's breasts in her mouth.

Michelle sighed. "You do make a nice point."

"Baby, you have gorgeous points," Hunter said, nibbling on Michelle's erect nipple.

Michelle laughed. "I love you, Hunter."

Hunter smiled at Michelle. "I love you, too, and intend to show you just how much."

Michelle laughed again and used her height advantage to roll Hunter onto her back. "Not if I beat you to it."

"It's a win-win either way," Hunter said, pulling her face down for a passionate kiss.

†

Hunter was curled in Michelle's arms, her hand stroking softly across her stomach, when the silence was broken by Michelle's stomach growling.

"I think your beast demands to be fed," Hunter teased.

"I could eat after working up an appetite," Michelle replied. "I don't know what we have to cook, but I'm burnt out on restaurant eating after that trip.

Hunter climbed from the bed. "Let's go search our options." She reached for Michelle's hand, and they entered the kitchen.

"We really need to go grocery shopping," Michelle said as she stared into the refrigerator.

"Yes, we do," Hunter agreed after reviewing items in the pantry. "We've got chips."

"We have cheese slices. The bread is fresh enough to make grilled cheese. Will that hold you tonight until we can shop tomorrow?"

"Yes. We can make an order and call it in for pickup after practice tomorrow," Hunter said. "Just a small order since we're flying to Chicago later this week."

"I'll make the sandwiches if you make a list," Michelle offered.

"Eggs and bread, for sure. What meals would you like on Thursday?"

"Some deli meats for sandwiches. Add some boneless chicken breasts and yellow rice. I make a mean baked chicken casserole. Some asparagus to roast and salad ingredients. That will hold us until we get back from Chicago. We can make a larger list for the next few days when we return."

"When will we head to Phoenix?" Hunter asked.

"Our flight is Wednesday morning. We start practice that afternoon. We'll fly home Sunday after the game."

"Will the rest of the team get time off during the break?"

Michelle nodded. "With strict orders from Coach to rest and eat well. We can't afford another injury."

Hunter was reminded of Carly's knee injury. "I think Carly's scheduled for knee surgery in the morning. Isn't she married?"

"Yes. Carly's husband, Steve, will be with her. He will let us know how she's doing."

"That's good. That's a tough injury," Hunter said. "Rehab will take months, right?"

"Yes, it will. Carly will surely miss the rest of this season and maybe longer."

"I hope we can get Alisha tuned up and ready to start," Hunter said.

Michelle nodded as she plated the sandwiches. "I know Coach was pretty disappointed in her performance during the game. It was a simple assignment." Michelle took their plates to the table.

"Trying too hard to impress Coach backfired on her."

"You got to listen and follow simple instructions."

Hunter swallowed a bite of the sandwich. "I think she got Coach's message loud and clear."

†

"Damn, it's good to be home," Michelle said as they entered the bedroom after tending to a load of laundry.

Hunter waited for Michelle to stretch out before placing her head on Michelle's chest. "There's no place I'd rather be than right here."

"Did you remember to place our grocery order?"

"I did. While you picked up the kitchen. It will be ready between four and five tomorrow. If we finish practice early, we can stop for frozen yogurt on the way."

"Now you're singing my tune," Hunter said. "Good night."

Michelle chuckled. "I'll be dreaming of frozen yogurt now."

"We will make it happen," Hunter promised.

CHAPTER FIFTEEN

"We're up early and ready for practice. Should we have yogurt before practice?" Michelle asked.

"That's a great suggestion. It's only a shoot-around today after the meeting, right?"

"Yep." Michelle smiled. "Let's go."

They arrived at the practice facility with fifteen minutes to spare. "Should we change first to be ready for practice?" Hunter asked.

"No. Coach said to come directly to the video room."

"We'd better follow instructions then." Hunter grinned.

Most of the team were seated around the large conference table when they entered. Carson was placing bottles of water in front of each chair. She saved two seats beside her for Michelle and Hunter.

After everyone had settled into their seats, Coach started the meeting. "I got a call from Carly's husband, Steve, earlier, and the damage was worse than expected. The surgery went well, but she will miss the rest of the season."

"Can we visit?" Carson asked.

"She's only in the hospital for tonight. Then she'll head home. Maybe we can arrange a video call before the game tomorrow night," Coach suggested.

"I bet she'd like that," Carson agreed.

"In light of her injury, I have made some recommendations to the front office, and they agreed with my suggestions. We must replace Carly for the rest of the season and potentially longer." Coach reached into a box beside her and held up a jersey with the number fifteen. "I would like to take this opportunity to welcome our newest team member to the squad." Coach turned the jersey toward the team.

Hunter gasped when she saw her last name on the jersey. "What? How, Coach?"

"Because I am brilliant," she teased. "When I signed you up for the practice team, I listed you as a developmental player, which allowed me to promote you to a full roster slot."

"Hell yes," Michelle said, slapping Hunter on the back.

"Congratulations," Carson added, and the rest of the team voiced their approval.

"I appreciate your work ethic and attention to detail when running plays. Carson will still play point, but I anticipate you getting significant playing time," Coach said.

"Thank you for the opportunity," Hunter said. She couldn't hold back the tears any longer.

"I know you will make the most of it," Coach replied. "Back to business. Does anyone have any questions before we hit the court?"

When no one answered, Coach said, "I'll see you on the court in fifteen minutes. It will be a light shoot-around. No contact. I want everyone rested for tomorrow's game. We'll shoot for an hour and a half, and then I'll see you back for the game at four tomorrow." She looked at Hunter. "Stay back for a minute."

When they were alone in the room, Coach looked at Hunter. "You won't start tomorrow night but will go in for Alisha if she doesn't play well. I feel that I owe her that."

"I understand, Coach. I'll fill whatever role you need me to."

"I know you will give me a hundred-ten percent. Do you have any questions?"

"No, Coach. I think I'm still in shock."

"Stop by my office after practice so we can update your contract."

Hunter stood and hugged Coach. "Thanks."

"Go before I change my mind," Coach teased.

†

The team clapped when she entered the locker room. Hunter walked to her locker and stopped when she saw it was empty. She looked at Sandy with confusion.

Sandy pointed across the room. "Congratulations on being promoted."

Hunter looked at the lockers on the team side of the room and saw her Jersey hanging on a hook. "Thanks, Sandy."

"You're all set with practice uniforms and game day gear."

Hunter walked over to her new locker, which was beside Michelle's.

218

"Congrats, Rooks," Michelle said, pulling her into a hug.

"Thank you," Hunter replied with tears in her eyes.

"Get the lead out, and let's get to work," Carson said, smiling at Hunter. "We must run you through the plays to ensure you've got them down."

Hunter nodded and changed into the practice uniform before walking out to begin stretching. Michelle sat down beside her. "Pinch me so I know I'm not dreaming."

Michelle reached over to pinch her arm. "You are definitely not dreaming."

Coach entered the gym. "I want Alisha and Hunter to alternate running the plays with the starters," she instructed.

Hunter had memorized every play the team ran, and when it was her turn, she executed each one perfectly. She stood back and watched Alisha as she missed several key points to the plays. Carson made her go through each one until she had the routes down.

"Okay, let me see some good shooting," Coach said.

Hunter jogged to the far end of the court with half of the team. She was fed balls to work on her three-point shooting and practiced driving to the basket on Dan.

"You've got this, Hunter." Dan grinned. "You will light this place up tomorrow night. Atlanta won't know what hit them."

"Thanks for the vote of confidence, Dan."

†

After dressing, Hunter told Michelle, "I have to stop by Coach's office for a few minutes. I won't be long."

"Take your time. No need to hurry." Michelle smiled.

"We're going for dinner to celebrate," Carson said.

"What about our groceries?"

"You can take them home and meet me at the condo," Carson said.

"We can change and be back in town in no time." Michelle grinned.

"Sounds perfect. I'll see you in a few."

Hunter knocked on Coach's door.

"Come on in." Coach nodded to a seat next to her at the table. She pushed two pages over to Hunter. "The amendment to your contract. Read over it carefully and sign, please."

Hunter read through the document and was surprised by the increase in salary. Her hand felt shaky as she signed her contract.

Coach nodded and signed underneath her signature.

"Tomorrow will be a big night for you. Atlanta has no information on you from scouting reports, so if you have a hot hand tomorrow, I want your debut spectacular. Alisha is not sharp enough for the role, but you are ready."

"Thanks, Coach."

"I think Carson and Michelle are taking you to dinner tonight. Eat a great meal and be rested and hydrated for tomorrow."

"I hope I can sleep tonight," Hunter said. "I still can't believe this is happening."

"I bet Michelle will help you sleep tonight," Coach teased, making Hunter blush. "Just don't pull any muscles."

"Got it, Coach."

"Hang on, and I'll make you a copy."

"How did you pick my jersey number?"

"It was your number when you played, right? High school and college."

"I can't believe you remembered that."

"I've had my eyes on you for years," Coach said, handing her the copy. "Have fun tonight."

"Thanks."

†

Michelle was waiting for her in the hallway. "Let's roll."

Hunter's face hurt from smiling so hard.

"I can't wait to play with you," Michelle said. "You're going to be fantastic."

"I don't want to disappoint you or Coach."

"You won't, so don't overthink things. Let your instincts take over."

"I can't wait to tell Mom and Jim."

"Call them," Michelle said.

"I'll wait until we get home."

"I'll put the groceries away and change clothes while you call," Michelle said.

†

"Hey, Mom," Hunter said when her mom answered. "I know it's early, but I've got news to share that can't wait."

"No problem. What's up, honey?"

"You need to watch tomorrow night's game. I'm going to be playing."

"What?" she heard her mom call out.

Hunter explained Carly's injury and being promoted to the team roster. "I won't start tomorrow night, but Coach says I will play significant minutes."

"Oh, honey. That's such great news. I am so excited. When do you play at home on the weekend next? Jim and I will come watch in person."

"Not until after the All-Star break," Hunter replied. "We play in LA again in a few weeks. That would be closer for you."

"Close doesn't matter. I can't wait to watch you play again."

"I'm so excited," Hunter said. "Carson and Michelle are taking me out to celebrate tonight."

"I won't keep you then. I will definitely be watching tomorrow. I'll print out a schedule, too, so Jim and I can plan to see some of your games."

"Thanks, Mom. Love you."

"Love you too, and I am so proud of you, Hunter. Call after the game if you can."

"I will, Mom. Goodnight."

†

"Damn, I've never known someone who can fill a pair of jeans like you," Michelle said.

Hunter smiled. "Have you looked in the mirror lately? You are one sexy woman."

Michelle pulled Hunter into her arms and kissed her passionately.

"Wow. I felt that one down to my toes." Hunter grinned. "We'd better leave now if we are going to dinner. Another one of those, and we'll end up in bed."

"I'll save them for later then," Michelle said, leading Hunter out of the bedroom.

Hunter was giddy with excitement as she climbed into the Jeep. Life had taken such an incredible turn since she arrived in Vegas. Not only had she found the woman of her dreams that she was deeply in love with, but she also had an opportunity to fulfill a dream of playing professionally. Even if it was for a limited time, Hunter was determined to make the most of the experience.

†

Carson and Michelle treated her to one of the best steak dinners of her life, and when they returned home, Michelle made good on her promise, making love with Hunter until the early morning. Hunter's anxiety about playing in her first game was forgotten as Michelle wrapped her in her arms, and they drifted off to sleep.

CHAPTER SIXTEEN

"Good morning," Michelle said after waking Hunter with a kiss.

Hunter squinted at the light coming in the window. "What time is it?"

"It's nine-thirty."

"Oh, my word. Why did you let me sleep so late?"

"Um, we were up quite late, and you needed to rest." Michelle grinned. "How did you sleep?"

"Obviously, pretty hard if I didn't realize you had left the bed," Hunter said, wiping the sleep from her eyes.

"Because your body needed it," Michelle replied. "I've got an early lunch in the oven for us. I brought you coffee, too." She handed Hunter the cup.

"Thanks. I didn't mean to sound grumpy," Hunter said, sipping.

"I know. You're usually awake before me, so I let you sleep in for a change. It was a bit selfish of me, too."

"How so?"

"Because I know you will bounce off the walls, excited about tonight, once you're fully awake."

"Damn. You know me too well already," Hunter replied.

"I have a plan. After we eat, we can relax to allow our food to settle. Then we can shower and dress for the game. I thought we might stop for some frozen yogurt as well. By then, there may be someone who can let us in at the arena."

"I'm sorry. I'm so excited and nervous about tonight."

"There is nothing to apologize for. I was heaving my guts before my first game. I hope you don't have a nervous stomach."

"Thankfully, no. Just an overabundance of energy," Hunter said.

"We need to find a way for you to store that for the game. What did you do before?"

"I used headphones and listened to music until it was time to dress and warm up. Once I get on the court, I'm settled."

"What kind of music?" Michelle asked.

"Don't laugh."

"I won't," Michelle promised.

"Carol King and Pheobe Snow."

"Those are perfectly mellow tunes. I have headphones you can use, and we can load some music onto your phone while we wait for lunch." Michelle smiled. "Alexa, play Carol King."

Michelle left the bedroom as the music started to play. She returned with a pair of noise-cancelling headphones and Hunter's cell phone. "I've added my Apple Music account to your phone. Download what you want, and I'll pair your phone to the headphones."

"Thank you." Hunter started downloading music.

†

Hunter entered the kitchen to find Michelle swaying to the music as she poured them glasses of tea. She walked up behind Michelle and wrapped her arms around her waist. "Something smells terrific."

"It's my baked chicken casserole and roasted asparagus. There's a salad in the fridge if you want to bring it to the table."

"Sure." She kissed Michelle's cheek and walked to the fridge.

"How are you feeling?"

"Very chill. Thank you."

"I love your choice of music. A little before our time, but it's calming and beautiful."

"Mom played the *Tapestry* album frequently at home. That's how I came to be introduced. Pheobe was an extra bonus."

"Your mom has great taste in music."

"I'll be sure to tell her you approve." Hunter grinned as Michelle placed the casserole and asparagus on the table.

"Let's eat."

"This is delicious," Hunter told Michelle. "Where did you learn how to cook like this? Did your mom teach you?"

"Heaven's no. She ran me out of her kitchen all the time. I'm a self-taught cook. Well, Google recipes also had a part to play in it."

"You seem to enjoy cooking."

226

"It's very relaxing for me. I love making special meals for the people in my life."

"That's lucky for me. I can cook some basics, but nothing that tastes this good."

"We can work on cooking more together if you'd like," Michelle offered.

Hunter looked up from her plate. "I'd like that. I enjoy spending time with you."

"We eat out so often during the season. There's nothing I like more than to come home to home-cooked meals. It is even more enjoyable now to share them with you."

"You had me with the sweet tea," Hunter said. "Last night's meal was spectacular, but the steaks you cook are just as good."

Michelle's smile lit up her face. "You are so good for my ego."

"I meant that sincerely," Hunter replied.

"Thank you. I didn't make dessert since we will stop for yogurt."

"That's perfectly fine with me. I think I've become addicted."

"Then I will gladly continue to feed your addiction. I love it, too."

"Will we still go to breakfast after the game?"

Michelle nodded. "It's a Carson tradition."

"That is also fine with me. I love the breakfast there."

†

"Damn, you look sexy," Michelle said when Hunter joined her in the living room.

"Thanks. My girlfriend dresses me well," Hunter teased. She cocked her head. "Are my outfits okay since I'm now on the roster?"

"Very much so, but you know I love to shop," Michelle said. "We can make a few upgrades if you like. I think some suits would look fabulous on you."

"Maybe when we return from Chicago, we can shop for a few," Hunter suggested.

Michelle rubbed her hands together. "I know just the place."

Hunter picked up the headphones. "Are we stopping for yogurt?"

"Yes, we are. We still have time," Michelle said.

†

Hunter placed the headphones on when they left the yogurt shop. She was beginning to feel anxious. "Do you mind?" she asked Michelle, pointing to the headphones.

"Not at all." Michelle drove the short distance to the arena and pulled into the players' lot. She reached for Hunter's hand as they entered the building. The photographers were already gathered and started snapping photos as they walked past. Michelle felt Hunter's hand move as she attempted to pull away, but she locked their fingers together and offered Hunter a reassuring smile.

Hunter relaxed, and they entered the locker room. It was no surprise they were the first to arrive. "Would you mind if I suit up and sit on the bench for a few minutes?"

"Not at all," Michelle said. "I'll wait for you here." She leaned over to kiss Hunter. "This is your night. Enjoy every minute of it."

228

When Hunter had dressed in her uniform and warm-up gear, Michelle nodded. "That looks fantastic on you."

"Thanks. I'll be back soon." Hunter picked up her headphones and walked to the tunnel. She had made the walk several times, but this was her first as an official player. Her eyes surveyed the enormity of the arena and knew that in less than two hours, every seat would be filled with energized fans. She sat on the sidelines in one of the chairs and looked at the scoreboard. It had already been programmed with team names, and she felt her heart race. *This is really happening. The next time I step on this court, I will be a player in the WNBA. Fantastic.* She listened to several songs with her eyes closed.

Coach walked in and sat beside Hunter. She tapped her shoulder, and Hunter's eyes flew open.

"Are you ready to set this place on fire?"

"Yes, Coach. I am."

"I anticipate sending you in early, so get loose and stay loose."

"Got it, Coach."

"Come then, and let's get your teammates fired up."

Hunter turned off her headphones and stored them in her locker with her phone as the group was huddling in the room.

"Tonight is our night to set this place on fire. I want you to go out there and show Atlanta they can't come into our house and win. Get warm. Hell, get hot, and we'll meet back just before the intros."

Carson reached her hand into the center of their circle. "You heard the lady. Let's get hot."

"One, two, three. Get hot," the team shouted and left the locker room. At the end of the tunnel, the players jogged onto the court.

Hunter sat beside Michelle to stretch, and her eyes glimmered with excitement. Fans were pouring into their seats with thirty minutes to go.

"You good?" Michelle asked.

"Yes. Relaxed and ready to go."

†

The starters were introduced, and their warm-up gear was removed while the Atlanta team was introduced. Hunter left her pants and jacket on to keep her muscles warm. As the game began, she felt on top of the world, and Vegas jumped out to a quick lead.

"Hunter," Coach called. "Get ready."

Hunter removed her warm-ups and waited for Coach's signal. "Go check-in and you'll enter on the next game stoppage."

Hunter had barely checked in when the referee signaled for her to enter the game. Hunter was surprised when she heard her name over the PA system.

"Vegas fans. Let's give a warm welcome to our newest player, Hunter James," he said.

The crowd applauded her entry into the game as Hunter jogged down the court and was high-fived by Carson. "You got this."

Hunter nodded as her heart thumped in her chest. She was glad to start on the defensive end, and when she picked up her player, the woman was casually dribbling up the court. Hunter timed her move perfectly and stripped the ball from her hands. She rushed down the court and found Carson open for an easy layup. The crowd roared as they ran back down the court.

One of Atlanta's post players hit a short jumper, and Carson took the inbound pass and brought the ball down the court.

"You're doing great," Michelle said as she hustled past her.

Carson passed the ball to Hunter, who dropped the ball inside to Michelle. She was tied up when Hunter's defender went to help out, leaving Hunter open for a three. Michelle found her open, and Hunter let the shot fly. Hunter's heart pounded as the ball approached the basket and dropped through the rim perfectly.

"Hell, yes," Hunter yelled and fist-pumped the air. Hunter glanced at the smile on Coach's face as she rushed back down the court.

"Hunter James, ladies and gentlemen. I think we will hear that name called out often," the announcer said.

Hunter and Carson hit another three-point shot each to build the lead to eight after the first quarter. Hunter took a long drink of Gatorade and listened closely to Coach.

"Their guards are sagging back to help their bigs down low, so I want you two to light them up outside if they don't come out on you. When they do, drop the ball into the post." She looked at Hunter and Carson. "Got it?"

Hunter nodded. "Yes, Coach."

"Don't hesitate to shoot. You are doing great."

Hunter's confidence grew with every shot. She and Carson were perfect from behind the arc when the half ended.

"You gals are killing it," Michelle said, placing an arm loosely around Hunter's shoulder as they walked off the court. "How are you feeling?"

"Great," Hunter said. "It feels fantastic to be playing again."

"You're playing an amazing first game," Carson said.

Hunter used the restroom and sat next to Michelle. She took a bottle of water and downed half in a long drink. "Thanks. I needed that."

"Atlanta wasn't prepared for what we're giving them. They must shut down the threes if they plan to make a game of this. That will provide us with the advantage under the basket. Time for our bigs to go to work. Let's double this fifteen-point lead and send them home wondering what hit them."

As they walked back onto the court, Hunter looked at Michelle. "It's time to 'kiss it,'" she teased. "They don't have the defense to stop you."

"Bring it," Michelle replied. "I might even try another three." She grinned.

"Step out, and I'll drive to pull your defender off and send you the ball," Hunter said. "Bend and lift."

"Got it," Michelle said, draining a shot from the corner during warm-ups.

When they returned to the bench, Coach approached Hunter. "You feeling good? I don't want you playing fatigued."

"My feet aren't touching the court," Hunter said.

"You're doing great. If we still have a big lead in the fourth, I'll return Alisha to rest you and give her some playing time."

Hunter nodded. "Thanks, Coach."

†

Hunter was proud of Michelle, who dropped several short step-back jumpers. She smiled when she saw her drop out to the corner and drove toward the lane. When Michelle's defender tried to cut her off, Hunter made a no-look pass to Michelle in the corner. She saw Michelle release the shot and turned to block out for a rebound. Michelle's shot dropped cleanly through the nylon.

With only seconds to go, Hunter stole a pass and found Michelle racing down the court. She lobbed a pass into her, and Michelle slammed a dunk home, barely missing the player's face who tried to guard her.

The horn sounded, and they returned to the bench.

"Alisha is going in for you, but keep your jacket on to stay warm in case Atlanta makes a run," Coach told her. "Great game."

"Thanks," Hunter replied and pulled on her jacket. After the break, she sat and felt her energy drain from her as her adrenalin returned to normal. She had played well but wasn't sure she could go another quarter.

Atlanta made a small run in the fourth, but the game ended with Vegas up twenty. Hunter joined the line to congratulate the Atlanta team. When the Atlanta coach shook her hand, she leaned in to speak to Hunter. "I don't know where you came from, but will you please go back? You destroyed my guards tonight."

Hunter recognized this as a high compliment and smiled. "Thanks, Coach."

Carson and Michelle were waiting for her at the end of the bench. As they started toward the tunnel, Hunter was shocked to hear fans calling her and asking for an autograph. Hunter smiled, accepting an ink pen, and began signing a variety of objects, from shirts to balls and a young girl's ball cap. Hunter was happy to walk into the locker room when the crowd thinned.

The team cheered loudly when Carson and Hunter entered. "You two slayed them tonight," one of the players said.

Coach held up the stat sheet. "Settle down," she said, and the players took seats. "Carson, another excellent game for you with thirty points, five assists, and two steals. However, tonight, the game ball goes to Hunter for a debut game of twenty-six points, eight assists, and four steals. Welcome to the W." Coach tossed Hunter the game ball.

Hunter's tears blurred her vision as her teammates congratulated her. She held out the ball and asked each of them to sign it. Carson took it first. *Your first great game of many to come.* She dated the ball and added the score before passing it to Michelle.

"Great teamwork all around, ladies. I hope you take that win into Chicago and give them a good dose. Celebrate tonight, and I'll see you for practice tomorrow at three. Wheels up, Friday at ten."

Coach left the locker room to allow her team to celebrate. She met with the press to see who they wanted to interview for tonight's game. She was delighted when they requested Hunter, Carson, and Michelle to join her on the podium. "I'll be right back."

Coach returned to the locker room. "Carson, Hunter, and Michelle to the interview podium for a press conference."

Hunter looked shocked. She turned to Carson. "What do I do?"

"Just answer their questions," Carson replied. "I'll jump in and help if needed, but you got this, Rooks," she teased.

Michelle draped a towel over Hunter's shoulder. "Let's do this."

Hunter followed her teammates and Coach into the interview room and sat on the podium.

"Great game, Coach," one of the reporters hollered. "We all want to know where your newest superstar came from. No one was expecting her caliber of play tonight, especially Atlanta," he added to a round of laughter.

"Hunter joined us a few weeks ago as a developmental player on the practice squad. She'd been away from the game for a few years but wanted to join us to get back on the court. The unfortunate injury to Carly opened that door, and bringing her up was easy."

"We would certainly agree it was a wise move. Hunter, how did it feel to be back in the game?"

Hunter cleared her throat. "I'd like to thank Coach for giving me an opportunity. It felt great to be playing again."

"Carson, you two seemed to have some good dynamics going tonight. How did you play so well together after such a short time?"

"Hunter and I have battled against each other since high school. She's a natural on the floor, as you all witnessed tonight. Coach instructed us to light them up behind the arc, and tonight, we were both red hot."

"I'd say so. Fifty-six points between the two of you. What an incredible game."

"Fantastic dunk tonight, Michelle. You are really expanding your range. To what do you attribute your new shots?"

"Hunter pushed me hard on the practice squad and has been drilling me on step-back jumpers and three-point shooting. I'm not confident on my three-pointers yet, but I'm getting there."

"You have a tough Chicago game coming up this weekend, Coach. Will we see Hunter on the starting squad?"

"I believe the odds are very likely that you will."

"This is Vegas, baby. We love those odds," another reporter called out.

"Welcome, Hunter. We certainly look forward to more games like tonight."

"Thank you. I will give this team my best," Hunter answered.

"Tonight was certainly a great team effort. Good luck in Chicago, ladies. Enjoy your celebration."

"Thank you all," Coach said and led her players from the podium.

"That wasn't too bad, now was it?" she teased Hunter.

"I survived." Hunter grinned.

"Hit the showers, and I'll see you tomorrow."

†

"Here are the three amigos. Great game tonight," Polly, their usual server, said when they entered. She winked at Hunter. "I didn't know I had been serving the secret weapon all this time."

"It worked out well that I could join these two on the court," Hunter said, blushing.

"I'd say so. You three demolished Atlanta tonight. Dessert is on me."

"Thanks, Polly," Carson said as she sat at their table.

"Coffee, for starters?" Polly asked.

"Sounds great," Carson answered.

"So, what's it going to be tonight, ladies?"

"Pancakes, and lots of them," Michelle said. "With a ham steak on the side."

"You got it. Hunter, for you?"

"Pancakes and ham sound good. Could you make them blueberry?"

"Absolutely. For you, Captain?"

"I'd like a ham and cheese omelet with rye toast and orange juice."

"Juice for you ladies?"

"Apple," they both answered.

"I'll have your coffee out in just a minute."

†

"I don't think you could have played a better game tonight," Carson told Hunter. "We are all proud of you."

"Thanks. It felt great."

"I was surprised when Coach rested you for the fourth quarter," Michelle said.

Hunter smiled. "I think she realized I had run out of adrenalin. I was starting to feel gassed."

"Now that your first game is under your belt, your adrenalin will become more regular," Michelle said. "It's good she didn't push you. It's too easy to get injured when you're fatigued."

Carson nodded. "Coach will never ask you to play more than you have in the tank. She expects us to let her know when we need a break."

"I hope my endurance will continue to improve," Hunter said.

"You played a lot of minutes for a first game. Be proud of yourself. We are," Michelle stated.

"Thanks, you two. Would you mind if I step out and call Mom before it gets too late?"

"Go ahead. I'll guard your pancakes," Carson replied.

†

Hunter stepped outside and leaned against Michelle's Jeep after she dialed home.

Her mom answered on the second ring and put her on speaker. "Hey, honey. Jim's here, too. You played an incredible game tonight."

"Thanks. It felt great."

"You are a natural," Jim said. "I can't wait to watch you in person."

"Just let me know when you're coming. I'm a hot shot now and can get you free tickets," Hunter joked.

"We've already started planning trips around your schedule," Elizabeth said.

"We'll be in Vegas for your next weekend game, and I think we've agreed on LA, Phoenix, and Seattle so far," Jim added.

"Did you see the post-game interviews? Please tell me I didn't sound like a complete goober."

"No, you were very professional. It's like you have done this many times," Jim said.

"I'll admit, I was scared to death."

"You couldn't tell. You did a great job."

"Thank you. I need to cut this short. Dinner just arrived. I'll give you a call this weekend, okay?"

"Good luck in Chicago," Jim said.

"Love you, honey."

"Love you, too, Mom. Goodnight, and thanks for watching."

†

Polly cleared the dishes from the table. "What's it going to be for dessert, ladies?"

"Do you have coconut cream pie?" Michelle asked.

"Of course."

"I'll take a warm slice of apple," Carson said.

"Hunter?"

"I couldn't dream of eating another bite right now."

"What do you like? I'll make yours to go."

"Banana cream if you have it."

"Too easy," Polly said and returned behind the counter.

When she returned with Michelle's pie and Hunter's in a box, she turned to Carson. "Do you want ice cream with your pie?"

"Not this time," Carson replied.

"This is too good. Do you want a bite?" Michelle offered.

"Thanks, but no. I should not have eaten that last pancake," Hunter groaned.

Polly brought Carson's pie. "Can I get you ladies anything else?"

"Just the check, Polly." Michelle smiled and handed her a credit card.

"Can I at least leave the tip?" Hunter asked.

"No, I'll put a nice one on the bill to cover the pie and extras," Michelle said.

"Thanks for another great meal."

"My pleasure," Michelle said.

239

†

"We'll see you tomorrow at practice," Michelle said when they left the restaurant.

"Have a good night," Hunter told her friend.

"You too. Don't stay up too late celebrating," Carson teased.

"Funny. I'm fading fast," Hunter replied.

"Drive safe," Michelle said and started the Jeep. She reached for Hunter's hand. "I am so proud of you."

"Thank you. That means the world to me," Hunter said.

"You mean the world to me. Let's go home and snuggle. We can pack for Chicago and enjoy a leisurely meal tomorrow night. Do you like barbequed chicken?"

"I like chicken any way you cook it," Hunter said.

"Let's make a quick order when we get home, and I'll grill some tomorrow. We have salad left, and I can make some baked beans or macaroni salad. Or both," Michelle said.

"I'll make the macaroni salad while you grill," Hunter offered.

"You have a deal." Michelle smiled.

†

Hunter brushed her teeth and climbed in beside Michelle. "So, how did it feel signing autographs and being interviewed?"

"I was surprised by both. The fans were genuinely excited to have my autograph."

"You are an instant success. I thought you interviewed well, too."

"It was comforting to have you and Carson beside me."

"I don't think I've ever seen Coach smile so much as she did tonight," Michelle said. "She is extremely proud of you."

"I can't thank her enough for giving me a chance."

"I believe she is as happy as you that you are on the team. I think that's a good start for your career."

"What do you think the odds are that I will be offered a contract next season?"

"Coach will do everything she can to get you signed. Especially if you continue to play this well."

"I will give it my all to make it happen."

"I know you will," Michelle said. "Are you ready for some sleep?"

"Yes and no," Hunter answered with a grin.

"Rest tonight. That kind of adrenalin leaves you exhausted. We can make love tomorrow night," Michelle replied.

Hunter sighed as she snuggled into Michelle and was sound asleep within minutes.

CHAPTER SEVENTEEN

The Chicago trip ended with a hard-fought victory. The team played well against an aggressive defense, and Hunter scored thirty. The game turned into a statement game with her when she was aggressively fouled by her defender, who clipped her with an elbow, creating a small cut over her eyebrow. The defender was given a flagrant one technical foul, and while Hunter was receiving medical care, Carson made the foul shots, and Vegas scored another basket.

"It's just a minor cut," Hunter told the Coach. "Some glue and Steri-Strips, and I'll be ready to return."

Coach frowned. "No signs of a concussion?" she asked the medical staff.

"None," they responded.

Hunter sighed. "I need to go back in, Coach. I need to let Chicago and the rest of the league know I won't be bullied."

Coach shook her head and smiled. "Just don't get hurt worse. Go check in."

"I may get a foul called on me," Hunter warned.

"Make it worth it," Coach grinned.

At the next stoppage of play, Hunter returned to the game. She found the perfect opportunity to send her message a few plays later. She passed the ball in the corner to Michelle, who returned the pass to her. This opened up the lane for Hunter to drive to the basket. Her defender was late in reacting and stepped into Hunter's path. Instead of altering her path, Hunter plowed into the player and sent her sliding across the end line on her ass. The ref blew her whistle, pointed at the defender, and called a foul for blocking.

The Chicago player jumped to her feet and rushed the ref, letting out a string of profanities over the call. The ref blew her whistle again and ejected the player from the game. Her coach had to escort her from the court, stopping the game temporarily.

Carson huddled the team on the court. She couldn't hold back her grin as she looked at Hunter. "I believe she got your message. You take the shots."

Hunter walked to the foul line amid booing from the crowd. The ref had her whistle hand near her mouth when she approached Hunter to hand her the ball.

"Way to give her a dose of her own medicine," she told Hunter.

Hunter could only nod as she received the ball and made the free throws. The replacement player gave Hunter a wide berth, and she scored ten more points before the game ended.

"That was a gutsy play," Michelle told her as they left the court.

"I had to send a message," Hunter answered.

"Received loud and clear." Michelle laughed. "Great game. How's the head?"

"I'm fine, I've had worse." She looked at Michelle. "Thanks for not storming over and pounding her into the court."

"Carson cut me off and got me to cool down. I know you don't need my protection, but damn, that pissed me off."

"You and I know I will be tested as a rookie."

"Maybe teams will think twice in the future. You sure nailed her ass."

Hunter grinned. "Even the ref thought it was a good move."

"I wondered what she said to you on the line."

"It was good I gave her a dose of her own medicine."

"That's true, but we will play them again. You'll need to watch your back when we do."

"I will definitely keep my eyes on her. I know I just made an enemy."

"We've all got your back," Michelle said, placing an arm around her shoulder protectively. "Come on. You've got autographs to sign."

†

The flight home was quick, and when they landed, most of the team went into relaxation mode for the All-Star game break. They wouldn't play again until Washington came to town after the break. Michelle and Carson were playing in the game, and Coach was one of the assigned coaches, so they would fly out again Wednesday morning to Phoenix.

The All-Star events were exciting, and Carson won the three-point shooting contest and was rewarded with a nice check. The game was reasonably evenly matched, but the Western Conference team won by four. The food and events were fun. Hunter enjoyed sharing them with her teammates and Coach.

"That was a fun trip," Coach said when they landed. "It's good to be home."

"We'll see you at three tomorrow for practice," Carson told her as they collected their bags.

"Don't remind me. It's back to the grind tomorrow. I've got game films from Washington and Minnesota to review."

"Anything we need to be overly concerned about?" Michelle asked.

"I'm not sure yet," Coach said. "I'll let you know tomorrow." She stepped out to hail a cab.

"I'll go get the car and pick you up in a few," Carson said.

"Almost home, babe," Michelle said.

"Do we have the last game for Washington recorded?" Hunter asked.

"I'm sure we do. Minnesota's, too, if you want to watch them. We can stretch out on the couch and watch them in comfort."

"Would you mind?"

"Not if you don't care if I fall asleep," Michelle joked. "Playing ball is much more exciting than watching it on television."

"I understand. You don't have to watch if you'd rather do something else."

"Hmm. I may do some baking," Michelle said.

"That works for me. Here we go."

They placed their bags in the trunk and climbed inside. Carson had the AC blasting cold air, and it was cooling down nicely.

"What are your plans for the rest of the day?" Carson asked.

"I was thinking about watching some games to get a heads up on Washington and Minnesota. Michelle is going to do some baking."

"Want some company watching the games?"

"Sure," Hunter replied.

"I can cook a pot of spaghetti tonight if you'll stay for supper."

"You don't mind me crashing your party?"

"Heck no. We'll slip into comfy clothes and relax for the rest of the day."

"I've got some shorts and a T-shirt in my bag."

"It's settled then," Hunter replied. "Do we have garlic bread?"

"In the freezer, waiting to be cooked." Michelle grinned.

†

Carson rummaged through her bag for clothes and followed Michelle and Hunter inside. "I can't believe we are just three weeks from starting the playoffs," she said when she was sitting beside Hunter.

"We should still be in first place, then," Michelle said.

"I think Coach is worried about Minnesota," Carson said. "They have been on a winning streak, too."

"At least we get them at home," Hunter said. "Mom and Jim are coming for that game."

Michelle smiled. "That will be exciting, to have them here. Will they stay with us?"

Hunter shook her head. "Jim has already got them booked at a casino. I'm sure we will see plenty of them."

"Maybe they can join us for a steak dinner Saturday night. You too, Carson," Michelle said.

"I'll propose that to Mom. I think Jim may have entered a poker tournament."

"If so, we can watch, hit some jackpots, and have dinner in town with them."

"You can always grill for us on Sunday after they've gone," Hunter suggested.

"Let's plan on that then." Michelle smiled. "Cake or brownies?"

Hunter looked at Carson. "Both, please," Hunter replied. "Are you ready to watch some games?"

"Let's start with Minnesota, if you don't mind."

†

"I can see why Coach is concerned. The Lynx are looking pretty strong," Carson said.

"We will have to pressure their guards to keep the ball outside. Their post-play was decent against New York." Hunter looked over at Michelle, who was watching from behind the counter. "You are going to have your hands full. She plays aggressive."

"I'll do my best to keep the ball out of her hands. I can force her to the baseline. That will also cut down her angles."

Carson nodded and looked at Hunter. "Their guards sag back on help defense. If they don't come out to contest, you and I should have a field day."

"If you two stay hot, we won't have to worry about offensive rebounds," Michelle said.

"That's the plan," Hunter said and high-fived Carson.

Hunter switched games. "Washington looks depleted," she said. "Not much help coming off the bench."

†

After dinner, Hunter walked Carson out to her car. "Are you okay? You seem down."

Carson chuckled. "I was getting spoiled with you living with me. It was nice to have someone at home to talk with. I'm happy that you and Michelle are doing well, but it makes me miss Stacy more."

"I can understand that, but I hope you know you can join us anytime or call if you want to talk. Michelle loves cooking, and the more the merrier, she says."

"I don't want to encroach on your time together."

"You wouldn't be encroaching on us. We can take turns cooking if you want. One night at your place and then one out here."

"I might have to bring home take-out. I don't have Michelle's cooking skills."

"That's fine, too." Hunter pulled Carson into a hug. "You know we love you."

"Yeah, I do. I love you guys, too."

"The season will be over before we know it, and Stacy will be home," Hunter told her.

"See you tomorrow."

"Get some rest. We've got a big week ahead of us."

"Yes, we do."

†

Michelle handed Hunter a glass of tea when she joined her on the couch. "Everything okay?"

"Carson's feeling a bit lonesome. I assured her we'd do more stuff together until Stacy comes home after the season ends."

"I think there is more to it than that. We discussed the new league during one of our meetings at the All-Star game. There are rules adopted that may change our decisions."

"Like what?" Hunter asked.

"For the inaugural season, only thirty players will be invited to play on six teams of five. Teams will rotate instead of remain constant."

"Like the Athletes Unlimited sports?" Hunter asked.

"Very similar. Most games will be played in Miami, but not all."

"I think Carson is worried Stacy won't be selected. Her team hasn't had a great season. She may not want to go if Stacy doesn't."

Hunter smiled at Michelle. "I hope you know I'd be fine if you got selected and I didn't. I'd still want you to play."

"That goes both ways. I'd be there to watch you. I wish they would have allowed teams to join together."

"Maybe in a few years they will, if it's successful," Hunter said.

"I'm not crazy about potentially being on different teams," Michelle said.

Hunter took Michelle's face in her hands. "Let's see how things pan out. If we choose not to participate, we can enjoy the off-season together."

"We could do a lot more traveling," Hunter said. "Money isn't an issue for us. The extra salary would be a bonus, but it won't affect our choices."

"No, it won't. I will follow you anywhere," Hunter said.

"I just don't want it to hurt your chances of getting drafted," Michelle said.

"My dream has come true by playing this season. I have proved to myself I am good enough to play, and that's all I need. If I don't make a roster, Coach would hire me back on the practice team."

"Or offer you a coaching spot," Michelle said. "I'd really enjoy playing together for a few years, though."

"Only time will tell, but please know no matter what changes, I always want to be with you."

"That is true for me, too. I love you."

"Come to bed, and you can show me how much," Hunter teased.

†

"Could we go see Walter and Betty this morning before practice? I'd like to invite them to Friday's game."

"Sure. That's no problem," Michelle answered. "We can shower, head out now, and have lunch in town."

"Thanks," Hunter answered.

†

Hunter's heart lodged in her throat when she saw the 'Sold' sign in front of the store and no sign of Walter on his bench. "This can't be good," she said as she unfastened her belt and rushed to the door.

Betty was sitting behind the counter when she entered.

"What's going on?" Hunter asked. "You've sold the store?"

Betty offered her a weak smile. "Walter passed away last week, and I am moving to Arizona to live with our youngest. I'm sorry. I didn't know how to contact you."

Hunter rushed around the counter and hugged her tightly. "I'm so sorry. When?"

"Last Monday. He woke up and said he wasn't feeling well. He passed not long after we got to the hospital. He knew his time was near and left this for you." Betty reached for an envelope, and Hunter opened it carefully. With tears in her eyes, she read the note Walter had written.

My Dearest Hunter,

Something tells me we won't be visiting again, so I wanted to tell you how proud I am that you have made your dreams come true. We've watched every game and couldn't be more happy for you. My heart is touched that you and Michelle have found one another, and I hope your love will be forever. Betty and I made arrangements for the store to be sold months ago, and she promised she would move in with one of the kids when my time came, so I hope that will happen. I have one final favor to ask. I would like for my ashes to be spread at the waterfall, and I know Betty won't have the strength to do it. It was always a special place for us and home to many good memories. Would you be so kind as to spread my ashes for us? I would greatly appreciate the gesture, as I know Betty would be grateful for your help.

Our short time together brought me great joy, and I want you to know I will be watching over you. Give em hell on the

*court and love Michelle for all you're worth. Time passes all
too quickly.*
    With love,
    Walter

"Walter wants me to spread his ashes at the waterfall.
Are you good with that?" Hunter asked Betty.

"He talked about it for weeks. I would appreciate it if you
would do this for us."

"Of course. I would be honored."

Betty handed Hunter a steel urn. "Do you have time
today?"

Hunter nodded. "Yes, we will take care of this now and
return the urn to you."

"Thank you both, so much. You meant the world to
Walter."

Hunter turned to Michelle, and they left the store. "I hope
you don't mind a side trip."

"Of course not," Michelle said. She drove Hunter to the
waterfall and parked the Jeep. "Do you want my company?"

"Yes, but I want you to read his note first." Hunter
handed Michelle the envelope as her tears returned. She
stepped out of the Jeep, cradling the urn to wait for Michelle.

When Michelle joined her, she took Hunter's hand as
they walked to the waterfall.

"What he said was beautiful," Michelle finally spoke.

"Yes, it was. I just hate we couldn't say goodbye."

"That's what we are doing now," Michelle said softly.
"Fulfilling his last wish."

Hunter nodded and removed the lid from the urn,
releasing some ashes as they walked the trail to the falls.
Hunter poured out the remaining contents when they walked

behind the flow, and the breeze carried them into the water. She returned the lid and watched the ashes disappear into the water. "Goodbye, my friend," she whispered. Hunter held Michelle's hand until all the ashes were washed away.

Michelle pulled her into a hug. "Walter would be happy you did this for them." She kissed Hunter softly and held out her hand.

†

Hunter returned inside to deliver the urn to Betty. "Thank you for allowing me to do this."

"Walter wouldn't want you to be sad over his death. He had a great life; part of his happiness was meeting you. He was very proud of you."

Hunter wrote down her number. "Please stay in touch and let us know how you're doing."

"I will. The kids will be here this weekend to take me home. Good luck to the two of you."

"Thank you." Hunter hugged Betty and walked out of the store.

Michelle smiled when she climbed inside the Jeep. "You okay?"

"Yeah. I just wasn't expecting that news. Walter left happy, so we should be, too."

"I agree," Michelle said and pulled onto the highway. "Can you eat?"

Hunter nodded. "I've wanted to try our breakfast place for something other than breakfast."

"They have awesome country-fried steak. Why don't you call Carson to meet us there?"

Hunter nodded and called Carson.

†

"That was a great lunch," Hunter said. "This one is my treat." She offered her card to the server.

"Sorry, miss, but your lunch has already been paid for," the server said.

"What?" Hunter asked.

"A gentleman asked to pay your bill. He said to tell you all you've been playing great. He left after picking up a to-go order."

"Well, that was nice of him," Hunter said. "I wish I could thank him."

"Keep winning," the server said and walked away.

"Don't be surprised. That happens often when we're spotted out during the day. It's the local's way of saying thanks," Carson said.

"I guess I'm not meant to treat you today," Hunter said.

"There's always yogurt after practice," Michelle replied.

"Or take out at my place tonight. I'm feeling up for Chinese," Carson teased.

"You are both on," Hunter said.

†

The Washington game was a complete run away after the first three quarters, and Coach pulled the starters for the fourth. Hunter was happy that the second team got well-deserved playing time and experience. They could be called upon to assist in the play-offs and needed to be sharp.

After the game, Coach addressed the team. "Tonight was an easy game for us compared to Friday's game. Minnesota must beat us to move into second place, so they will hit us with everything they've got. Eat well and get some rest. I'll see you for the shoot-around tomorrow. Hunter and Carson, you're on tap for interviews tonight."

"Knock 'em dead," Michelle teased Hunter.

"I'll be back soon." She followed Carson and Coach from the locker room.

†

Hunter was relieved when most of the questions were proposed to Coach. She and Carson sipped water while they awaited their turn.

"Hunter. You have been lighting up the court, averaging twenty-five points a game. How do you plan to continue this streak?"

Hunter wiped the sweat from her face. "By continuing to follow our game plan. Coach studied our opponents and gave us goals for each game. Our games will become more challenging as the competition intensifies for playoff berths. We are confident that if we follow our plan, our chances of success will remain high."

"Carson. You two have made a formidable backcourt for the team. Do you anticipate continuing to score big from beyond the arc?"

"I hope we continue to light it up from three, but we are also prepared and capable of driving to the basket to score. Our post players are doing a remarkable job under the basket and remain aggressive on both ends of the court."

"Any predictions from either of you for Friday's game?"

"Hopefully, a W will seal our seating in first place in the conference," Carson said.

255

"Scores?"

Hunter smiled. "Doesn't matter as long as we're up by one when the horn sounds."

"Thanks, ladies. Good luck, Friday night."

When the press conference ended, Coach smiled at them. "Good job. I'm glad you didn't give them a score prediction."

"I'd hate to eat my words if it turned out badly. A win is a win as long as we're on top by one."

Carson smiled. "Well spoken. When did you get so smart?"

"It must be the company I'm keeping," Hunter teased.

Coach shook her head. "Good grief. I don't know which of you is worse. Go shower, and I'll see you tomorrow."

"Goodnight, Coach."

"Pancakes, here we come," Carson said.

†

"When is your mom arriving this weekend?" Carson asked after swallowing a bite of pasta.

"She and Jim will be here by noon tomorrow," Hunter replied. "We'll have time to meet them for lunch, and then they can check in and freshen up before the game."

"We plan to take them to the diner if you'd care to join us," Michelle said.

Carson laughed. "She's got you hooked on the country-fried steak, right?"

"Guilty as charged. We need a lot of calories for tomorrow's game," Michelle clarified. "We could do pasta again if you'd rather."

"No, the diner is perfect for me," Carson said.

"Is Jim playing in the poker tournament?" Michelle asked.

"Yes. It starts at eight. I told Mom we would watch for a while and then hit some slots. We hope he wins all day, and we can celebrate with a nice dinner," Hunter said.

Michelle looked at Carson. "We're still on for steaks with you at our place on Sunday, right?"

"I'll be there early afternoon with a dessert," Carson replied.

†

"Are you ready to head home?" Michelle asked.

Hunter nodded. "Early night tonight since we can't sleep in tomorrow. Meet us at the diner at one?"

"I'll be there," Carson said, then walked to her car.

Hunter climbed in beside Michelle. "I've got my belly full of good food. All I need is a good snuggle with you, and I'll be out like a light."

"Are you excited for your mom to be at the game?"

"It's been a long time since she's seen me play. I hope we have a great game."

"We will," Michelle assured her. "I feel it in my bones."

"It would be nice to start the playoffs with a bye." Hunter fell silent. "So after tomorrow, we have road games in Atlanta, Connecticut, and LA, and then we're done with the regular season?"

"That's it. If nothing changes, we will open our playoff with the winner of Seattle and LA. The Connecticut game will be challenging, but even a loss will not change our status."

"That's good to know. I hope we can win the rest of our games, but it takes the pressure off to know we can afford to lose one."

Michelle activated the garage door opener. "Do we have clothes all set for tomorrow?"

"We do. I took care of that today while you shopped," Hunter answered.

"We can just climb into bed, then?"

"That's the plan." Hunter smiled. "We'll be up early for breakfast, shower, dress, and head into town to meet Mom and Jim."

"Where are we meeting them?"

"At the casino hotel in the lobby at noon. Jim arranged for an early check-in time."

"Maybe we test our luck if we get there early," Michelle said.

"That's a good possibility. I'm always lucky with you."

Michelle draped an arm around Hunter. "That is so sweet. Do you want something to drink before we hit the sack?"

"Will you split some tea with me?"

"You know I will," Michelle said. "I'll be right behind you."

CHAPTER EIGHTEEN

"We're a half hour early. The lobby has some slots. Do you want to play there so we can keep an eye out for your mom?"

"That works for me." Hunter found an interesting-looking game that had a view of the front door. "Is this good for you?"

"It is. That's one of my favorite games," Michelle said. "Let's fire them up."

Hunter placed a twenty in the machine and started betting. She started hitting minor wins and then hit a nice one. "I'm cashing out. I don't want to use all my luck today."

"I'll wait for you here," Michelle said, playing both machines. She doubled her bet on the machine Hunter had just left and started laughing when she hit the jackpot. Michelle cashed out her machine and waited for the machine to give her a total. She was still smiling when Hunter returned.

"No, you didn't."

"Yes, love, I did. I continued playing your machine and hit the jackpot. Will you exchange this for me, and by then, I should know what the winnings are here?"

Hunter cashed in the voucher and returned. Michelle hit the payout button, and a seven-hundred-dollar voucher appeared in the slot. "Lunch and dinner are on me." She smiled.

"Do you play poker?"

"Not well. Why?"

"Good. I'd hate to lose you to the tournament tomorrow," Hunter teased.

"No chance of that. You have to enter and qualify before you get offered a seat."

"That's good to know," Hunter said. "Let's go cash you out."

Elizabeth rushed into Hunter's arms when she came through the front door. "It's so good to see you. You look terrific."

"Thanks, Mom."

Elizabeth hugged Michelle. "You're looking pretty sharp also."

"Thanks. How was the ride?"

"Long, but I'm glad we are here. Jim's getting us checked in."

"I'll get the valet to bring the Jeep around," Michelle said. "It may take a few minutes."

Jim waved at Michelle and hugged Hunter. "How are you? You look great."

"I'm good, thanks. I hope you two are hungry."

"I can always eat."

"The valet is taking our bags to the room, so we can leave when you are ready," Jim said.

"Michelle is getting the Jeep brought around. We got here early and decided to try our luck."

"How'd you do?" Elizabeth asked.

"I did good, but Michelle hit big, so no arguing when she pays for lunch today, okay?"

"I won't argue. Should we wait outside with Michelle?" Jim asked.

"Sure, the diner isn't far from here. Are you excited about the tournament?"

"I am. But not as excited as about watching you play tonight," Jim answered.

"When you arrive at the arena, go to the box office. The tickets are in your name," Hunter told her mom.

†

Carson had already got them a table when they arrived at the diner.

"This is my lucky day," Jim said. "I am surrounded by beautiful women."

"Very smooth, honey," Elizabeth said.

"I know what you two are having," Mary, the server, said. "What about the rest of y'all?"

"Anything but breakfast," Carson said and then explained. "This is our post-game breakfast stop."

"Okay. So what's their usual?" Jim asked her.

"Country fried steak, corn, green beans, and mashed potatoes," Mary answered. "With pie for dessert."

"You're spot on, Mary." Michelle smiled.

"That sounds delicious. I'll have that, too," Jim said.

"I'd like the club with fries," Elizabeth said.

"And for you, missy?" Mary said, tapping on her order pad.

"The club sounds good with a side of pasta salad and fries," Carson said.

"Look at you," Michelle teased.

"I'm still stuffed from all the pasta we ate last night." Carson grinned.

"Drinks?" Mary looked at Carson. "Water, water, water."

"Coke for me," Jim said.

"Make it two," Elizabeth answered.

"Easiest order I've had all day. Be right back with your drinks."

"I take it you eat here often?" Her mom grinned.

"About once a week for lunch. Every home game for dinner. It's kind of our tradition," Hunter explained.

†

"The gates open at five, and the game starts at seven, so you have plenty of time before the game to relax," Hunter told Jim when they left the restaurant. "Do you know where the arena is?"

"Yes, I've been there before for a hockey game," Jim answered.

"We'll see you at the game then," Hunter said.

"Good luck, ladies. Kick some butt tonight," Jim said.

"That's the plan." Michelle grinned.

†

When they arrived at the arena, the team bus for Minnesota was parked in the lot. The Lynx were late in finishing their shoot-around before the game.

"I hope they wore themselves down," Carson said as they entered the locker room.

"That would be nice," Michelle said.

Hunter had put her headphones on and was listening to her music.

"She seems pretty chill today," Carson said.

"Looks are deceiving. Hunter's nervous about playing in front of her mom. She'll flip the switch once we hit the court and be all business."

"I hope so," Carson said and started dressing.

†

Both teams played well, and Vegas was up by two at the half. Coach looked around at her team. "We're playing well, but so are they. We will have to dig a little deeper in the second half. Stay tough on defense and keep firing those threes. Michelle, if your defender doesn't come out on you, you too. They won't be expecting that from you."

"Got it, Coach," Michelle answered.

"Hydrate, potty, and I'll see you back on the court."

Carson looked at her teammates. "We've got this. We just need to stay the course. Their guards are dropping back on defense, so we will light them up. That should open the floor and allow us to get the ball down low when they have to come out on us."

†

Minnesota took a short lead in the third, but Hunter rained four threes to take the lead going into the final quarter. They were up by four with three minutes left when the unimaginable happened. Carson was driving into the lane and misstepped, twisting her ankle. An injury time-out was called to give her medical attention.

"I'm okay. It's just a sprain," Carson assured Coach.

Carson limped severely as she was assisted to the bench.

"Take her back for x-rays and get her icing," Coach told the staff. "Alisha, get checked in."

Alisha ran to the scorer's table.

Coach looked at Hunter. "You're going to have to take over at the point. Protect the ball and use as much clock as you can." Hunter nodded and Coach continued. "If you can get the ball inside, do it. They will probably double you now that Carson is out of the game."

Hunter looked at Michelle. "Go for the corner, but if you can't break out, it's time to 'kiss it.'"

"Damn, I love when you say that." Coach chuckled. "You know what to do, so go do it."

"Okay, tight defense. Don't give them anything easy. Make them work for it. Alisha, the guard will drive on you being fresh into the game. Cut her off or run her into the baseline so we can double her." She looked at her bigs. "Time to work those boards hard, especially on defense. Don't give them a second chance. Let's do this," Hunter said and broke the huddle. She draped her arm around Alisha. "No threes. Got it?"

"Got it, Hunter."

Hunter picked up the point guard when she came across half-court, making her waste valuable time before setting up their shot. The center had been blazing hot all night, missed a short jumper, and Michelle grabbed the rebound. The defense swarmed her, and she barely got the ball into Hunter's hands. Hunter slowly brought the ball down the court to eat up the clock, and Michelle rushed to her favorite spot. Hunter drove toward the basket and the defense collapsed to halt her drive. She whipped a pass out to Michelle, and with two seconds remaining on the shot clock, Michelle launched a three.

"Yes," Michelle fist pumped after the shot fell, and she rushed down the court.

Alisha was too slow to contest a shot, but thankfully, the guard was inside the arc, and it was only a two-point shot.

"You've got to get out faster," Hunter reminded Alisha.

Hunter brought the ball down the court, and when she was trapped, her only option was to pass to Alisha. Alisha caught the pass and faked a drive to the basket. Hunter was impressed when Alisha pulled the ball back out and dropped a jumper for two in the final second. "Hell, yes."

They were under two minutes, and Hunter knew Minnesota would start fouling them soon. Their point dropped a three, and the Lynx were within two possessions. Michelle stepped out to inbound the ball, and Hunter was smothered by the defense. Alisha rushed down the court to assist, and her defender went for the steal but was unsuccessful and fouled her.

Alisha went to the line and missed the first shot but sank the second. Minnesota called a time-out to advance the ball.

"No threes," Coach said. "Hunter, I want you on the inbound pass to Michelle. I'm fine if they foul either of you, but if you can, get across half-court. Expect them to foul the rest of the game."

Alisha missed her assignment, and the guard scored two.

Three-point lead. Hunter grabbed the ball and lobbed it into Michelle, who found her racing down the sideline. The guards were still down court from guarding Michelle, and no one came out to stop the ball. She stopped at the top of the key and waited until three seconds were left before taking the shot. Hunter held her breath when the shot hit the back of the rim, lifting straight into the air and falling through. She turned and waved Michelle back on defense as the inbounds pass was long. They were in a two-on-one break with Michelle. She stepped out to stop the ball, but the guard quickly passed to her teammate, and no one could reach her in time to contest the shot.

They are back to a three-point lead. Hunter passed the ball to Michelle, who was immediately fouled. "You got this," she told Michelle as they walked down the court. Hunter stopped at midcourt, prepared to defend a long pass.

Michelle made both free throws and set up to defend the inbound pass. The player tried lobbing the ball past Michelle, and she swatted the ball out to Hunter. As the guards rushed to foul her, Michelle was left open. Hunter hurled the ball. "Kiss it," she called out.

Michelle caught the pass, stepped back, and kissed the shot off the glass for a two-pointer.

Hunter called out, "No fouls," with only twelve seconds left to play. Her teammates knew it wouldn't be enough even if they scored a quick three. The first shot missed wide, and the rebounder tipped the ball in for two as the horn sounded. It was close, but Vegas had pulled off the win.

Michelle rushed to Hunter, picked her up, and spun her around. When she placed her back on the court, she laughed. "Damn, that was close."

"Too close," Hunter agreed. "Great shooting."

"I had a great teacher," Michelle said.

After shaking hands, Hunter jogged toward the locker room to check on Carson. A group of fans were waiting for autographs. "I'll be right back," she told them.

Carson stretched her leg out on the bench, loaded with a large ice pack. She looked up at Hunter. "Did we win?"

"Yes, but it was close. How's your ankle?"

"A mild sprain, but I'll be on crutches a few days. I should be good for next week."

"That's great news."

Hunter could hear the fans chanting her name. She looked at Carson.

"Go, I'm fine. I'll see you after."

†

Hunter rushed back through the tunnel and stopped when she saw most of the fans on their feet calling her name. She was stunned for a few seconds, then lifted her hand to wave to them, and the crowd started applauding. She found Michelle signing autographs and rushed over.

Pens and objects were thrust toward her as fans requested autographs. "How's Carson?" Michelle asked.

"According to her, a mild sprain. Nothing broken. Ice and crutches this weekend."

Once the crowd thinned, Coach called them into the locker room. "I got a few more gray hairs tonight, but you held on to the win. I'm very proud of you. Alisha, you did well for coming in cold."

"Thanks, Coach."

"Hunter and Michelle are requested for interviews. We'll meet on Monday for a light practice before we fly to Atlanta on Tuesday. Rest and rehydrate. She looked at Carson. Are you okay to shower?"

"I'm helping her, Coach," Sandy said.

"Thanks, Sandy."

†

The questions started firing once they took their seats in the press room. "Great win tonight, Coach. Can you give us an update on Carson?"

"The x-rays were negative and indicated a mild sprain. Crutches and lots of ice this weekend. I may hold Carson out of the Atlanta game for another few days of rest, but she'll be ready for Connecticut."

"That's your last big hurdle of the regular season, correct?'

"Yes, and they are playing well right now."

"Hunter, what got you so fired up tonight?"

"My mom is in the crowd tonight, and I wanted to play well for her and my friend, Walter, who passed away last week."

"I'm sorry for your loss, but forty points tonight was certainly a performance he would be proud of."

"Forty?"

Coach looked at the stat sheet. "Forty for you and thirty-two for Michelle."

"You really took over the game when Carson went out. You were incredible."

"Thanks, but Michelle and the rest of the team were a big help."

"I think we should nickname Michelle 'Ice,'" one said. "You were so chill taking the free throws with the game on the line, and that step-back jumper was perfection."

"Coach tasked us with holding on for the win, and we managed to do that under Hunter's leadership."

"The crowd was amazing tonight and wouldn't stop calling your name until you gave them a curtain call. How did that make you feel, Hunter?"

"It was incredible. That's never happened before, and it made me feel so proud of the team and the fans of my new home."

"We hope it will be your home for many years."

"I do, too," Hunter answered.

"Three more games left in the regular season. Will this team maintain first place going into the playoffs?"

"That's the goal, and we're confident we can make it happen," Michelle said.

"Thanks, ladies. Time for you to go celebrate," Coach said to dismiss them.

"Do you have time for a few more questions, Coach?"

"Go ahead, Tom."

"There is great hope that Hunter will remain on the roster after this season. What are the odds of that happening?"

"Expanding the league next year will open more opportunities for players who aren't bound by a contract. We will have a limited number of players we can mark as safe from expansion teams. I will advocate for Hunter to remain on our side of the ball. She's got such great skill and heart. I wouldn't look forward to playing against her."

"We certainly wouldn't want to see that either. Do you think this team can take it all this year?"

"We're certainly peaking at a good time. I think it's highly possible, especially having a home-court advantage. We must pack the arena every game to show the players how much they mean to this community."

"I think tonight was an excellent start to that. Vegas fever is running high right now. Have you ever seen the crowd this fired up?"

"No, but it's an excellent feeling, and the players appreciate the support. If nothing else, I'd like to spend a few minutes with my team."

"Thanks, Coach. Good luck next week."

†

"Yes, you are, and that's final," Coach heard when she entered the locker room.

"Whoa, what's going on?" she asked Carson.

"These two knuckleheads insist I go home with them for the weekend. I don't want to be treated like an invalid."

Coach smiled. "That's the perfect solution. I know they will make you rest and ice that ankle."

"I can do that alone at home," Carson complained.

"Let me make it simple. Do you wish to play next week?"

"Of course I do, Coach."

"Then spend the weekend with Hunter and Michelle or ride the bench."

"But you can't do that," Carson cried out.

"I am the coach, and I decide who plays and who rides the pine. If I don't have the assurance that you are healed enough to play, I won't take the chance of creating more permanent damage."

"Damn, that's not fair. Hunter's family is in town," Carson groaned.

"So, you are stuck with me as a nursemaid. Hunter can still be with her family." Michelle grinned.

"Fine then, since I don't have any other choice. I will be ready to play next week, Coach."

"I will leave that up to the medical staff."

"Let's shower and get out of here before she blows a gasket," Michelle told Hunter.

"I'm still going to breakfast tonight," Carson grumbled.

"On crutches," Hunter called on her way to the shower.

Coach smiled at Carson. "You know they love you."

"Yeah, yeah, I know."

"Stay off that foot, and I'll see you Monday for an eval."

"Yes, Coach."

Sandy helped Carson finish dressing and got her crutches.

"Damn, I hate these things."

"We have a wheelchair if you'd prefer," Sandy replied.

"Hell no."

"Where are your keys? I'll pull your car up close while Hunter checks in with her mom and Jim," Michelle said.

"In my bag," Carson huffed.

"I'll get them started toward the diner and be right back," Hunter said.

"You can drive Carson, and I'll follow in the Jeep," Michelle said.

†

"Carson is staying with us this weekend, so we'll meet you at the diner as soon as we load her up."

"Is she going to be okay?" Elizabeth asked.

"She claims it's a mild sprain, but we can keep her off it and iced to help her heal quicker."

"If you need to stay with her tomorrow, we understand."

Hunter shook her head. "No. Michelle is staying home to keep her in line. I'll be there tomorrow to support Jim and visit with you."

"Okay, we'll meet you at the diner and go ahead and get a table," Elizabeth said.

"Ask for the large corner booth if it's available so Carson can prop her leg. Ask if Polly is working, and you can tell her what's happened. She'll take care of us."

†

Hunter returned to the locker room as Carson was fitted for a boot. "Damn, I hate these things," she complained.

"I know it's uncomfortable, but it will help stabilize your ankle. Can we take Carson to the parking lot in a wheelchair to save her steps on crutches?"

"Yeah, let me grab one," Sandy said.

"I am not an invalid," Carson growled.

"No, but you are a very grumpy patient. Take the ride. It's a long walk to the parking lot on crutches," Hunter pleaded.

"All right," Carson relented, and was assisted into the wheelchair.

"I'm sending freezable ice packs and prescription-strength anti-inflammatory meds home with her. Keep it elevated and ice at least once an hour when she's awake this weekend for twenty minutes."

"Got it." Hunter took the bag of supplies. "Let's get you out of here."

Sandy pushed the wheelchair to Carson's car and helped her inside.

"I'll get the Jeep and be right behind you." Michelle jogged toward her vehicle.

"Thanks for the help, Sandy," Carson said as Hunter climbed into the driver's seat.

"Have a restful weekend, and I'll see you Monday." Sandy closed the door behind Carson.

†

Polly was serving coffee to Elizabeth and Jim when Carson entered on crutches. "Good grief, Carson."

"I'm okay, Polly. It's just a mild sprain," Carson replied.

"You need to take care of that and get healed. The playoffs are coming up." Polly winked. "You three want coffee?"

"Yes, please," Michelle said as Carson settled into the booth with her right leg propped.

"That was a great game tonight, ladies," Jim said. "You had me on the edge of my seat that fourth quarter."

"Minnesota gave us a good game," Hunter agreed.

Polly returned to take their orders. "Pancakes and lots of them for you three?"

"I'm going with French toast and bacon," Carson said. "With some fresh fruit."

"Okay, ham steaks for you two?"

"Yes, please," Michelle answered.

"The pancakes must be fabulous, so I'll have those, too, with ham," Jim said.

Elizabeth smiled at Polly. "You can double Carson's order for me, please."

"Do I need to bring a bag of ice or a stack of towels for your ankle?"

Carson smiled at her. "I've been icing. I'll be okay until I get home, but thanks, Polly."

"Uh, Polly?" Michelle said.

"Yes?"

"Make sure I get the check tonight."

"Got it." Polly nodded.

"That's not necessary. You got lunch."

"Courtesy of the hotel's casino. I hit a nice jackpot before you arrived, so that was our agreement."

"I do love free food." Elizabeth smiled. "Thank you, Michelle."

†

Once Carson was settled in the car, Hunter turned to her mom. "I'll text you when I arrive so you can tell me where to find you."

"Are you sure you're not needed at home?"

Hunter looked at Carson. "Michelle will make sure she stays out of trouble."

"Hey, now. I'm right here." Carson laughed.

"Have a good night and good luck tomorrow, Jim," Hunter said.

"Be careful going home."

†

Michelle helped Carson in the bathroom while Hunter gathered pillows from the couch to prop her foot. Carson was relieved to remove the boot and sighed at the swelling and bruise that had formed.

"We need to ice again," Michelle said.

"Probably so."

Michelle looked at Hunter. "I've got an icepack already frozen, so I'll grab one and put these others in to chill. Will you place a towel under her foot?"

"Will do," Hunter said.

"Will you bring me my phone? I'm sure I've missed a few calls from Stacy," Carson said.

"Sure," Hunter grabbed her bag and found the phone before walking to the bathroom for a towel.

Michelle gently placed the ice pack on Carson's ankle. "I'll be back in twenty to remove it. Tell Stacy hello from us. Do you need more medicine?"

"It will wait until you return." Carson smiled at them. "Thank you both for taking care of me."

"We're the three amigos," Hunter reminded her.

†

Hunter started the timer on her watch. "Let's go get ready for bed," she told Hunter as they left the room.

"If you take out two pills, I'll make us some water," Hunter said.

"On it, boss," Michelle teased and kissed Hunter. "I failed to tell you earlier with all the chaos, but I am proud of how you stepped into the leader role tonight. I don't think we would have won if you hadn't taken control."

"Thanks. It was too close for comfort," Hunter said. "You were pretty amazing yourself tonight."

"We make a great team," Michelle said.

"Yes, we do."

†

Carson was nearly asleep when they entered to remove the ice and administer her meds.

"I won't hear you if you call out, but Hunter will." Michelle smiled. "Let us know if you need anything."

"If you have to get up, please use the crutches," Hunter said. "I'll check on you in the morning before I leave."

"Thanks." Carson nodded, and they left the room.

"What time do you need to leave in the morning?" Michelle asked.

"I don't think it will hurt to miss the tournament opening, so by eight," Hunter answered.

"I'll make you some breakfast while you shower and dress."

"Nothing heavy. Maybe some toast and fruit," Hunter said. "Will you wait to eat with Carson?"

"I thought I would, but I'll have coffee with you."

"Good," Hunter answered and snuggled into Michelle.

CHAPTER NINETEEN

Hunter crept into the room to check on Carson. She was sleeping soundly, so Hunter didn't wake her. She brushed her teeth and returned to the kitchen to kiss Michelle.

"Do you want to take the Jeep?" Michelle asked.

"Naw, I'm going to burn Carson's gas. If she wakes up and needs something from home, I'll have her keys to get in. Call if she does, and I'll bring it home tonight."

"What about dinner? We were supposed to go out with Jim and your mom?"

"I'll see if they will come out here. I can pick up some take-out to bring home. They can go ahead and pick up the trailer and save a trip out in the morning. I know they will leave early to beat some of the heat."

"Have fun today, and don't worry about Carson. She's going to be fine."

"I know she's in good hands, but I'll call later to check on you."

†

Hunter found her mom quickly and sat beside her to watch the game. "I didn't know Jim is a poker player."

"He loves it and tries to play several tournaments a year. He's actually pretty good," her mom said. "He always comes home with winnings."

"That's a good thing. Do you go with Jim often?"

Elizabeth shook her head. "This is my second time."

"Can I be nosy and ask something personal?"

"Are you wondering if we will get married?"

"Yeah. Jim makes you happy."

"Possibly after we both retire. But what we have now works for both of us. We do love one another, but I don't think we necessarily need to be married."

"There's no rush, but I was curious."

"Have you and Michelle discussed marriage?"

Hunter looked at her mom. "We are still too new as a couple to talk about marriage. I think she would be the one if I got married. She's good for me."

"You make an adorable couple, and it's easy to see how much you love each other."

"Thanks, Mom. We really do."

†

"Excuse me, miss," a gentleman said as he approached them. "Could I bother you for an autograph? My daughter claims she is your best fan and would die to have you autograph something for her.

"Hang on a second." Hunter left and returned a few minutes later with a souvenir Vegas mini basketball from the casino gift shop. "What's her name?"

"Ashley," he said.

"How old is Ashley?"

"She's twelve. She watched the game last night and screamed through the house when you pulled out the win. We've watched every game together this season. I tried to get tickets, but every game was sold out."

"We have one more game at home. It's on a Wednesday. Would she be able to attend?"

"Absolutely," he said.

"How many in the family?"

"Just the three of us," he answered.

"Your last name?" she asked as she wrote on the ball.

"Taylor."

"Please tell Ashley there will be three tickets under her name at the box office for that game, and I expect her to cheer loudly," Hunter said. She finished signing her name and handed him the ball.

"Thank you so much," he said, tears filling his eyes. "Ash will be over the moon."

"Please tell her to wait for me after the game, okay?"

"Are you kidding? I'll have to drag her out of the arena. Thank you so much."

"My pleasure. See you soon."

Elizabeth smiled at her. "That was very kind of you."

"The people here have been very kind to me. It's nice to give a little back."

†

When they stopped the games for a rest break, Jim approached them. "How's it going," Elizabeth asked.

"Good, so far. I pulled a complex table of players, but I'm up sixty grand so far. Eighth place at present."

"Congratulations."

"Thanks. Will you and your mom have some lunch and maybe play some slots? I hope to play until the final table, so it may be late before we finish."

"Michelle and I want you to come for a late dinner after the tournament. I'll grab some Chinese take-out, and you can hook up your trailer. That will save you a trip out in the morning."

"That sounds like a great plan," Jim said. "He reached for his wallet to offer Hunter money."

"I've got this. You go win this thing. We'll be back later."

Jim kissed Elizabeth and walked back to his table.

"What would you like for lunch?"

"Do you still like sushi?" Elizabeth asked. "I can't convince Jim to try it."

"I love it, and I know just the spot."

†

Hunter led her mom through the casino to a row of restaurants. When they entered her favorite sushi spot, she was greeted by the host.

"Great game last night. You're the new hero."

"Thank you. I'm glad you enjoyed watching."

He pointed to the big screen television on the wall. "The whole restaurant was watching. Bar sales went big time after the win. Your dinner on me, please."

"Not necessary," Hunter said.

"I insist. Just take care of your server," he said, leading them to a table.

Elizabeth looked at her. "Does that happen often?"

Hunter smiled. "Increasingly so. The team brings in substantial revenue for the city, and owners and shopkeepers take excellent care of us."

"Good afternoon, Ms. James," the server said as she handed them a menu. "What can I bring you to drink?"

"A Coke for me, please," Hunter answered.

"Would you mind if I have sake?" her mom asked.

"Go for it." Hunter grinned.

"I bring you the best." The server nodded and returned to the bar.

"What do you recommend?"

"I usually have sushi and either the teriyaki chicken or the steak," Hunter replied.

"Both sound good," Elizabeth said.

"Then we order both and share. Do you have a favorite roll?"

"I like the spicy crab," Elizabeth answered, "but I'm open to trying anything."

"Okay, I'll order for us."

The waitress returned with their drinks. "Are you ready to order?"

Hunter gave her their order and took a sip of her drink. "How's the sake?"

"Very nice. Would you like some?"

Hunter shook her head. "It gives me a headache, but thank you."

†

Two rolls of sushi and two meals later, Hunter pushed back her plate. "I honestly can't eat another bite."

"That was a fantastic meal," Elizabeth said.

The server came to clear their plates. "May I offer you something else?"

"No, but it was all very delicious."

"Should I package the sake to go?" she asked when she picked up the half-full bottle.

"Yes. That was too good to waste," Elizabeth said.

"Bring it tonight. Michelle and Carson will help you finish it off," Hunter replied.

"I will then. Jim doesn't enjoy the taste either."

The server returned with a box with the sake inside. "Is there anything else?"

Hunter shook her head, removing a fifty from her wallet. "For you. Thank you for great service."

"Thank you," she answered with a bow.

Hunter looked at her mom. "I need to walk." She grinned. "Let's see if we can find some machines we like."

†

They played the slots, and Hunter turned to her mom when the pots slowed down. "Let's cash out and go check on Jim."

282

She texted to check on Carson, and Michelle answered that they were both doing fine.

"The girls okay?" Elizabeth asked.

"They haven't killed each other, so that's a plus." Hunter chuckled.

Hunter looked up at the leaderboard and pointed it out to her mom. "He's doing great. Up to fourth now."

They took seats as close as they could and watched Jim play. Elizabeth frowned when Jim lost a second hand in a row. "Maybe we should wander around the casino some more. He seemed to do better while we were gone."

"Let's go then."

They strolled through row after row of slot machines until Hunter spotted one of her favorite games.

"I have a feeling," Hunter said, sitting at the machine. She placed a fifty in the machine next to where her mom sat. "Let's win some money." She placed another fifty in her machine and started spinning.

Elizabeth squealed when she hit a minor jackpot. "Should I quit or keep playing?"

"Double your bet and keep playing," Hunter suggested.

Hunter followed her own advice, and almost simultaneously, they hit for a significant win. Her mom had hit for two thousand, and Hunter had hit for twenty-five hundred.

"Now, we should quit." Hunter chuckled. They removed their vouchers and walked to the payout window.

Hunter tucked her winnings into her pocket. "I don't think we're to blame for the bad luck." She grinned. As they were walking back to the poker room, Hunter saw one of the self-serve photo booths. She reached for her mom's hand. "Come with me."

They climbed inside the booth and snuggled together after Hunter fed the money into the slot. Several photos were taken rapidly, causing them to blink and laugh. When the camera stopped, they watched the timer, and Hunter laughed when the images slid from the machine. "Those are hilarious. Should we take some serious shots?"

"Do you think we can?" Elizabeth asked.

"We can try," Hunter said, sliding another bill into the machine.

Serious only lasted for two clicks, and they both started laughing again. Hunter plucked the photo strips from the machine and handed one of each to her mom. "It was worth a shot."

"I love them," Elizabeth said.

Hunter slipped an arm around her mom while they walked through the casino. "This has been a great day. Thank you for spending it with me."

"I've had a blast with you. I hope we will have more days like this soon."

"We will make it happen," Hunter said.

†

When they entered, Jim was leaving the table. He shook the hands of the two remaining men and turned to find them. Elizabeth waved to him.

"How'd you do, honey?"

"Third place, but I'm good with that. Let me collect my winnings, and I'll be right back."

"Do you need some time to freshen up before coming to the house?"

"Jim will probably change into jeans and boots," Elizabeth said. "We won't take long."

"I'll go ahead and pick up some take-out. Do you have any preferences in food?"

"No, we both love Chinese."

"Let me have your phone, and I'll plug in my address. Come when you're ready."

"That sounds good. Jim is probably starving."

"He won't be for long. I'll see you soon."

Hunter walked outside to request her car and called in a large food order while she waited.

†

Jim and her mom were exiting the bike when Hunter pulled up beside them.

"That's perfect timing." Hunter smiled at her mom.

"Good grief, were you expecting to feed an army?" Jim asked when he picked up an armful of bags.

"Mom said you'd be starving," Hunter teased. "We can eat leftovers tomorrow for lunch if there are any."

"I'm hungry, but carrying this is a workout." Jim grinned.

Michelle heard them arrive and rushed out to take some of the bags. "Someone must be hungry." She winked at Hunter.

"I wanted to get a good variety. Besides, we'll have instant lunch tomorrow, so we can be lazy," Hunter told her and leaned in for a kiss.

"Somehow, I don't see you two being lazy," Elizabeth said.

"She's right, we've got laundry to do and packing for next week's trip," Michelle reminded her.

"Hey, Carson," Hunter said when they entered. "How are you feeling?"

"I think I've lost the feeling in my ass. Michelle hasn't let me off the couch today except to pee."

"Good job, honey," Hunter said. "Has she been a good patient?"

"Except for the moaning and groaning," Michelle teased.

"Whatever you brought smells great," Carson called from her couch. "I'm suddenly hungry."

"Hobble yourself over here then, and let's eat. Mom even brought some sake to share with you."

"Tell me you didn't eat sushi without me?" Michelle feigned hurt.

"On the house, too. The owner said bar sales skyrocketed after we won last night."

"It sure was good, too," Elizabeth added.

"Oh, don't rub it in," Michelle teased. She looked at Jim. "How did you do?"

"I placed third and brought home forty-five thousand. Not bad for a day's play."

"I hope you aren't carrying that much," Michelle frowned.

"Goodness no. I had the casino wire it into my poker account at my bank."

"Smart. You can get knocked in the head for much less," Michelle said.

"We did pretty good today, also." Her mom winked at Hunter.

"Tell me more." Michelle smiled.

Hunter grinned. "We may have come home with a few thousand more and free sushi today."

"Hunter had a feeling after we ate lunch, and that feeling paid off well," Elizabeth said.

Michelle placed food on the table. "Sounds like a great day all around."

"It was perfect," Elizabeth replied.

"Jim, what are you and I drinking?" Hunter asked. "I've got tea, soda, or water."

"I'll have a soda," he answered.

Hunter handed glasses to Michelle for the sake and brought two sodas to the table. "I guess I may have overdone it a bit."

Carson laughed. "You know it won't go to waste around here." She looked at Elizabeth. "We've been known to wake up at three for seconds on Chinese."

"Yeah, we have." Hunter smiled, remembering good times.

†

They talked for several hours until Jim stood and stretched. "I hate to leave good company, but we must start early in the morning. It's been a great weekend, and I hope we can do it again soon. Minus the crutches." He winked at Carson.

"That sounds like fun. You are welcome anytime if you want to stay here with us," Michelle offered.

"Thank you," Elizabeth said and hugged Michelle and Carson.

"Let me pull the trailer out, and we'll get you hooked up," Hunter told Jim. "I only got to use the gear twice, but I appreciate you loaning it to me."

"Maybe we can hook up and do some traveling after the season," Jim suggested as they attached the trailer to his bike.

"I'd like that," Hunter said and hugged him. She turned to her mom. "Call to let me know you've made it home, okay?"

"I will. Good luck next week. We'll see you in LA."

"I'm looking forward to it, Mom. Be safe."

†

Hunter watched them ride away and returned inside. Michelle was putting away leftovers. "I am so freaking full," Carson groaned from the couch.

"Time to ice?" Hunter asked.

"Yes, after I take this damn boot off."

"See if there's a game on. I'll bring a towel and ice pack," Michelle called from the kitchen.

"Atlanta and Indiana or Connecticut and New York?" Hunter asked.

"New York," Michell replied. "We know everything we need on Atlanta."

Michelle placed the ice pack on Carson and sat next to Hunter. "Well, that's a different starting lineup."

"Who's missing?"

"Connecticut's center. Unless she's shrunk several inches, I wonder if she's injured?"

Hunter pulled out her phone to check the injury updates on her favorite sports channel. "Hmm, she listed day-to-day for a lower back sprain."

"We should still prepare for her. She can be a beast on the glass." Michelle draped an arm over Hunter. "Their power forwards are strong, too."

At the end of the first quarter, the two teams were tied. Hunter removed the ice pack. "Does anyone want anything from the kitchen?"

"Just you," Michelle said.

"Oh, that's sickeningly sweet," Carson teased Michelle.

"It is, isn't it?" Hunter said and leaned down to kiss Michelle. "I love every minute of it." Her phone pinged with a text, and Hunter reached for her bag to answer. The photo booth strips flew onto the floor, and Michelle picked them up.

Thanks again for a great weekend. Love you.

Love you too, Mom. Goodnight.

Michelle held up the photos. "It looks like you two were having a good time."

"We had a great day. I hadn't realized how much time I had missed with my mom. It was nice just being silly and having fun."

"Those photos say it all." Michelle passed them over to Carson. "Pre or post sake?"

"Post, we were walking back to the poker room."

"Cute," Carson said and handed them back to Hunter.

†

After the game ended, they got Carson to bed. "We've got to get you healed. We need you for Connecticut,"

Michelle said. "Atlanta, we can handle. The Sun is a whole different story."

"I'll be ready. Coach wants to bench me for Atlanta to rest, but I don't like the thought."

"We need you at one hundred percent," Hunter said. "Alisha and I can handle the Atlanta guards."

"I know you can, but I cringe whenever Alisha gets the ball in her hands. This isn't college ball, and she's struggling to adapt."

Hunter smiled at Carson. "The only way she's going to improve is if she gets court time, and Atlanta's the perfect game to make that happen."

"I know, but it still doesn't mean I have to like it." Carson pouted.

"All you need to focus on right now is getting that ankle ready to play," Michelle said. "We don't play the Sun until Friday, so that gives you time unless you tweak it."

"I'm following orders," Carson said. "I hope I can lose the crutches on Monday."

"I think that's probable," Michelle said.

"Do you need me to do some laundry for the trip?" Hunter asked.

"No, I've got a ton of clothes. You can help me pack on Monday after practice."

"Will you stay with us on Monday, and we can take your car to the airport?" Michelle asked.

"Are you offering me a choice?" Carson grinned.

"Not really, but it sounded like a nice offer to me," Michelle said.

"It will make things easier, so yes."

"Thank you. We will try to sleep in tomorrow, but holler if you need anything," Hunter said.

"What's that for you? Eight?" Carson asked.
"Maybe longer," Michelle answered.
"Goodnight, you two."
"Goodnight, Carson."

CHAPTER TWENTY

The Atlanta game was routine for Vegas, and even Carson admitted Alisha did an excellent job. The game in Connecticut was anything but routine, and it took a long last-second shot from Hunter to win. Hunter was glad they were not scheduled to fly out until the following day. She was exhausted and barely made it through the post-game meal.

When they returned to the room, she changed into sleep clothes and climbed into bed. Michelle and Carson were still in the bathroom, and Hunter was fast asleep when they entered the bedroom.

"Isn't she the cutest?" Michelle whispered.

"She played her ass off tonight after carrying the load in Atlanta. She deserves a great night's sleep," Carson replied. "Goodnight."

Michelle crept into the bed and wrapped her arms around Hunter. She barely stirred except to snuggle into Michelle.

†

"Sorry I went out on you last night," Hunter said the following day in the shower with Michelle.

"You've played your heart out this week, and your body was exhausted. I hope you can nap on the flight home today. You know you can ask Coach for a day off from practice if you need to rest."

"I'll be fine by Wednesday's game. It's the last one of our regular season," Hunter assured her.

"Don't forget you owe a twelve-year-old a signed T-shirt after the game."

"Sandy's already gotten all the signatures and will place it in my locker Wednesday," Hunter answered.

"Sandy's a gem. That's for sure," Michelle replied. "Did you hear Carly's going to join us on the bench for the last game?"

"That's fantastic. How's the rehab going?"

"Not as quickly as she hoped, but she's progressing."

"Good," Hunter replied.

Michelle could sense the trepidation coming from Hunter. "If she returns next season, it still looks good for you. It may be a sixth man, but you would still get playing time."

Hunter continued drying. "I know, but nothing is promised after the season ends."

"Have faith," Michelle said, and Hunter offered her a weak smile.

†

Hunter reclined her seat and fell asleep shortly after taking off. Michelle walked to the restroom and was stopped by Coach on her way back.

"Is she okay?"

"This week has exhausted her, but she'll be good by Wednesday. I told her she could request a day off, but Hunter wouldn't miss practice. I think the season's end and the uncertainty also weigh on her. She was excited to hear Carly would be on the bench with us Wednesday, but I think that hit home with her hard."

"Thanks for sharing that with me. Hunter's played her ass off these last few games. Two of them, we wouldn't have won without her."

"I agree. Hunter has told me she would be fine going back on the practice team to stay in Vegas, but deep down, I know that's not what she wants. She's got a taste for the game again, and I think she deserves more."

"She's certainly earned it," Coach said. "I'll do my best."

"Hunter knows that too, Coach. She appreciates you going out on a limb for her."

"We'll go easy at practice this week, but make sure she rests. We need her best for the playoffs."

"I will," Michelle replied. She returned to her seat and kicked back with Hunter to watch her sleep.

†

The coach was true to her word, and her practices were light. Hunter seemed more rested on Tuesday. The game on Wednesday should be easy, as they had dominated Washington in their last two games. Hopefully, Coach would play some reserves since it was the last home game of the season.

"Did you remember to add the Taylors' family for tickets at the box office?" Michelle asked over her bowl of cereal.

"All taken care of," Hunter said.

"I know that will be one happy young lady." Michelle smiled. "How are you feeling today?"

"Amped up and ready to go," Hunter said.

"This will be a great game for you tonight. You and Carson slayed them with three-pointers last time."

"As long as we win, that's all that matters," Hunter replied.

"Are you excited to see your mom and Jim Friday?"

"Yes. I've talked with Mom almost every day since they went home. I hope they can make it for a playoff game."

"I would almost guarantee they will be in the stands. They are proud of you, too."

Michelle and Hunter curled up on the couch, watching a movie until it was time to prepare for the game.

"That is one of my favorite outfits on you," Michelle said when Hunter slipped a suit jacket over her shoulders. "You look incredible, and if we didn't have a game to win, I'd take you back to bed right now."

Hunter's smile beamed. "You are such a smooth talker."

"Maybe, but you know I mean every word I said. You are my beautiful love."

"I must have had some good karma stored up to find your love," Hunter said.

"Face it. We are just meant to be." Michelle pulled her in for a deep kiss. "Damn, we'd better get out of this bedroom."

"Let's go," Hunter said and took Michelle's hand.

†

The crowd roared when they entered the arena and didn't stop until the final buzzer. Hunter scored thirty points before the Coach started substituting players. When Alisha came in for her, Hunter received a standing ovation from the crowd, and tears filled her eyes as she hugged Coach and walked to the end of the bench.

Carson and Michelle were next and were met with the same raucous applause. The fans loved this team, and the team loved them. Hunter found Ashley sitting with her parents in the stands, her face glowing excitedly. Hunter hadn't noticed until she stood up to cheer, but Ashley wore a miniature version of Hunter's game jersey.

Damn, I will miss this.

After the game, Ashley raced to the railing on the front row to wait for Hunter. Hunter finished congratulating her teammates and took the signed shirt off her shoulder. As she approached Ashley, she held the shirt for her to see.

"Everyone signed it for you," Hunter said.

"Oh, my God. That is so perfect. Thank you, Hunter."

"You're welcome. You held up your bargain, too. I heard you cheering all game."

Ashley took the T-shirt and looked at Hunter. "May I hug you?"

Hunter reached out her arms and pulled Ashley in for a hug. "Ask your dad if he wants a picture."

"Heck, yes, he does," her dad proudly answered.

Ashley turned around to face him with her arm draped over Hunter. He snapped several photos and smiled. "She will never forget this night."

"I won't either," Hunter replied. "Thanks for coming."

"Good luck in the playoffs. I'll be cheering for you," Ashley said.

"I know you will. We need all your help," Hunter said.

The crowd was getting anxious for Hunter to sign autographs. "I need to go."

"Thanks, Hunter."

"You're welcome," Hunter answered before taking a pen to begin signing autographs.

†

When she entered the locker room, Coach smiled. "Three guesses who the press wants to talk to tonight?"

"Hunter, Hunter, Hunter," came the team's chant.

"Just me?" Hunter asked.

"Coach, too." Carson smiled.

"Turn the television on so we can watch this," Michelle said.

Hunter turned and walked to the press room with Coach.

"Great game tonight."

"Thanks, Coach. It felt good."

Hunter sat next to Coach on the podium.

"Great win, ladies."

"Thanks," Coach said. "It was a great way to end the regular season. We have one game left in LA, and then we will get revved up to host the playoffs."

"You've sealed the bye game, correct, Coach?"

"Yes, we clenched that after the game with the Sun."

"You played an excellent game that night, Hunter. Hell, you've played excellent since you stepped on the court. How do you feel about the good news?"

Hunter's smile turned into a look of confusion. "What? That we got a bye? That's wonderful for us."

"No, there is a rumor about you making big waves," a woman said.

Of fuck. The cat's out of the bag now. Lord, not tonight.

Coach cleared her throat. "We haven't had a chance to discuss it yet."

"Do you care to share more on it, Coach?"

Coach turned to Hunter. "Just before game time, I got a call from the front office. It was a direct message from the owners' group. They said, and I quote, 'Sign Hunter to a contract for next year before she leaves Vegas.' They were so impressed by your play and the way this town loves you. Again, I quote, 'Whatever it takes, sign her.'"

It took several seconds for Coach's comment to sink in. Suddenly, Hunter jumped up with her arms in the air. "Are you freaking kidding me?"

"It's on every casino marquee in town," one reporter said. "So, you'd better make the deal."

"What do you think? Want to join us next year?" Coach asked.

"Hell, yes," Hunter said and hugged Coach. "Thank you, Coach."

"Thank you for a great season." Coach chuckled.

"We're not done yet." Hunter grinned. "We've got a championship to win."

"Congratulations, Hunter. We thank you, and the city of Vegas thanks you."

"Okay, we have celebrating to do."

"And a contract to write," someone yelled.

"Yes, that too." Coach smiled.

†

"I'm sorry I couldn't tell you before the game, but I needed your feet on the ground." Coach slipped an arm around her shoulder as they returned to the locker room.

"That's okay, Coach. I'm still in shock, so that was a good call. Thank you."

"You've earned it." Coach smiled. "I'll have a contract for you tomorrow."

The team erupted when they returned to the locker room. Congratulations rained down upon Hunter. Tears flowed from many eyes as they hugged and celebrated her success with a glass of champagne.

"Where did this come from?" Coach asked as she raised a glass.

"It was delivered by one of the casinos at halftime," Sandy said.

†

As they sat down at the diner, Hunter's phone rang.

"Congratulations on the great news tonight," Elizabeth said. "We saw the interview after the game.

"Thanks, Mom. I think I'm still in shock."

"I would expect so. We are very proud of you. Enjoy your pancakes, and we'll see you this weekend."

"Congratulations on making the team," Polly said. "I'm glad they are doing right by you."

"Thanks, Polly."

"Your usuals tonight?"

"Yes, please," Carson said.

†

Michelle took Hunter in her arms after making love. "I hope the great news tonight will relieve some of your stress over what happens at the end of the season."

Hunter was still trying to catch her breath. She nodded. "Yes, I promise to relax and not worry so much."

"Thank you. I hate seeing you stressed."

"I know it was weighing on me emotionally and physically," Hunter admitted.

"Let's get some sleep. We're all set to fly to LA tomorrow. We can have a nice breakfast before heading to Carson's. Can you eat some French toast?"

"I love your French toast," Hunter said as her hand traced the contours of Michelle's abs.

"Good night then," Michelle whispered, pulling the covers over them.

†

They landed in LA by midafternoon and rode the bus to the hotel.

"We'll meet in the lobby at six to go to dinner and relax. Tomorrow, we have a ten o'clock shoot-around, and then we will have a nice pregame meal." Coach handed out room keys. "Is your family coming into town tonight?" she asked Hunter.

Hunter smiled. "No, they will be here tomorrow."

"Invite them to join us for the pregame meal if you'd like. We fly out after the game tomorrow night, so that would give you time to visit. When you get settled, will you come to my room so we can review your contract?"

"Sure, Coach. I'll see you soon," Hunter said as they entered the elevator.

"Whoa, it's like a freezer in here," Carson said as they entered the room. "Do you mind if I cut it down for a while?"

"Not at all," Hunter said. "Coach has asked me to come to her room to review my contract."

"Unpack and be on your way. Don't keep the woman waiting," Michelle said.

"First things first," Hunter said, disappearing into the bathroom.

When she returned, she looked at Michelle. "You are going to love that shower."

"I hope it's made for tall people." Michelle laughed. "I felt like I needed to kneel in Atlanta."

"It will be perfect for you. We can try it out later." Hunter smiled.

†

Hunter knocked on Coach's door. When she opened the door, Hunter asked, "Did I give you enough time?"

"Yes, you did. Come, have a seat with me. Do you want water?"

"Sure, thanks."

"I know yesterday's news might have surprised you, but I'm happy for the end result. Did you see the front page of the paper this morning?"

"No, I haven't, Coach."

"Not just the sports section's front page, but the entire front page." Coach placed a folded newspaper in front of Hunter.

Hunter opened the paper and saw a half-page image of last night's press conference with the tag, *No Freakin Way* in bold letters.

"I can't believe I blurted that out."

"Five hundred copies of that photo will be given out at our first playoff game. Be prepared to do some signing."

"Should I pre-sign them?"

"No, part of the fan's joy is getting the live signature," Coach said. "You can take that copy. I have five more at home. I'm sure that's not the document you are interested in reading, though." Coach placed a folder in front of Hunter. "A contract for next year's season with the first option to extend it for two more. The owners were generous with the salary for a second-year player to demonstrate your value to the team. Read over it and let me know if you have any questions."

Hunter read through several pages, and her eyes widened when she saw the salary. She looked up at Coach. "It was never about the money. I would have taken the practice team salary just to be able to play."

"That's ridiculous. You've earned every penny of it, and next year, I will have you for the entire season. Trust me, I will squeeze every possible ounce of talent from you."

"Thank you for believing in me, Coach."

"Thank you for putting your heart into every game. I know you worried each one could be your last, but now you know it won't be. You have many more to come in a Vegas uniform."

Hunter picked up the pen and signed the contract.

"I'll make a copy for you when we return to Vegas," Coach said. "Do you have any questions?"

"Just one? Would you be disappointed if we didn't play in the new league in the off-season?"

"Not at all. Why?"

"The rules coming out are much different than we expected, and we question if we shouldn't wait a year or two to join."

"I think that would be a sound decision. Enjoy your off-season with family and loved ones. The facilities will be available to you to keep in shape and prepare for next season. I had hoped that it would have been an opportunity for exposure for you to hit the radar of other teams in the league, but you no longer need that. You have a home in Vegas."

"For a long time, I hope. Maybe sitting beside you when my playing time is done."

"You will make a helluva coach." She smiled at Hunter.

Hunter stood and hugged Coach. "Thanks. I'll see you later."

†

Hunter played the best game of her career, and after the game, when she was signing autographs, she looked up to see a familiar face. "Officer Collins?"

"No, just Sheila. I've been sent on a mission. You nearly caused a riot a few weeks ago."

"How's that?"

"I was working the swing shift, and your first game was on television in the office. I called over the PA system for Big Dee to change the recreation room television channel to 98. She had been playing cards and walked over to take the remote from the Queen Fembot, who protested loudly that they were watching that ridiculous Bachelorette show. They started shouting until Big Dee's glare silenced them. When she changed channels, you were about to take a three-point shot. I could hear her shout, 'Well, I'll be damned. Hunter's doing it.' When she learned you were playing here tonight, she begged me to get her an autograph. You know, Big Dee doesn't beg for anything."

Hunter reached for the program Sheila had opened to her photograph and wrote:

Big Dee, #1 in my heart,
Living the dream. Thanks for watching!
Hunter #15

Hunter handed her the program.

Sheila smiled. "She's going to love that. Will you do one more?" She handed Hunter her game ticket. "For me."

"Absolutely." Hunter took the ticket and added her autograph in the limited space. "Thank you for coming tonight. Tell the ladies hello for me."

"I will. Congratulations on the new contract. You can bet we will be watching every game. Even the Fembots are fans now that they recognized you."

Hunter smiled. "That I would need to see to believe."

Sheila smiled. "Continue living that dream. That's a handsome partner I've seen you with. Take care of each other."

"We will," Hunter replied.

The young girls were screaming for Hunter. "Get back to work."

EPILOGUE

Michelle and Hunter were stretched out on the bed three months later with an extensive roadmap between them. Michelle looked up at Hunter and smiled.

"You know when most pro teams are asked what they are going to do after winning a championship, they say go to Disney World," she teased.

"Been there, done that, bought the T-shirt many years ago. We're going to Alaska, baby!" Hunter laughed. "In two days, we will pick up the RV we've rented for two months and be on our way."

"Are you disappointed we aren't taking your bike and camping?" Michelle asked.

"Heavens no. Have you checked out all the luxuries that RV has? It even has a shower for tall people."

"I'm glad your mom and Jim will join us for part of the trip," Michelle added.

"Mom considered retiring early, but Jim couldn't get it to work for him. I'm sure we will have more chances to spend time together."

"Are you okay with our decision not to join the new league?"

"All I want is to spend as much time with you as possible. We'll start with Alaska, and who knows where we will end up after that. Maybe a tropical island with umbrella drinks," Hunter said.

"I know it will be several months before we get our championship rings," Michelle paused and pulled out a velvet box from under her pillow. "I was wondering. Hunter James, would you marry me?"

"Are you freakin' kidding me? I would love to marry you, Michelle Thomas."

"I want you to know there's no rush for a date, but I am one hundred percent committed to spending the rest of my life with you. It can be six months or six years from now if that's what you wish."

Michelle slipped the ring on Hunter's finger and leaned into a kiss. "You are my forever person."

ABOUT THE AUTHOR

Ali Spooner lives in beautiful northwest Florida with several fur babies. Ali's writing began as a hobby, and with the assistance of the Affinity Rainbow Publishing team, her love of storytelling has advanced to a new level.

Ali's characters are primarily everyday people, from cowgirls to psychics. Ali also has created a few supernatural characters in her paranormal series. Several of her thirty-plus books have been Amazon-rated number-one choices and always include a happily ever after. Ali's hobbies include photography, reading, travel, college sports, and spending time with family and friends.

OTHER AFFINITY BOOKS

The Kitten Trap by Annette Mori
Inspired by the classic movie, *The Parent Trap*, two adorable black kittens, Midnight and Onyx, play matchmakers for their human mothers, Mac and Carmen. Struggling with the complexities of farm life, Mac can barely believe her beautiful girlfriend, Carmen, has agreed to move to the drafty old farmhouse to live with her and her beloved Pops. When Carmen is forced to leave the farm to care for her ailing mother, Midnight and Onyx as well as Mac and Carmen must struggle with the difficult separation. Just when it appears Carmen and Onyx may come back home to the farm, cruel fate raises a further challenge, one that will need the help of two mischievous kittens to overcome.

To Autumn by Katie M Hall
Sixteen-year-old Robyn Gale, along with her younger sister Anne, is sent away for the summer holidays of 1997 to

stay with her grandmother at a caravan park in Devon. Robyn's had a tough few months: trying to cope with the fallout of their mother's attempted suicide, messing up her GCSEs, and finding herself attracted to girls. Perhaps getting away from her real life is just what she needs…she can focus on finding a boyfriend, watching *Neighbours,* and swimming. A solid plan, until she meets charismatic Australian lifeguard, Autumn, and her life is turned even more down under.

Fairytail Farm by Ali Spooner

Dr. Hill McCall and her wife Alice dreamed of developing a sanctuary for unwanted cats and dogs to live out their lives as a retirement project. Hill has secretly worked on the project for months when a wealthy benefactor surprises her with a large donation, allowing Hill to be more aggressive with the project's opening. A group home operator approaches Hill about summer volunteer positions for four girls as Fairytail Farm becomes more than just a sanctuary for the animals. It creates an environment of love and kindness for the animals and all that support the project. Several love stories develop from first love to mature couples who have found their forever person. Fairytail Farm is more than a dream come true. It is a home for happily ever afters.

The Love Demand by Annette Mori

In the dazzling realm of reality television, where love and drama entwine in a complicated dance as old as time, a groundbreaking series emerges that transcends the ordinary. *The Love Demand* is not your typical reality show. Lacey Fellows isn't sure she wants to subject herself to further humiliation, however, on the off chance her girlfriend may agree to accept a second marriage proposal, Lacey reluctantly consents to participating in the new reality show. What she doesn't count on is meeting a kindred spirit—one she can't seem to shake from her thoughts. Jaimie would do almost anything for her girlfriend, including following her to the ends of the earth and participating in a conniving television show that puts her in front of a camera, which happens to be her least favorite place. Her girlfriend, Sabina, hasn't met a camera she doesn't like. They couldn't be more opposite, but Jaimie still hopes Sabina will want marriage, kids, and the whole shebang. The last thing she expects is to fall in love with someone else. Let the games begin.

Sullivan's Trace by Ali Spooner

Micah "Sully" Sullivan has settled into a solitary life at the family horse ranch after her father's death. When her long-term vet, Doc Barton, plans to retire, his granddaughter, Bryn, arrives to take over his practice. An attack on one of Sully's prized horses throws Sully and Bryn into a whirlwind as they fight to save the young animal. Just as Sully is becoming comfortable with her growing attraction to Bryn, tragedy occurs, and her brother and his wife are killed in an accident. Sully's solitary life drastically changes when a family of three is born.

Love Sins by Annette Mori

Jessica Green's life is predictable and boring. As the chief engineer for Solar Flair, her career is right on track. Her love life, not so much. The last thing she expects is a call from her estranged father's attorney. Too curious to ignore the message, she can't resist meeting with him and discovering more about specific instructions related to his estate, as well as the letter her father left for her. Rattled by what she finds at her father's home, she promptly dials 911.

Special Agent Amanda Forrester is perplexed by a call to join a homicide investigation until she arrives at the scene and learns the victim is not only a serial killer but an elite assassin the authorities have been after for years. To Amanda's increasing irritation, the daughter recognizes a picture of the last target and insinuates herself into the investigation. As the case takes a surprising turn, Amanda finds she has landed smack dab in the middle of a complicated and dangerous situation. The facts lead her to a puzzle weaving together the recent suicide of a wealthy businessman with the activities of several prominent politicians. Amanda must join forces with a mysterious organization and the persistent woman she finds increasingly hard to resist. Her instinct to protect the alluring and vulnerable Jessica Green kicks into high gear, taking the reader on a roller-coaster journey for the last book in *The Next Generation* series.

A Wild Moon Rises by Jen Silver

Successful author, Malory G Holmes, has had a rough year. Wounded by an emotional breakup and writer's block she returns home after eight months travelling to discover the startling results of a DNA test. Apparently, through her mother's side, she is related to a baronet with an estate in Briarbay, Northumberland. She decides to visit the place to find out more about this unknown side of her family.

Selene Wylde is content with life, running a bookshop in the small hamlet of Briarbay. She also looks after her father, Reginald, who is grieving over the recent death of his husband, Sir Alan Guyatt. Reginald is worrying about his claim to stay at Briarbay Hall as the Will of Sir Alan has not yet been found.

With the arrival in her shop of a very attractive, well-known writer, Selene's world begins to tilt alarmingly. Malory and Selene become entangled in a web of secrets and deceptions with the added complication of a rapidly growing attraction.

eBooks, Print, Free eBooks

Visit our website for more publications available online.

https://affinityebooks.com/

Published by Affinity Rainbow Publications
A Division of Affinity eBook Press NZ LTD
Canterbury, New Zealand

Registered Company 2517228

www.ingramcontent.com/pod-product-compliance
Lightning Source LLC
Chambersburg PA
CBHW071531260626
47170CB00002B/592